Snared in a web of lust and sorcery by the Lady Synelle, his life sought both by Karela, fierce woman bandit, and by Antimides, who seeks the throne of Ophir, only Conan of Cimmeria stands between the world and the bloody malevolence of the horned god, Al'Kiir.

"Robert Jordan is one of the few writers to successfully capture much of the spirit of Howard's original character."

—*Science Fiction Chronicle*

"Robert Jordan is an excellent, colorful action writer . . . sensual, detailed, action/suspense oriented. Robert E. Howard would approve."

—*Science Fiction Review*

Look for these other TOR Books by Robert Jordan

CONAN THE DEFENDER
CONAN THE DESTROYER
CONAN THE INVINCIBLE
CONAN THE MAGNIFICENT
CONAN THE TRIUMPHANT
CONAN THE UNCONQUERED
CONAN THE VICTORIOUS (trade edition)

Conan the Triumphant

BY

ROBERT JORDAN

A TOM DOHERTY ASSOCIATES BOOK

This is a work of fiction. All the characters and events portrayed in this book are fictional, and any resemblance to real people or incidents is purely coincidental.

CONAN THE TRIUMPHANT

First trade printing: October 1983
First mass market printing: April 1985

A TOR Book

Published by Tom Doherty Associates
8-10 West 36 Street
New York, N.Y. 10018

Cover art by Boris Vallejo

ISBN: 0-812-54242-8
CAN. ED.: 0-812-54243-6

Printed in the United States of America

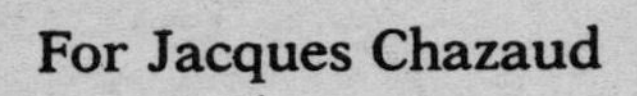

For Jacques Chazaud

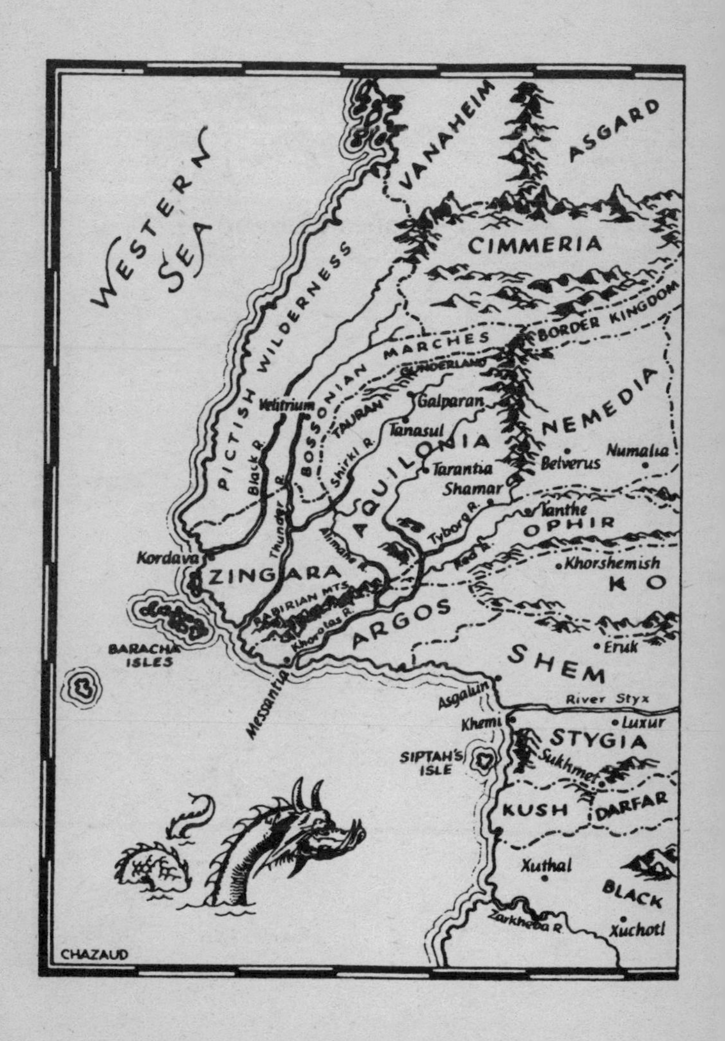
WESTERN SEA
VANAHEIM
ASGARD
CIMMERIA
PICTISH WILDERNESS
BORDER KINGDOM
BOSSONIAN MARCHES
GUNDERLAND
Velitrium
TAURAN
Galparan
Tanasul
NEMEDIA
AQUILONIA
Shirki R.
Black R.
Thunder R.
Tarantia
Shamar
Belverus
Numalia
Tybor R.
Ianthe
OPHIR
Kordava
ZINGARA
Alimane R.
Red R.
Khorshemish
RABIRIAN MTS.
Khorotas R.
ARGOS
BARACHA ISLES
Messantia
SHEM
Eruk
Asgalun
River Styx
Khemi
Luxur
STYGIA
SIPTAH'S ISLE
Sukhmet
KUSH
DARFAR
Xuthal
BLACK
Xuchotl
Zarkheba R.
CHAZAUD

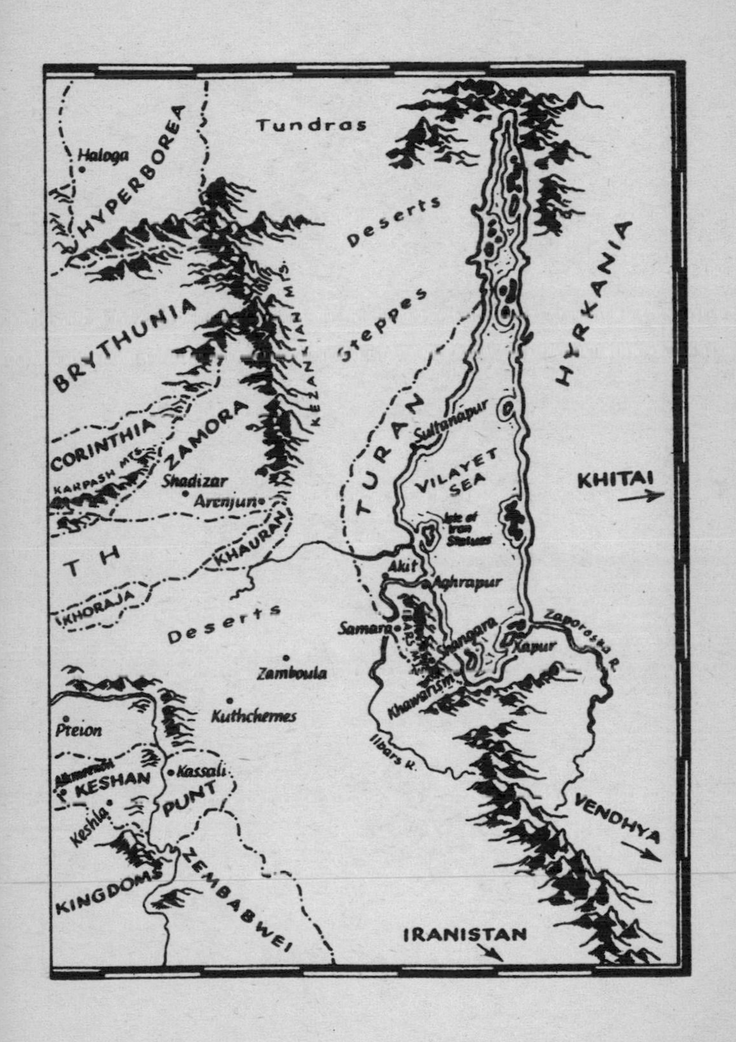
Tundras
Haloga
HYPERBOREA
Deserts
Steppes
BRYTHUNIA
KEZANKIAN MTS.
HYRKANIA
CORINTHIA
ZAMORA
TURAN
Sultanapur
KARPASH MTS.
Shadizar
Arenjun
VILAYET SEA
KHITAI
Isle of Iron Statues
KHAURAN
TH
Akit
Aghrapur
KHORAJA
Deserts
Samara
Shangara
Zaporoska R.
Xapur
Khawarizm
Zamboula
Kuthchemes
Preion
Kassali
KESHAN
PUNT
Keshla
Ilbars R.
VENDHYA
KINGDOMS
ZEMBABWEI
IRANISTAN

Conan

The Triumphant

Prologue

The great granite mound called Tor Al' Kiir crouched like a malevolent toad in the night, wearing a crown of toppled walls and ruined columns, memories of failed attempts by a score of Ophirean dynasties to build there. Men had long since forgotten the origin of the mountain's name, but they knew it for a place of ill luck and evil, and laughed at the former kings who had not had their sense. Yet their laughter was tinged with unease for there was that about the mountain that made it a place to avoid even in thought.

The roiling black clouds of the storm that lashed Ianthe, that sprawling golden-domed and alabaster-spired city to the south, seemed to center about the mountain, but no muffled murmur of the thunder that rattled roof-tiles in the capital, no flash of light from lightnings streaking the dark like dragons' tongues, penetrated to the depths of Tor Al'Kiir's heart.

The Lady Synelle knew of the storm, though she could not hear it. It was proper for the night. Let the heavens split, she thought, and mountains be torn asunder in honor of *his* return to the world of men.

Her tall form was barely covered by a black silk tabard, tightly belted with golden links, that left the outer curves of breasts and hips bare. None of those who knew her as a princess of Ophir would have recognized her now, dark eyes glittering, beautiful face seemingly carved from marble, spun-platinum hair twisted about her head in severe coils and bearing a coronet of golden chain. There were four horns on the brow of that coronet, symbol that she was High Priestess of the god she had chosen to serve. But the bracelets of plain black iron that encircled her wrists were a symbol as well, and one she hated, for the god Al'Kiir accepted only those into his service who admitted themselves to be his slaves. Ebon silk that hung to her ankles, the hem weighted by golden beads, stirred against her long, slender legs as, barefoot, she led a strange procession deeper into the mountain through rough-hewn passages, lit by dark iron cressets suggesting the form of a horrible, four-horned head.

A score of black-mailed warriors were strange enough, their faces covered by slitted helmets bearing four horns, two outthrust to the sides and two curling down before the helmet, making them seem more demons than men. The quillons of their broadswords were formed of four horns as well, and each wore on his chest, picked out in scarlet, the outline of the monstrous horned head only hinted by the fiery iron baskets suspended by chains from the roof of the tunnel.

Stranger still was the woman they escorted, clothed in Ophirean bridal dress, diaphanous layers of pale cerulean silk made opaque by their number, caught at the waist with a cord of gold. Her long hair, black as a raven's wing, curling about her shoulders, was filled with the tiny white blossoms of the tarla, symbol of purity, and her feet were bare as a sign of humility. She stumbled, and rough hands grasped her arms to hold her erect.

"Synelle!" the black-haired woman called woozily. A hint of her natural haughtiness came through her drug-induced haze. "Where are we, Synelle? How did I come here?"

The cortege moved on. Synelle gave no outward sign that she had heard. Inwardly her only reaction was relief that the drug was wearing off. It had been necessary in order to remove the woman from her palace in Ianthe, and it had made her easier to prepare and bring this far, but her mind must be clear for the ceremony ahead.

Power, Synelle thought. A woman could have no real power in Ophir, yet power was what she craved. Power was what she would have. Men thought that she was content to order the estates she had inherited, that she would eventually marry and give stewardship of those lands—ownership in all but name—to her husband. In their fools' blindness they did not stop to think that royal blood coursed in her veins. Did ancient laws not forbid a woman taking the crown, she would stand next in succession to the childless King now on the throne in Ianthe. Valdric sat his throne, consumed with chivying his retinue of sorcerers and physicians to find a cure for the wasting sickness that killed him by inches, too busy to name an heir or to see that, for this failure to do so, the noble lords of Ophir struggled and fought to gain the seat his death would vacate.

A dark, contented smile touched Synelle's full red lips. Let those proud men strut in their armor and tear at one another like starving wolfhounds in a pit. They would wake from their dreams of glory to find that the Countess of Asmark had become Queen Synelle of Ophir, and she would teach them to heel like whipped curs.

Abruptly the passage widened into a great, domed cavern, the very memory of which had passed from the minds of men. Burning tapers on unadorned walls hacked from the living stone lit the smooth stone floor, which bore only two tall, slender wooden posts topped with the omnipresent four-horned head. Ornament had been far from the minds of those who had burrowed into a nameless mountain in a now forgotten age.

They had meant it as prison for the adamantine figure, colored like old blood, that stood dominating the grotto, as it would have dominated the greatest place ever conceived. A statue it seemed, yet was not.

The massive body was as that of a man, though half again as tall as any human male, save for the six claw-tipped fingers on each broad hand. In its malevolent, horned head were three lidless eyes, smouldering blackly with a glow that ate light, and its mouth was a broad, lipless gash filled with rows of needle-sharp teeth. The figure's thick arms were encircled by bracers and armlets bearing its own horned likeness. About its waist was a wide belt and loinguard of intricately worked gold, a coiled black whip glistening metallically on one side, a monstrous dagger with horned quillons depending on the other.

Synelle felt the breath catch in her throat as it had the first time she had seen her god, as it did each time she saw him. "Prepare the bride of Al' Kiir," she commanded.

A choking scream broke from the bridal-clothed woman's throat as she was hurried forward by the guards who held her. Quickly, with cords that dug cruelly into her soft flesh, they bound her between the twin posts on widely straddled knees, arms stretched above her head. Her blue eyes bulged, unable to tear themselves away from the great form that overtowered her; her mouth hung silently open as she knelt, as if terror had driven even the thought of screaming from her.

Synelle spoke. "Taramenon."

The bound woman started at the name. "Him, also?" she cried. "What is happening, Synelle? Tell me! Please!" Synelle gave no answer.

One of the armored men came forward at the summons, carrying a small, brass-bound chest, and knelt stiffly before the woman who was at once a princess of Ophir and a priestess of dark Al'Kiir.

Muttering incantations of protection, Synelle opened the chest and drew out her implements and potions, one by one.

As a child had Synelle first heard of Al'Kiir, a god forgotten by all but a handful, from an old nurse-maid who had been dismissed when it was learned what sort of evil tales she told. Little had the crone told her before she went, but even then the child had been enraptured by the power said to be given to the priestesses of Al'Kiir, to those women who would pledge their bodies and their souls to the god of lust and pain and death, who would perform the heinous rites he demanded. Even then power had been her dream.

Synelle turned from the chest with a small, crystal-stoppered vial, and approached the bound woman. Deftly she withdrew the clear stopper and, with its damp end, traced the sign of the horns on the other woman's forehead.

"Something to help you attain the proper mood for a bride, Telima." Her voice was soft and mocking.

"I don't understand, Synelle," Telima said. A breathy quality had come into her voice; she tossed her head with a gasp, and her hair was a midnight cloud about her face. "What is happening?" she whimpered.

Synelle returned the vial to its resting place in the chest. Using powdered blood and bone, she traced the sign of the horns once more, this time in broad strokes on the floor, with the woman at the posts at the horns' meeting. A jade flask contained virgin's blood; with a brush of virgin's hair she anointed Al'Kiir's broad mouth and mighty thighs. Now there was naught left save to begin.

Yet Synelle hesitated. This part of the rite she hated, as she hated the iron bracelets. There were none to witness save her guards, who would die for her, and Telima, who would soon, in one way or another, be of no import to this world, but she herself would know. Still it must be done. It must.

Reluctantly she knelt facing the great figure, paused to take a deep breath, then fell on her face, arms outspread.

"O, mighty Al'Kiir," she intoned, "lord of blood and death, thy slave abases herself before thee. Her body is thine. Her soul is thine. Accept her submission and use her as thou wilt."

Trembling, her hands moved forward to grasp the massive ankles; slowly she pulled herself across the floor until she could kiss each clawed foot.

"O, mighty Al'Kiir," she breathed, "lord of pain and lust, thy slave brings thee a bride in offering. Her body is thine. Her soul is thine. Accept her submission and use her as thou wilt."

In ages past, before the first hut was built on

the site of Acheron, now eons gone in dust, Al'Kiir had been worshipped in the land that would become Ophir. The proudest and most beautiful of women the god demanded as offerings, and they were brought to him in steady streams. Rites were performed that stained the souls of those who performed them and haunted the minds of those who witnessed them.

At last a band of mages vowed to free the world of the monstrous god, and had the blessings of Mitra and Azura and gods long forgotten placed on their foreheads. Alone of that company had the sorcerer Avanrakash survived, yet with a staff of power had he sealed Al'Kiir away from the world of men. That which stood in the cavern beneath Tor Al'Kiir was no statue of the god, but his very body, entombed for long ages.

Two of the guards had removed their helmets and produced flutes. High, haunting music filled the cavern. Two more stationed themselves behind the woman kneeling between the posts. The rest unfastened their scabbarded broadswords from their belts and began to pound the stone floor in rhythm to the flutes.

With boneless sinuosity Synelle rose and began to dance, her feet striking the floor in time with the pounding of the scabbards. In a precise pattern she moved, cat-like, each step coming in an ancient order, and as she danced she chanted in a tongue lost to time. She spun, and weighted black silk stood straight out from her body, baring her from waist to ankles. Sensuously she dipped and swayed from the looming shape of the god to the kneeling woman.

Sweat beaded Telima's countenance, and her eyes were glazed. She seemed to have lost awareness of her surroundings and she writhed uncontrollably in her bonds. Lust bloomed on her face, and horror at the realization of it.

Like pale birds Synelle's hands fluttered to Telima, brushed damp dark hair from her face, trailed across her shoulders, ripped away one single layer of her bridal garb.

Telima screamed as the men behind her struck with broad leather straps, again and again, crisscrossing from shoulders to buttocks, yet her jerking motions came as much from the potion as from the lashing. Pain had been added to lust, as required by the god.

Still Synelle danced and chanted. Another layer of diaphanous silk was torn from Telima, and as her shrieks mounted the chant wove into them, so that the cries of pain became part of the incantation.

The figure of Al'Kiir began to vibrate.

Where neither time, nor place, nor space existed, there was a stirring, a half awakening from long slumber. Tendrils of pleasurable feeling caressed, feeble threads of worship that called. But to where? Once appetites had been fed to satiation. Women had been offered in multitudes. Their essences had been kept alive for countless centuries, kept clothed in flesh forever young to be toys for the boundless lusts of a god. Memories, half dreams, flickered. In the midst of eternal nothingness was suddenly a vast floor. A thousand women born ten thousand years before danced nude. But they were merely shells, without interest. Even a god could not keep frail human essence alive forever. Petulance, and dancers and floor alike were gone. From whence did these feelings come, so frequently of late after seemingly endless ages of absence, bringing with them irritating remembrance of what was lost? There was no direction. A shield was formed and blessed peace descended. Slumber returned.

Synelle slumped to the stone floor, panting from her exertions. There was no sound in the cavern except for the sobs of the midnight-haired beauty kneeling in welted nudity.

Painfully the priestess struggled to her feet. Failure again. So many failures. She staggered as she made her way to the chest, but her hand was steady as she removed a dagger that was a normal sized version of the blade at the god's belt.

"The bowl, Taramenon," Synelle said. The rite had failed, yet it must continue to its conclusion.

Telima moaned as Synelle tangled a hand in her black hair and drew her head back. "Please," the kneeling woman wept.

Her sobs were cut off by the blade slashing across her throat. The armored man who had borne the chest thrust a bronze bowl forward to catch the sanguinary flow.

Synelle watched with disinterest as final terror blazed in Telima's eyes and faded to the glaze of death. The priestess's thoughts were on the future. Another failure, as there had been so many in the past, but she would continue if a thousand women must die in that chamber. She would bring Al'Kiir back to the world of men. Without another glance at the dead woman, she turned to the completion of the ceremony.

1

The long pack train approaching the high crenellated granite walls of Ianthe did not appear to be moving through a country officially at peace. Twoscore horsemen in spiked helms, dust turning their dark blue wool cloaks gray, rode in columns to either side of the long line of sumpter mules. Their eyes constantly searched even here in the very shadow of the capital. Half carried their short horse-bows at the ready. Sweaty-palmed muledrivers hurried their animals along, panting with eagerness to be done now that their goal was in sight.

Only the leader of the guards, his shoulders

broad almost to the point of busting his metal jazeraint hauberk, seemed unconcerned. His icy blue eyes showed no hint of the worry that made the others' eyes dart, yet he was as aware of his surroundings as they. Perhaps more so. Three times since leaving the gem and gold mines on the Nemedian border, the train had been attacked. Twice his barbarian senses had detected the ambush before it had time to develop, the third time his fiercely wielded broadsword smashed the attack even as it began. In the rugged mountains of his native Cimmeria, men who fell easily into ambush did not long survive. He had known battle there, and had a place at the warriors' fires, at an age when most boys were still learning at their father's knees.

Before the northeast gate of Ianthe, the Gate of Gold, the train halted. "Open the gates!" the leader shouted. Drawing off his helm, he revealed a square-cut black mane and a face that showed more experience than his youth would warrant. "Do we look like bandits? Mitra rot you, open the gates!"

A head in a steel casque, a broken-nosed face with a short beard, appeared atop the wall. "Is that you, Conan?" He turned aside to call down, "Swing back the gate!"

Slowly the right side of the iron-bound gate creaked inward. Conan galloped through, pulling his big Aquilonian black from the road just inside to let the rest of the train pass. A dozen mail-clad soldiers threw their shoulders behind the gate as soon as the last pack-laden mule ran by. The huge wooden slab closed with a hollow boom, and a great bar, thicker than a man's body, crashed down to fasten it.

The soldier who had called down from the wall appeared with his casque beneath his arm. "I should have recognized those accursed eastern helmets, Cimmerian," he laughed. "Your Free-Company makes a name for itself."

"Why are the gates shut, Junius?" Conan demanded. "Tis at least three hours till dark."

"Orders, Cimmerian. With the gates closed, perhaps we can keep the troubles out of the city." Junius looked around, then dropped his voice. "It would be better if Valdric died quickly. Then Count Tiberio could put an end to all this fighting."

"I thought General Iskandrian was keeping the army clear," Conan replied coolly. "Or have you just chosen your own side?"

The broken-nosed soldier drew back, licking his thin lips nervously. "Just talking," he muttered. Abruptly he straightened, and his voice took on a blustering tone. "You had better move on, Cimmerian. There's no loitering about the gates allowed now. Especially by mercenary companies." He fumbled his casque back onto his head as if to give himself more authority, or perhaps simply more protection from the Cimmerian's piercing gaze.

With a disgusted grunt Conan touched boot to his stallion's ribs and galloped after his company. Thus far Iskandrian—the White Eagle of Ophir, he was called; some said he was the greatest general of the age—had managed to keep Ophir from open civil war by holding the army loyal to Valdric, though the King seemed not to know it, or even to know that his country was on the verge of destruction. But if the old general's grip on the army was falling. . . .

Conan scowled and pressed on. The twisted maze of maneuverings for the throne was not to his liking, yet he was forced to keep an understanding of it for his own safety, and that of his company.

To the casual observer, the streets of Ianthe would have showed no sign that nobles' private armies were fighting an undeclared and unacknowledged war in the countryside. Scurrying crowds filled narrow side streets and broad thoroughfares alike, merchants in their voluminous robes and peddlers in rags, silk-clad ladies shopping with retinues of basket-carrying servants in tow, strutting lordlings in satins and brocades with scented pomanders held to their nostrils against the smell of the sewers, leather-aproned apprentices tarrying on their errands to bandy words with young girls hawking baskets of oranges and pomegranates, pears and plums. Ragged beggars, flies buzzing about blinded eyes or crudely bandaged stumps, squatted on every corner—more since the troubles had driven so many from their villages and farms. Doxies strutted in gilded bangles and sheer silks or less, often taking a stance before columned palaces or even on the broad marble steps of temples.

Yet there was that about the throng that belied

the normalcy of the scene. A flush of cheek where there should have been only calm. A quickness of breath where there was no haste. A darting of eye where there was no visible reason for suspicion. The knowledge of what occurred beyond the walls lay heavily on Ianthe even as the city denied its happening, and the fear that it might move within the walls was in every heart.

When Conan caught up to the pack train, it was slowly wending its way through the crowds. He reined in beside his lieutenant, a grizzled Nemedian who had had the choice of deserting from the City Guard of Belverus or of being executed for performing his duty too well, to the fatal detriment of a lord of that city.

"Keep a close watch, Machaon," the Cimmerian said. "Even here we might be mobbed if this crowd knew what we carried."

Machaon spat. The nasal of his helm failed to hide the livid scar that cut across his broad nose. A blue tattoo of a six-pointed Kothian star adorned his left cheek. "I'd give a silver myself to know how Baron Timeon comes to be taking this delivery. I never knew our fat patron had any connections with the mines."

"He doesn't. A little of the gold and perhaps a few gems will stay with Timeon; the rest goes elsewhere."

The dark-eyed veteran gave him a questioning look, but Conan said no more. It had taken him no little effort to discover that Timeon was but a tool of Count Antimides. But Antimides was supposedly one of the few lords of Ophir *not* maneuvering to ascend the throne at the death of the King. As such he should have no need of secret supporters, and that meant he played a deeper game than any knew. Too, Antimides also had no connection with the mines, and thus as little right to pack-saddles loaded with gold bars and chests of emeralds and rubies. A second reason for a wise man to keep his tongue behind his teeth till he knew more of the way things were, yet it rankled the pride of the young Cimmerian.

Fortune as much as anything else had given him his Free-Company in Nemedia, but in a year of campaigning since crossing the border into Ophir they had built a reputation. The horse archers of Conan the Cimmerian were known for their fierceness and the skill of him who led them, respected even by those who had cause to hate them. Long and hard had been Conan's climb from a boyhood as a thief to become a captain of mercenaries at an age when most men might only dream of such a thing. It had been, he thought, a climb to freedom, for never had he liked obeying another's commands; yet here he played the game of a man he had never even met, and it set most ill with him. Most ill, indeed.

As they came in sight of Timeon's palace, a pretentiously ornamented and columned square of white marble with broad stairs, crowded between a temple of Mitra and a potter's works, Conan suddenly slid from his saddle and tossed his reins and helmet to a surprised Machaon.

"Once this is all safely in the cellars," he told his lieutenant, "let those who rode with us have until dawn tomorrow for carousing. They've earned it."

"The baron may take it badly, Conan, you leaving before the gold is safely under lock and key."

Conan shook his head. "And I see him now, I may say things best left unsaid."

"He'll likely be so occupied with his latest leman that he'll not have time for two words with you."

One of the company close behind them laughed, a startling sound to come from his sephulcral face. He looked like a man ravaged nearly to death by disease. "Timeon goes through almost as many women as you, Machaon," he said. "But then, he has wealth to attract them. I still don't see how you do it."

"If you spent less time gaming, Narus," Machaon replied, "and more hunting, perhaps you'd know my secrets. Or mayhap it's because I don't have your spindly shanks."

A dozen of the company roared with laughter. Narus' successes with women came with those who wanted to fatten him up and nurse him back to health; there seemed to be a surprising number of them.

"Machaon has enough women for five men," laughed Taurianus, a lanky, dark-haired Ophirean, "Narus dices enough for ten, and Conan does enough of both for twenty." He was one of those who had joined the company since its arrival in Ophir. But nine of the original score remained. Death had done for some of the rest; others had simply tired of a steady diet of blood and danger.

Conan waited for the laughter to subside. "If Timeon's got a new mistress, and it's about time for him to if he's running true to form, he'll not notice if I'm there or no. Take them on in, Machaon." Without waiting for a reply the Cimmerian plunged into the crowd.

Other than staying away from Timeon until he was in better temper, Conan was unsure of what he sought. A woman, perhaps. Eight days the journey to the mines and back had taken, without so much as a crone to gaze on. Women were forbidden at the mines; men condemned to a life digging rock were difficult enough to control without the sight of soft flesh to incite them, and after a year or two in the pits the flesh would not have to be that soft.

A woman, then, but there was no urgency. For a time he would simply wander and drink in the bustle of the city, so different even with its taint from the open terror that permeated the countryside.

Ophir was an ancient kingdom; it had coexisted with the mage-ridden empire of Acheron, gone to dust these three millenia and more, and had been one of the few lands to resist conquest by that dark empire's hordes. Ianthe, its capital, might have been neatly planned and divided into districts at some time in its long history, but over the centuries the great city of spired towers and golden-domed palaces had grown and shifted, winding streets pushing through haphazardly, buildings going up wherever there was space. Marble temples, fronted by countless rows of fluted columns and silent save for the chants of priests and worshippers, sat between brick-walled brothels and smoking foundries filled with the clanging of hammers, mansions and alabaster between rough taverns and silversmiths' shops. There was a system of sewers, though more often than not the refuse thrown there simply lay, adding to the effluvia that filled the streets. And stench there was, for some were too lazy even to dispose of their offal in the sewers, emptying chamber pots and kitchen scraps into the nearest alley. But for all its smells and cramped streets, for all its fears, the city was alive.

A trull wearing a single strip of silk threaded through her belt of coins smiled invitingly at the big youth, running her hands through her dark curls to lift well-rounded breasts, wetting her lips for the breadth of his shoulders. Conan answered her inviting smile with one that sent a visible shiver through her. Marking her as likely for later, though, he moved on, the doxy's regretful gaze following him. He tossed a coin to a fruit-girl and took a handful of plums, munching as he went, tossing the seeds into a sewer drain when he saw one.

In the shop of a swordsmith he examined keen blades with an expert eye, though he had never found steel to match that of his own ancient broadsword, ever present at his side in its worn shagreen scabbard. But the thought of a woman rose up in him, the memory of the whore's thighs. Perhaps there was some small urgency to finding a woman after all.

From a silversmith he purchased a gilded brass necklace set with amber. It would go well on the neck of that curly-head wench, or if not her, about the neck of another. Jewelry, flowers and perfume, he had learned, went further with any woman, be she the most common jade of the streets or a daughter of the noblest house, than a sack of gold, though the trull would want her coins as well, of course. The perfume he obtained from a one-eyed peddler with a tray hung on a strap about his scrawny neck, a vial of something that smelled of roses. Now he was ready.

He cast about for a place to throw the last of his plum pits, and his eye fell on a barrel before the shop of a brass smith, filled with scraps of brass and bronze obviously ready for melting down. Lying atop the metallic debris was a bronze figure as long as his forearm and green with the verdigris of age. The head of it was a four-horned monstrosity, broad and flat, with three eyes above a broad, fang-filled gash of a mouth.

Chuckling, Conan straightened the statuette in the barrel. Ugly it was, without doubt. It was also naked and grotesquely male. A perfect gift for Machaon.

"The noble sir is a connoisseur, I see. That is one of my best pieces."

Conan eyed the smiling, dumpy little man who had appeared in the doorway of the shop, with his plump hands folded over a yellow tunic where it was strained by his belly. "One of your best pieces, is it?" Amusement was plain in the Cimmerian's voice. "On the scrap heap?"

"A mistake on the part of my apprentice, noble sir. A worthless lad." The dumpy fellow's voice dripped regretful anger at the worthlessness of his apprentice. "I'll leather him well for it. A mere two gold pieces, and it is—"

Conan cut him off with a raised hand. "Any more lies, and I may not buy it at all. If you know something of it, then speak."

"I tell you, noble sir, it is easily worth—" Conan turned away, and the shopkeeper yelped. "Wait! Please! I will speak only the truth, as Mitra hears my words!"

Conan stopped and looked back, feigning doubt. This fellow, he thought, would not last a day among the peddlers of Turan.

There was sweat on the shopkeeper's face, though the day was cool. "Please, noble sir. Come into my shop, and we will talk. Please."

Still pretending reluctance, Conan allowed himself to be ushered inside, plucking the figure from the barrel as he passed. Within, the narrow shop was crowded with tables displaying examples of the smith's work. Shelves on the walls held bowls, vases, ewers and goblets in a welter of shapes and sizes. The big Cimmerian set the statuette on a table that creaked under its weight.

"Now," he said, "name me a price. And I'll hear no more mention of gold for something you were going to melt."

Avarice struggled on the smith's plump face with fear of losing a purchaser. "Ten silvers," he said finally, screwing his face into a parody of his former welcoming expression.

Deliberately Conan removed a single silver coin from his pouch and set it on the table. Crossing his massive arms across his chest, he waited.

The plump man's mouth worked, and his head moved in small jerks of negation, but at last he sighed and nodded. "Tis yours," he muttered bitterly. "For one silver. It's as much as it is worth to melt down, and without the labor. But the thing is ill luck. A peasant fleeing the troubles brought it to me. Dug it up on his scrap of land. Ancient bronzes always sell well, but none would have this. Ill favored, they called it. And naught but bad luck since it's been in my shop. One of my daughters is with child, but unmarried; the other has taken up with a panderer who sells her not three doors from here. My wife left me for a carter. A common carter, mind you. I tell you, that thing is. . . ." His words wound down as he realized he might be talking himself out of a sale. Hurriedly he snatched the silver and made it disappear under his tunic. "Yours for a silver, noble sir, and a bargain greater than you can imagine."

"If you say so," Conan said drily. "But get me something to carry it through the streets in." He eyed the figure and chuckled despite himself, imagining the look on Machaon's face when he presented it to him. "The most hardened trull in the city would blush to look on it."

As the smith scurried into the back of his shop, two heavy-set men in the castoff finery of nobles swaggered in. One, in a soiled red brocade tunic, had had his ears and nose slit, the penalties for first and second offences of theft. For the next he would go to the mines. The other, bald and with a straggly black beard, wore a frayed wool cloak that had once been worked with embroidery of silver or gold, long since picked out. Their eyes went immediately to the bronze figure on the table. Conan kept his gaze on them; their swords, at least, looked well tended, and the hilts showed the wear of much use.

"Can I help you?" the shopkeeper asked, reappearing with a coarsely woven sack in his hand. There was no 'noble sir' for this sort.

"That," slit-ear said gruffly, pointing to the statuette. "A gold piece for it."

The smith coughed and spluttered, glaring reproachfully at Conan.

"It's mine," the Cimmerian said calmly, "and I've no mind to sell."

"Two gold pieces," slit-ear said. Conan shook his head.

"Five," the bald man offered.

Slit-ear rounded on his companion. "Give away your profit, an you will, but not mine! I'll make this ox an offer," he snarled and spun, his sword whispering from its sheath.

Conan made no move toward his own blade. Grasping the bronze figure by its feet, he swung it sideways. The splintering of bone blended with slit-ear's scream as his shoulder was crushed.

The bald man had his sword out now, but Conan merely stepped aside from his lunge and brought the weighty statuette down like a mace, splattering blood and brains. The dead man's momentum carried him on into the tables, overturning those he did not smash, sending brass vases and bowls clattering across the floor. Conan whirled back to find the first man thrusting with a dagger held left-handed. The blade skittered off his hauberk, and the two men crashed together. For the space of a breath they were chest to chest, Conan staring into desperate black eyes. This time he disdained to use a weapon. His huge fist traveled more than half the length of his forearm, and slit-ear staggered back, his face a bloody mask, to pull shelves down atop him as he crumpled to the floor. Conan did not know if he was alive or dead, nor did he care.

The smith stood in the middle of the floor, hopping from one foot to the other. "My shop!" he wailed. "My shop is wrecked! You steal for a silver what they would have given five gold pieces for, then you destroy my place of business!"

"They have purses," Conan growled. "Take the cost of your repairs from—" He broke off with a curse as the scent of roses wafted to his nose. Delving into his pouch, he came out with a fragment of vial. Perfume was soaking into his hauberk. And his cloak. "Erlik take the pair of them," he muttered. He hefted the bronze figure that he still held in one hand. "What about this thing is worth five gold pieces? Or worth dying for?" The shopkeeper, gingerly feeling for the ruffians' purses, did not answer.

Cursing under his breath Conan wiped the blood from the figure and thrust it into the sack the smith had let drop.

With a shout of delight the smith held up a handful of silver, then drew back as if he feared Conan might take it. He started, then stared at the two men littering his floor as if realizing where they were for the first time. "But what will I do with them?" he cried.

"Apprentice them," Conan told him. "I'll wager they won't put anything valuable in the scrap barrel."

Leaving the dumpy man kneeling on the floor with his mouth hanging open, Conan stalked into the street. It was time and more to find himself a woman.

In his haste he did not notice the heavily veiled woman whose green eyes widened in surprise at his appearance. She watched him blend into the crowd then, gathering her cloak about her, followed slowly.

2

The *Bull and Bear* was almost empty when Conan entered, and the half-dread silence suited his mood well. The curly-haired trull had been leaving with a customer when he got back to her corner, and he had not seen another to compare with her between there and this tavern.

An odor of stale wine and sweat hung in the air of the common room; it was not a tavern for gentlefolk. Half a dozen men, carters and apprentices in rough woolen tunics, sat singly at the tables scattered about the stone floor, each engrossed in his own drinking. A single doxy stood with her back to a corner, not plying her trade but seeming rather to ignore the men in the room. Auburn hair fell in soft waves to her shoulders. Wrapped in layers of green silk, she was more modestly covered than most noble ladies of Ophir, and she wore none of the gaudy ornaments such women usually adorned themselves with, but the elaborate kohl of her eyelids named her professional, as did her presence in that place. Still, there was a youthful freshness to her face that gave him cause to think she had not long been at it.

Conan was so intent on the girl that he failed at first to see the graying man, the full beard of a scholar spreading over his chest, who muttered to himself over a battered pewter pitcher at a table to one side of the door. When he did, he sighed, wondering if the wench would be worth putting up with the old man.

At that moment the bearded man caught sight of Conan, and a drunken, snaggle-toothed grin split his wizened face. His tunic was patched in a rainbow of colors, and stained with wine and food. "Conan," he cried, gesturing so hard for the big youth to come closer that he nearly fell from his stool. "Come. Sit. Drink."

"You look to have had enough, Boros," Conan said drily, "and I'll buy you no more."

"No need to buy," Boros laughed. He fumbled for the pitcher. "No need. See? Water. But with just a little. . . ." His voice trailed off into mumbles, while his free hand made passes above the pitcher.

"Crom!" Conan shouted, leaping back from the

table. Some in the room looked up, but seeing neither blood nor chance for advantage all went back to their drinking. "Not again while you're drunk, you old fool!" the Cimmerian continued hastily. "Narus still isn't rid of those warts you gave him trying to cure his boil."

Boros cackled and thrust the pitcher toward him. "Taste. 'S wine. Naught to fear here."

Cautiously Conan took the proffered pitcher and sniffed at the mouth of it. His nose wrinkled, and he handed the vessel back. "You drink first, since it's your making."

"Fearful, are you?" Boros laughed. "And big as you are. Had I your muscles. . . ." He buried his nose in the pitcher, threw back his head, and almost in the same motion hurled the vessel from him, gagging, spluttering and spitting. "Mitra's mercies," he gasped shakily, scrubbing the back of a bony hand across his mouth. "Never tasted anything like that in my life. Must have put a gill or more down my gullet. What in Azura's name is it?"

Conan suppressed a grin. "Milk. Sour milk, by the smell."

Boros shuddered and retched, but nothing came up. "You switched the pitcher," he said when he could speak. "Your hands are swift, but not so swift as my eye. You owe me wine, Cimmerian."

Conan dropped onto a stool across the table from Boros, setting the sack containing the bronze on the floor at his side. He had little liking for wizards, but properly speaking Boros was not such a one. The old man had been an apprentice in the black arts, but a liking for drink that became an all-consuming passion had led him to the gutter rather than down crooked paths of dark knowledge. When sober he was of some use in curing minor ills, or providing a love philtre; drunk, he was sometimes a danger even to himself. He was a good drinking companion, though, so long as he was kept from magic.

"Here!" the tavernkeeper bellowed, wiping his hands on a filthy once-white apron as he hurried toward them. With his spindly limbs and pot belly, he looked like a fat spider. "What's all this mess on the floor? I'll have you know this tavern is respectable, and—"

"Wine," Conan cut him off, tossing coppers to clatter on the floor at his feet. "And have a wench bring it." He gestured to the strangely aloof doxy. "That one in the corner will do."

"She don't work for me," the tavernkeeper grunted, bending to collect the pitcher and the coins. Then he got down on hands and knees to fetch one copper from under the table and grinned at it in satisfaction. "But you'll have a girl, never fear."

He disappeared into the rear of the building, and in short moments a plump girl scurried out, one strip of blue silk barely containing her bouncing breasts and another fastened about her hips, to set a pitcher of wine and a pair of dented tankards before the two men. Wriggling, she moved closer to Conan, a seductive light in her dark eyes. He was barely aware of her; his eyes had gone back to the auburn-haired jade.

"Fool!" the serving wench snapped. "As well take a block of ice in your arms as that one." And with a roll of her lips she flounced away.

Conan stared after her in amazement. "What is Zandru's Nine Hells got into her?" he growled.

"Who understands women?" Boros muttered absently. Hastily he filled a tankard and gulped half of it. "Besides," he went on in bleary tones once he had taken a deep breath, "now Tiberio's dead, we'll have too much else to be worrying about. . . ." The rest of his words were drowned in another mouthful of wine.

"Tiberio dead?" Conan said incredulously. "I spoke of him not too hours gone and heard no mention of this. Black Erlik's Throne, stop drinking and talk. What of Tiberio?"

Boros set his tankard down with obvious reluctance. "The word is just now spreading. Last night it was. Slit his wrists in his bath. Or so they say."

Conan grunted. "Who will believe that, and him with the best blood claim to succeed Valdric?"

"Folk believe what they want to believe, Cimmerian. Or what they're afraid not to believe."

It had had to come, Conan thought. There had been kidnappings in plenty, wives, sons, daughters. Sometimes demands were made, that an alliance be broken or a secret betrayed; sometimes there was only silence, and fear to paralyze a noble in his castle. Now began the assassinations.

He was glad that a third of his Free-Company was always on guard at Timeon's palace. Losing a patron in that fashion would be ill for a company's reputation.

"Tis all of a piece," Boros went on unsteadily. "Someone attempts to resurrect Al'Kiir. I've seen lights atop that accursed mountain, heard whispers of black knowledge sought. And this time there'll be no Avanrakash to seal him up again. We need Moranthes the Great reborn. It would take him to bring order now."

"What are you chattering at? No matter. Who's next in line after Tiberio? Valentius, isn't it?"

"Valentius," Boris chuckled derisively. "He'll never be allowed to take the throne. He's too young."

"He's a man grown," Conan said angrily. He knew little of Valentius and cared less, but the count was a full six years older than he.

Boros smiled. "There's a difference between you two, Cimmerian. You've put two hard lifetimes' experience into your years. Valentius has led a courtier's life, all perfumes and courtesies and soft words."

"You're rambling," Conan barked. How had the other man read his thoughts? A fast rise had not lessened his touchiness about his comparative youth, nor his anger at those who thought him too young for the position he held. But he had better to do with his time than sit with a drunken failed mage. There was that auburn-haired wench, for instance. "The rest of the wine is yours," he said. Snatching up the sack with the bronze in it, he stalked away from the table, leaving Boros chortling into his wine.

The girl had not moved from the corner or changed her stance in all the time Conan had been watching her. Her heart-shaped face did not change expression as he approached, but her downcast eyes, blue as a northland sky at dawn, widened like those of a frightened deer, and she quivered as if prepared for flight.

"Share some wine with me," Conan said, motioning to a table nearby.

The girl stared at him directly, her big eyes going even wider, if such were possible, and shook her head.

He blinked in surprise. That innocent face might belie it, but if she wanted directness. . . . "If you don't want wine, how does two silvers take you?"

The girl's mouth dropped open. "I don't . . . that is, I . . . I mean. . . ." Even stammering, her voice was a soprano like silver bells.

"Three silvers, then. A fourth if you prove worth it." She still stared. Why was he wasting time with her, he wondered, when there were other wenches about? She reminded him of Karela, that was it. This girl's hair was not so red, nor her cheekbones so high, but she recalled to him the woman bandit who had shared his bed—and managed to disrupt his life—every time their paths had crossed. Karela was a woman fit for any man, fit for a King. But what use raking up old memories? "Girl," he said gruffly, "if you don't want my silver, say so, and I'll take my custom elsewhere."

"Stay," she gasped. It was an obvious effort for her to get the word out.

"Innkeeper," Conan bellowed, "a room!" The wench's face went scarlet beneath the rouge on her cheeks.

The spidery tapster appeared on the instant, a long hand extended for coin. "Four coppers," he growled, and waited until Conan had dropped them into his palm before adding, "Top of the stairs, to the right."

Conan caught the furiously blushing girl by the arm and drew her up the creaking wooden stairs after him.

The room was what he had expected, a small box with dust on the floor and cobwebs in the corners. A sagging bed with a husk-filled mattress and none-too-clean blankets, a three-legged stool, and a rickety table were all the furnishings. But then, what he was there for went as well in a barn as in a palace, and often better.

Dropping the sack on the floor with a thump, he kicked the door shut and put his hands on the girl's shoulders. As he drew her to him he peeled her silken robes from her shoulders to her waist. Her breasts were full, but upstanding, and pink-nippled. She yelped once before his mouth descended on hers, then went stiff in his arms. He could as well have been kissing a statue.

He drew back, but held her still in the circle of his arms. "What sort of doxy are you?" he demanded. "A man would think you'd never kissed a man before."

"I haven't," she snapped, then began to stammer. "That is, I have. I've kissed many men. More than you can count. I am very . . . experienced." She bared her teeth in what Conan suspected was meant to be an inviting smile; it was more a fearful rictus.

He snorted derisively and pushed her out to arms' length. Her hands twitched toward her disarrayed garments, then were still. Heavy breathing made her breasts rise and fall in interesting fashion, and her face slowly colored again. "You don't talk like a farm wench," he said finally. "What are you? Some merchant's runaway daughter without sense enough to go home?"

Her face became a frozen mask of arrogant pride. "You, barbarian, will have the honor of taking a noblewoman of Ophir to . . . to your bed." Even the stumble did not crack her haughty demeanor.

Taken together with her manner of dress—or undress, rather—it was too much for the Cimmerian. He threw back his head and bellowed his laughter at the fly-specked ceiling.

"You laugh at me?" she gasped. "You dare?"

"Cover yourself," he snapped back at her, his mirth fading. Anger sprouted from stifled desires; she was a tasty bit, and he had been looking forward to the enjoyment of her. But a virgin girl running away from a noble father was the last thing he needed, or wanted any part of. Nor could he walk away from her if she needed help, either. That thought came reluctantly. Softhearted, he grumbled to himself. That was his trouble. To the girl he growled, "Do it, before I take my belt to your backside."

For a moment she glared at him, sky-blue eyes warring with icy sapphire. Ice won, and she hastily fumbled her green robes back into place, muttering under her breath.

"Your name," he demanded. "And no lies, or I'll pack you to the Marline Cloisters myself. Besides the hungry and the sick, they take in wayward girls and unruly children, and you look to be both."

"You have no right. I've changed my mind. I do not want your silver." She gestured imperiously. "Stand away from that door."

Conan gazed back at her calmly, not moving. "You are but a few words away from a stern-faced woman with a switch to teach you manners and proper behavior. Your name?"

Her eyes darted angrily to the door. "I am the Lady Julia," she said stiffly. "I will not shame my house by naming it in this place, not if you torture me with red-hot irons. Not if you use pincers, and the knout, and . . . and. . . ."

"Why are you here, Julia, masquerading as a trull, instead of doing needlework at your mother's knee?"

"What right have you to demand . . . ? Erlik take you! My mother is long dead, and my father these three months. His estates were pledged for loans and were seized in payment. I had no relations to take me in, nor friends who had use for a girl with no more than the clothes on her back. And you will call me Lady Julia. I am still a noblewoman of Ophir."

"You're a silly wench," he retorted. "And why this? Why not become a serving girl? Or a beggar, even?"

Julia sniffed haughtily. "I would not sink so low. My blood—"

"So you become a trull?" He noted she had the grace to blush. But then, she did that often.

"I thought," she began hesitantly, then stopped. When she resumed her voice had dropped to a murmur. "It seemed not so different from my father's lemans, and they appeared to be ladies." Her eyes searched his face, and she went on urgently. "But I've done nothing. I am still . . . I mean . . . Oh, why am I telling any of this to you?"

Conan leaned against the door, the crudely cut boards creaking at his weight. If he were a civilized man, he would abandon her to the path she was following. He would have his will of her and leave her weeping with her coins—or cheat her of them, for that was the civilized way. Anything else would be more bother than she was worth. The gods alone knew what faction she might be attached to by blood, for all they had not helped her so far, or what faction he might offend by aiding her.

His mouth twisted in a grimace, and Julia flinched, thinking it was for her. He was thinking too much of factions of late, spending too much time delving the labyrinthine twists of Ophirean politics. This he would leave to the gods. And the wench.

"I am called Conan," he said abruptly "and I captain a Free-Company. We have our own cook, for our patron's kitchens prepare fussed-over viands not fit for a man's stomach. This cook, Fabio, needs a girl to fetch and serve. The work is yours, an you want it."

"A pot girl!" she exclaimed. "Me!"

"Be silent, wench!" he roared, and she rocked back on her heels. He waited to be certain she would obey, then nodded in satisfaction when she settled with her hands clasped at her throat. And her mouth shut. "Do you decide it is not too far beneath you, present yourself at Baron Timeon's palace before sunfall. If not, then know well what your future will be."

She let out one startled squeak as he took the step necessary to crush her to his chest. He tangled his free hand in her long hair, and his mouth took its pleasure with hers. For a time her bare feet drummed against his shins, then slowly her kicking stopped. When he let her heels thud to the floor once more, she stood trembling and silent, tremulous azure eyes locked on his face.

"And I was gentle compared to some," he said. Scooping up the sack containing the bronze, he left her standing there.

3

Boros was gone from the common room when Conan returned below, for which the Cimmerian was just as glad.

The spidery innkeeper rushed forward, though, rubbing his hands avariciously. "Not long with the girl, noble sir. I could have told you she'd not please. My Selina, now . . . ."

Conan snarled, and the fellow retreated hastily. Crom! What a day, he thought. Go out searching for a wench and end up trying to rescue a fool girl from her own folly. He had thought he had outgrown such idiocy long ago.

Outside the street was narrow and crooked,

little more than an alley dotted with muddy pot-holes where the cracked paving stones had been pried up and carried away, yet even here were there beggars. Conan tossed a fistful of coppers into the nearest out-thrust bowl and hurried on before the score of others could flock about him. A stench of rotted turnip and offal hung in the air, held by stone buildings that seemed to lean out over the way.

He had not gone far when it dawned on him that the mendicants, rather than chasing after him crying for more, had disappeared. Such men had the instincts of feral animals. His hand went to his sword even as three men stepped into the cramped confines of the street before him. The leader had a rag tied over where his right eye had been. The other two wore beards, one no more than a straggly collection of hairs. All three had swords in hand. A foot grated on paving stone behind the Cimmerian.

He did not wait for them to take another step. Hurling the bag containing the bronze at the one-eyed man, he drew his ancient broadsword and dropped to a crouch in one continuous motion. A blade whistled over his head as he pivoted, then his own steel was biting deep into the side of the man behind. Blood spurting, the man screamed, and his legs buckled.

Conan threw himself into a dive past the collapsing man, tucking his shoulder under, and rolled to his feet with his sword at the ready just in time to spit one-eye as he rushed forward with blade upraised. For an instant Conan stared into a lone brown eye filling with despair and filming with death, then one of the others was crowding close, attempting to catch the big Cimmerian while his sword was hung up in the body. Conan snatched the poignard from one-eye's belt and slammed it into his other attacker's throat. The man staggered back with a gurgling shriek, blood pumping through the fingers clutching his neck to soak his filthy beard in crimson.

All had occurred so quickly that the man impaled on Conan's blade was just now beginning to fall. The Cimmerian jerked his blade free as one-eye dropped. The first attacker gave a last quiver and lay still in a widening sanguinary pool.

The man with the straggly beard had not even had time to join the fight. Now he stood with sword half-raised, dark eyes rolling from one corpse to another and thin nose twitching. He looked like a rat that had just discovered it was fighting a lion. "Not worth it," he muttered. "No matter the gold, it's not worth dying." Warily he edged backwards until he came abreast of a crossing alley; with a last frightened glance he darted into it. In moments even the pounding of his feet had faded.

Conan made no effort to follow. He had no interest in footpads, of which the city had an overabundance. These had made their try and paid the price. He bent to wipe his sword, and froze as a thought came to him. The last man had mentioned gold. Only nobles carried gold on their persons, and he was far from looking that sort. Gold might be paid for a killing, though the life of a mercenary, even a captain, was not usually considered worth more than silver. Few indeed were the deaths that would bring gold. Except . . . assassination. With a shout that rang from the stone walls Conan snatched up the sack-wrapped statuette and was running in the same motion, encarmined blade still gripped in his fist. With him out of the way it might be easier to get through his company to Timeon. And that sort of killing had already begun. His massive legs pumped harder, and he burst out of the alley onto a main street.

A flower-girl, screeching at the giant apparition wielding bloody steel, leaped out of his way; a fruit peddler failed to move fast enough and caromed off Conan's chest, oranges exploding from his basket in all directions. The peddler's imprecations, half for the huge Cimmerian and half for the apprentices scurrying to steal his scattered fruit, followed Conan down the crowded street, but he did not slow his headlong charge. Bearers, scrambling to move from his path, overturned their sedan chairs, spilling cursing nobles into the street. Merchants in voluminous robes and serving girls shopping for their masters' kitchens scattered screaming and shouting before him.

Then Timeon's palace was in sight. As Conan pounded up the broad alabaster stairs, the two guards he had set on the columned portico rushed forward, arrows nocked, eyes searching the street for what pursued him.

"The door!" he roared at them. "Erlik blast your hides! Open the door!"

Hurriedly they leaped to swing open one of the massive bronze doors, worked with Timeon's family crest, and Conan rushed through without slowing.

He was met in the broad entry hall by Machaon and half a score of the company, their boots clattering on polished marble tiles. Varying degrees of undress and more than one mug clutched in a fist showed they had been rousted from their rest by his shouts, but all had weapons in hand.

"What happens?" Machaon demanded. "We heard your shouts, and—"

Conan cut him off. "Where is Timeon? Have you seen him since arriving?"

"He's upstairs with his new leman," Machaon replied. "What—"

Spinning, Conan raced up the nearest stairs, a curving sweep of alabaster that stood without visible support. Pausing only an instant Machaon and the others followed at a dead run. At the door to Timeon's bedchamber, tall and carved with improbable beasts, Conan did not pause. He slammed open the door with a shoulder and rushed in.

Baron Timeon leaped from his tall-posted bed with a startled cry, his round belly bouncing, and snatched up a long robe of red brocade. On the bed a slender, naked girl clutched the coverlet to her small yet shapely breasts. Ducking her head, she peered shyly at Conan through a veil of long, silky black hair that hung to her waist.

"What is the meaning of this?" Timeon demanded, furiously belting the robe about his girth. After the current fashion of the nobility, he wore a small, triangular beard on the point of his chin. On his moon face, with his found, protuberant eyes, it made him look like a fat goat. An angry goat, now. "I demand an answer immediately! Bursting into my chambers with sword drawn." He peered suddenly at the blade in Conan's hand. "Blood!" he gasped, staggering. He flung his arms around one of the thick intricately carved posts of his bed as if to hold himself erect, or perhaps to hide himself behind. "Are we attacked? You must hold them off till I escape. That is, I'll ride for aid. Hold them, and there'll be gold for all of you."

"There's no attack, Lord Timeon," Conan said hastily. "At least, not here. But I was attacked in the city."

Timeon glanced at the girl. He seemed to realize he had been far from heroic before her. Straightening abruptly, he tugged at his robe as if adjusting it, smoothed his thinning hair. "Your squabbles with the refuse of Ianthe have no interest for me. And my pretty Tivia is too delicate a blossom to be frightened with your tales of alley brawls, and your gory blade. Leave, and I will try to forget your ill manners."

"Lord Timeon," Conan said with forced patience, "does someone mean you harm, well might they try to put me out of the way first. Count Tiberio is dead this last night at an assassin's hand. I will put guards at your door and in the garden beneath your windows."

The plump noble's water blue eyes darted to the girl again. "You will do no such thing. Tiberio took his own life, so I heard. And as for assassins —" he strode to the table where his sword lay, slung the scabbard into a corner and struck a pose with the weapon in hand—"should any manage to get past your vigilance, I will deal with them myself. Now leave me. I have . . ." he leered at the slender girl who still attempted unsuccessfully to cover herself, "matters to attend to."

Reluctantly Conan bowed himself from the room. The instant the door was shut behind him, he growled, "That tainted sack of suet. An old woman with a switch could beat him through every corridor of this palace."

"What are we to do?" Machaon asked. "If he refuses guards. . . ."

"We guard him anyway," Conan snorted. "He can take all the chances he wants to with us to protect him, and he will so long as there's a woman to impress, but we cannot afford to let him die. Put two men in the garden, where he can't see them from his windows. And one at either end of this hall, around the corners where they can hide if Timeon comes out, but where they can keep an eye on his door."

"I'll see to it." The scarred warrior paused. "What's that you're carrying?"

Conan realized he still had the bronze, wrapped in its sack, beneath his arm. He had forgotten it in the mad rush to get to Timeon. Now he wondered. If the men who had attacked him had not been trying to open a way to the baron—and it now seemed they had not—perhaps they had been after the statuette. After all, two others had been willing to kill, and die, for it. And they had thought it worth gold. It seemed best to find out the why of it before giving Machaon a gift that might bring men seeking his life.

"Just a thing I bought in the city," he said. "Post those guards immediately. I don't want to take chances, in case I was right the first time."

"First time?" Machaon echoed, but Conan was already striding away.

The room Conan had been given was spacious, but what Timeon thought suitable for a mercenary captain. The tapestries on the walls were of the second quality only, the lamps were polished pewter and brass rather than silver or gold, and the floor was plain red tiles. Two arched windows looked out on the garden, four floors below, but there was no balcony. Still, the mattress on the big bed was goose down, and the tables and chairs, if plain varnished wood, were sturdy enough for him to be comfortable with, unlike the frail, gilded pieces in the rooms for noble guests.

He tossed the rough sacking aside and set the bronze on a table. A malevolent piece, it seemed almost alive. Alive and ready to rend and tear. The man who had made it was a master. And steeped in abomination, Conan was sure, for otherwise he could not have infused so much evil into his creation.

Drawing his dagger, he tapped the hilt against the figure. It was not hollow; there could be no gems hidden within. Nor did it have the feel or heft of bronze layered over gold, though who would have gone to *that* much trouble, or why, he could not imagine.

A knock came at the door while he was still frowning at the horned shape, attempting to divine its secret. He hesitated, then covered it with the sack before going to the door. It was Narus.

"There's a wench asking for you," the hollow-cheeked man said. "Dressed like a doxy, but her face scrubbed like a temple virgin, and pretty enough to be either. Says her name is Julia."

"I know her," Conan said, smiling.

Narus' mournful expression did not change, but then it seldom did. "A gold to a silver there's trouble in this one, Cimmerian. Came to the front and demanded entrance, as arrogant as a princess of the realm. When I sent her around back, she tried to tell me her lineage. Claims she's noble born. The times are ill for dallying with such."

"Take her to Fabio," Conan laughed. "She's his new pot girl. Tell him to put her peeling turnips for the stew."

"A pleasure," Narus said, with a brief flicker of a smile, "after the way her tongue scourged me."

At least one thing had gone well with the day, Conan thought as he turned from the door. Then his eye fell on the sacking covered bronze on the table, and his moment of jollity faded. But there were other matters yet to be plumbed, and the feeling at the back of his neck told him there would be deadly danger in doing so.

4

The sly-faced man who called himself Galbro wandered nervously around the dusty room where he had been told to wait. Two great stuffed eagles on perches were the only decoration, the amber beads that had replaced their eyes seeming to glare more fiercely than ever any living eagle's eyes had. The lone furnishings was the long table supporting the leather bag in which he had brought what he had to sell. He did not like these meetings; despite all the silver and gold they put in his purse, he did not like the woman who gave him the coin. Her name was unknown to him, and he did not want to know it, nor anything else about her. Knowledge of her would be dangerous.

Yet he knew it was not the woman alone who made him pace this time. That man. A northlander, Urian said he was. From whencever he came, he had slain five of Galbro's best and walked away without so much as a scratch. That had never happened before, or at least not since he came to Ophir. It was an ill omen. For the first time in long years he wished that he was back in Zingara, back in the thieves' warren of alleys that ran along the docks of Kordava. And that was foolish, for if he was not shortened a head by the guard, his throat would be slit by the denizens of those same alleys before he saw a single nightfall. There were penalties attached to playing both sides in a game, especially when both sides discovered that you cheated.

A light footstep brough him alert. *She* stepped into the room, and a shiver passed through him. No part of her but her eyes, dark and devoid of softness, was visible. A silver cloak that brushed the floor was gathered close about her. A dark, opaque veil covered the lower half of her face, and her hair was hidden by a white silk headcloth, held by a ruby pin, the stone as large as the last joint of his thumb.

The ruby invoked no shreds of greed within him. Nothing about her brought any feeling to him except fear. He hated that, fearing a woman, but at least her coin was plentiful. His taste for that was all the greed he dared allow himself with her.

With a start he realized she was waiting for him to speak. Wetting his lips—why did they dry so in her presence?—he opened his bag, spread his offerings on the table. "As you can see, my lady, I have much this time. Very valuable."

One pale, slender hand extended from the cloak to finger what he had brought, object by object. The brass plaque, worked with the head of the demon that so fascinated her, was thrust contemptuously aside. He schooled his face not to wince. Leandros had labored hard on that, but of late she accepted few of the Corinthian's forgeries. Three fragments of manuscript, tattered and torn, she studied carefully, then lay to one side. Her fingers paused over a clay head, so worn with age he had not been certain it was meant to be the creature she wanted. She put it with the parchments.

"Two gold pieces," she said quietly when she was done. "One for the head, one for the codexes. They but duplicate what I already have."

A gold for the head was good—he had hoped for no more than coppers at best—but he had expected two for each of the manuscripts. "But, my lady," he whined, "I can but bring you what I find. I cannot read such script, or know if you already possess it. You know not what difficulties I face, what expenses, in your service. Five of my men slain. Coin to be paid for thefts. Men to be—"

"Five men dead?" Her voice was a whipcrack across his back, though she had not raised it.

He squirmed beneath her gaze; sweat rolled

down his face. This cold woman had little tolerance for failure, he knew, and less for men who drew attention to themselves, as by leaving corpses strewn in the streets. He had Baraca as example for that. The Kothian had been found hanging by his feet with his skin neatly removed, yet still alive. For a few agonized hours of screaming.

"What have you been into, Galbro," she continued, her low words stabbing like daggers, "to lose five men?"

"Naught, my lady. A private matter. I should not have mentioned it, my lady. Forgive me, please."

"Fool! Your lies are transparent. Know that the god I serve, and whom you serve through me, gives me the power of pain." She spoke words that his brain did not want to comprehend; her hand traced a figure in the air between them.

Blinding light flashed behind his eyes, and agony filled him, every muscle in his body writhing and knotting. Helpless, he fell, quivering in every limb, bending into a backbreaking arch till only his head and drumming heels touched the floor. He tried to shriek, but shrieks could not pass the frozen cords of his throat, nor even breath. Blackness veiled his eyes, and he found a core within him that cried out for death, for anything to escape the all-consuming pain.

Abruptly the torment melted away, and he collapsed in a sobbing heap.

"Not even death can save you," she whispered, "for death is one of the realms of my master. Behold!" Again she spoke words that seared his mind.

He peered up at her pleadingly, tried to beg, but the words stuck in his throat. The eagles moved. He knew they were dead; he had touched them. But they moved, wings unfolding. One uttered a piercing scream. The other swooped from its perch to the table, great talons gripping the wood as it tilted its head to regard him as it might a rabbit. Tears rolled uncontrollably down his thin cheeks.

"They would tear you to pieces at my command," the veiled woman told him. "Now speak. Tell me all."

Galbro began to babble. Words spilled from his mouth like water from a fountain. The bronze figure, described in minute detail. How he learned of it, and the attempts to secure it. Yet even in his terror he held back the true description of the giant northlander. Some tiny portion of him wanted to be part of killing this man who had endangered him; a larger part wanted whatever the veiled woman might pay for the piece. Did she know how to obtain it without him she might decide his usefulness was at an end. He knew she had others like him who served her, and Baraca reminded him of the deadliness of her wrath. When his torrent of speech ended, he lay waiting in dread.

"I dislike those who keep things from me," she said at last, and he shivered at the thought of her dislike. "Secure this bronze, Galbro. Obey me implicitly, and I will forgive your lies. Fail. . . ."

She did not have to voice the threat. His whirling mind provided a score of them, each worse than the last. "I will obey, my lady," he sobbed, scrubbing his face in the dust of the floor. "I will obey. I will obey."

Not until her footsteps had faded from the room could he bring himself to stop the litany. Raising his head he stared wildly about the room, filled with joyous relief that he was alone and still alive. The eagles caught his eye, and he moaned. They were still again, but one leaned forward with wings half raised as if ready to swoop at him from its perch. The other still clung to the table, head swiveled to pierce him with its amber gaze.

He wanted to flee, yet he knew with a sinking feeling that he could not run far enough or fast enough to escape her. That accursed northlander was responsible for this. If not for him everything could have gone on as before. Rage built in him, comforting rage that overlaid his terror. He would make the northlander pay for everything that had happened to him. That big man would pay.

Synelle waited until she was in her palanquin—unadorned for anonymity—with the pale gray curtains safely drawn before lowering her veil. The bearers carried her from the courtyard of the small house where she had met Galbro without a word needed from her. Tongueless, so they could not speak of where they had borne her, they knew the need to serve her perfectly as well as did the sly-faced thief.

It was well she always went to these meetings prepared. A cloth on which Galbro had wiped his sweat, obtained by another of her minions, a few feathers plucked from the eagles, these had given her the means to quell the thief. She could rest at her ease knowing the man's soul was seared with the need for absolute obedience. And yet for once the gentle swaying of the platform did not lull her as she lolled on silken cushions.

Something about the sly little man's description of the bronze produced an irriating tickle in the back of her mind. She had encountered many representations of Al'Kiir's head, many medalions and amulets embossed with his head or the symbol of the horns, but never before a complete figure. It sounded so detailed, perhaps an exact duplicate of the actual body of the god. Her face went blank with astonishment. In one of the manuscript fragments she had gathered there was . . . something. She was sure of it.

She parted the forward curtains a slit. "Faster!" she commanded. "Erlik blast your souls, faster!"

The bearers increased their pace to a run, forcing their way through the crowds, careless of the curses that followed them. Synelle would do more than curse if they failed to obey. Within, she pounded a small fist against her thigh in frustration at the time it took to cross the city.

As soon as the palanquin entered the courtyard

of her mansion, before the bearers could lower it to the slate tiles, Synelle leaped out. Even in her haste hate flickered through her at the sight of the house. As large as any palace in the city, it still was not a palace. The white stuccoed walls and red-tiled roof were suitable for the dwelling of a merchant. Or a woman. By ancient law no woman, not even a princess, could maintain a palace within the walls of Ianthe. But she would change that. By the gods, if what she thought were true she would change it within the month. Why wait for Valdric to die? Not even the army could stand against her. Iskandrian, the White Eagle of Ophir, would kneel at her feet along with the great lords of Ophir.

Dropping her cloak for a serving maid to tend to, she raised her robes to her hips and ran, heedless of servants who stared at bare, flashing limbs. To the top floor of the mansion she ran, to a windowless room where only one other but herself was allowed, and that one with her mind ensorceled to forget what lay within, to die did anyone attempt to force the awful knowledge from her.

Golden sconces on the walls held pale, perfumed candles, yet all their light could not thrust back an air of darkness, the feel of a shrine to evil. Shrine it was, in a way, though there was no idol, no place for votive offerings. Three long tables, polished till they gleamed, were all the furnishings the room contained. On one were flasks of liquids that bubbled in their sealed containers or glowed with eery lights, vials of powders noxious and obscene, the tools of her painfully learned craft. The second was covered with amulets and talismans; some held awesome powers she could detect but not yet wield. Al'Kiir would give them to her.

It was to the third table she hurried, for there were the fragments of scroll, the tattered pages of parchment and vellum that she had slowly and carefully gathered over the years. There was the dark knowledge of sorceries the world had attempted to forget, sorceries that would give her power. Hastily she pawed through them, for once careless of flakes that dropped from ancient pages. She found what she sought, and easily read in a language dead a thousand years. She was perhaps the last person in the world capable of reading that extinct tongue, for the scholar who had taught her she had had strangled with his own beard, his wife and children smothered in their beds to be doubly sure. Death guarded secrets far better than gold.

An eager gleam lit her dark eyes, and she read again the passage she had found.

> Lo, call to the great god, entreating him, and set before the image, the succedaneum, the bridge between worlds, as a beacon to glorify the way of the god to thee.

She had thought this spoke of the priestess as bridge and beacon, placing herself before the image of Al'Kiir, but that which lay beneath the mountain was not an image. It was material body of the god. It must be the image that was to be placed before the priestess during the rites. The image. The bronze figure. It had to be. A thrill of triumph coursed through her as she swept from the room.

In the corridor a serving girl busily lighting silver lamps hung from the walls awkwardly made obeisence clutching her coal-pot and tongs.

Synelle had not realized how close the fall of darkness came. Twilight was almost on the city; precious time wasted away as she stood there. "Find Lord Taramenon," she commanded, "and bid him come to my dressing chamber immediately. Run, girl!" The serving girl ran, for the Lady Synelle's displeasures brought punishments best not thought of.

There was no need to ask if the handsome young lord was in her mansion. Taramenon wished to be king, a foolish desire for one with neither the proper blood lines nor money, and one he believed he had hidden from her. It was true he was the finest sword in Ophir—she had made a point of binding the best bladesmen of the land to her service—but that counted little in the quest for a throne. He followed Synelle in her own seeking because he believed in his arrogance that she would find it impossible to rule without a husband by her side, because he thought in his pride that he would be that husband. Thus he would gain his crown. She had done nothing to dissuade him from the belief. Not yet.

Four tirewomen, lithe matched blondes in robes that seemed to be but vapors of silk, paused only to bend knee before hurrying forward, moving as gracefully as dancers, as Synelle entered her dressing chamber. Her agents had gone to great efforts to find the four, sisters of noble Corinthian blood with but a year separating each from the next; Synelle herself had seen to the breaking and training of them. They followed her submissively and silently as she strolled about the room, removing her garments without once impeding her progress in any way. In nakedness more resplendant than any satins or silks, long-limbed, full-breasted and sleek, Synelle allowed them to minister to her. One held an ivory-framed mirror while another used delicate fur brushes to freshen the kohl on Synelle's eyelids and the rouge on her lips. The others wiped her softly with cool, damp clothes, and annointed her with rare perfume of Vendhya, priced at one gold coin the drop.

The heavy tread of a man's boots sounded in the antechamber, and the tirewomen scurried to fetch a lounging robe of scarlet velvet. Synelle refused to hold out her arms for them to slip it on until the steps were at the very door.

Taramenon gasped at the tantalizing flash of silken curves, quickly sheathed, that greeted his entrance. He was tall, broad of shoulders and deep of chest, with an aquiline nose and deep brown eyes that had melted the hearts of many women. Synelle was glad that he did not follow the fashion in beards, being rather clean shaven. She was also pleased to note the quickening of his breath as he gazed at her.

"Leave me," she commanded, belting tight the red satin sash of her robe. The girls filed obediently from the room.

"Synelle," Taramenon said thickly as soon as they were gone, and stepped forward as if to take her in his arms.

She stopped him with an upraised hand. There was no time for such frivolity, no matter how amusing it might usually be to make him writhe with a desire she had no intention of slaking. Her studies told her there were powers to be gained from allowing a man to take her, and dedicating that taking to Al'Kiir, but she knew Taramenon's plans for her. And she had seen too many proud, independent women give themselves to a man only to discover they had given pride and independence as well. Not for her listening breathlessly for a lover's footstep, smiling at his laughter, weeping at his frowns, running to tend to his wants like the meanest slave. She would not risk such an outcome. She would never give herself to any man.

"Send your two best swordsmen after yourself to find and follow Galbro," she said, "without allowing him to become aware of it. He seeks a bronze, an image of Al'Kiir the length of a big man's forearm, but it is too important to trust to him. When he has located it for them, they are to secure it and bring it to me at once. Do you understand, Taramenon? Are you listening?"

"I listen," he said hoarsely, a touch of anger in his voice. "When you summoned me to your dressing chamber, at this hour, I thought something other than an accursed figure was on your mind."

A seductive smile caressed her full lips, and she moved closer to him, until her breasts were pressed against him. "There will be time for that when the throne is secure," she said softly. Her slender fingers brushed his mouth. "All the time in the world." His arms began to come up around her, but she stepped smoothly out of his embrace. "First the throne, Taramenon, and this bronze you call accursed is vital to attaining that. Send the men tonight. Now."

She watched a multitude of emotions cross his face, and wondered yet again at how transparent were the minds of men. No doubt he thought his features unreadable, yet she knew he was adding this incident to a host of others, cataloguing the ways he would make her pay for them once she was his.

"It will be done, Synelle," he growled at last.

When he was gone her smile turned to one of ambition triumphant. Power would be hers. The smile became full-throated laughter. It would be hers, and hers alone.

5

The night streets of Ianthe were dark and empty, yet near the palace of Baron Timeon a shadow moved. A cloaked and hooded figure pressed itself to the thickly-ornamented marble walls, and cool green eyes, slightly tilted above high cheekbones, surveyed the guards marching their rounds among the thick, fluted columns of alabaster. All very well, those guards, but would he who lay sleeping within remember his own thief's tricks?

The cloak was discarded, revealing a woman in tight-fitting tunic and snug breeches of buttery leather, with soft red boots on her feet. Moonlight shimmered on titian hair tied back from her face with a cord. Quickly she undid her sword belt and refastened it with her Turanian scimitar hanging down her back, then checked the leather sack hanging at her side. Strong, slender fingers tested the niveous marble carvings of the wall, and then she was climbing like a monkey.

Below the edge of the flat roof she paused. Boots grated on slate tiles. He remembered. Yet for all the reputation this Free-Company was building in the country, they were yet soldiers. Those on the roof walked regular paths, as sentries in a camp. The measured tread came closer, closer. And then it was receding.

As agile as a panther, she was onto the roof, running on silent feet, losing herself in the shadows of two score chimneys. At the drop of the central garden around which the entire palace was arranged, she fell to her belly and peered down. There were the windows of his sleeping chamber. They were dark. So he did sleep. She would have expected him to be carousing with yet another in a long line of all too willing wenches. It was one of the things she remembered most about him, his eye for women and theirs for him.

Knowledge had been easily come by. Not even bribes had been necessary. All that had been required was for her to pretend to be a serving woman—though that had been no small a task in itself, given her lush beauty; serving maids with curves like hers soon found themselves promoted to the master's bed—and chat to the women of

Baron Timeon's palace in the markets. They had been eager to tell about the great house in which they served, about their fat master and his constantly changing parade of women, about the hard-eyed warriors who had hired themselves to him. Especially about the warriors they had been willing to talk, giggling and teasing each other about returning from the stable with hay covering the back of a robe and stolen moments in secluded corners of the garden.

She would have wagered there were guards in that garden as well as on the roof, but those did not worry her. From the leather sack she produced a rope woven of black-dyed silk, to the end of which was fastened a padded grapnel. The metal prongs hooked on the scrollwork along the roof-edge; the rope fell invisibly into the darkness below. It was just long enough to reach the window she sought.

A short climb downward, and she was inside the room. It was as black as Zandru's Seventh Hell. A dagger found its way into her hand . . . and she stopped dead. What if there were some error in her information? She did not want to kill the wrong man. She had to be sure.

Mentally cursing her own foolishness, she felt in the darkness for a table, for a lamp . . . and yes, a coal-box and tongs. She puffed softly on the coal till it glowed, held it to the wick. Light bloomed, and she gasped at the apparition on the table beside the brass lamp. Horned malevolence glared at her. It was but a bronze figure, yet she sensed evil in the thing, and primeval instinct deep within her told her that evil was directed at women. Could the man she sought have changed so much as to keep such monstrosity in his chamber? The man she sought!

Heart pounding, she spun, dagger raised. He still slept, a young giant sprawled in his slumber. Conan of Cimmeria. Soft-footed she crept closer to his bed, her eyes drinking him in, the planes of his face, the breadth of his shoulders, the massive arms that had. . . .

Stop, she commanded herself. How many wrongs had this man committed against her? She had lived on the plains of Zamora and Turan with the freedom of the hawk till Conan had come, and brought with him the destruction of her band of brigands. For his stupid male honor and the matter of a silly oath she had made him swear in a moment of anger, he had allowed her to be sold into slavery, into a zenana in Sultanapur. Every time the switch had kissed her buttocks, every time she had been forced to dance naked for the pleasure of the fat merchant who had been her master and his friends, all these could be laid at Conan's feet.

When at last she had escaped and fled to Nemedia, become the queen of the smugglers of that country, he had appeared again. And before he was done she must needs pack her hard-acquired wealth on sumpter animals and flee again.

She had escaped him, then, but she could not escape his memory, the memory of his building fires in her, fires that she came to crave like the smoker of the yellow lotus craved his pipe. That memory had hounded her, driven her into riotous living and excesses that shocked even the jaded court of Aquilonia. Only when all her gold was gone had she known freedom again. Once more she had taken up the life she loved, living by her wits and her sword. She had sought a new country, Ophir, and raised a new band of rogues.

How many months gone had the first rumors come to her of a huge northerner whose Free-Company was a terror to all who opposed him? How long had she tried to convince herself that it was not the same man who always brought ruin to her? Once more she found herself within the same borders as he, but this time she would not flee. She would be free of him at last. With a sob she raised the dagger high and brought it down.

A strange sound penetrated Conan's dreams—a woman's sob, he thought drowsily—and brought him awake. He had just time to see a shape beside his bed, see the descending dagger, and then he was rolling aside.

The dagger slashed into the mattress where his chest had been, and the force of the missed stab brought his attacker down on top of him. Instantly he seized the shape—the back of his brain noted a curious softness—and hurled it across the room. In the same motion he leaped from the bed, seized the worn leather-wrapped hilt of his broadsword and slung the scabbard aside. It was then that he saw his assailant clearly for the first time.

"Karela!" he exclaimed.

The auburn-haired beauty rising warily from the floor near the wall snarled at him. "Yes, Derketo blast your eyes! And would she had made you sleep just one moment more."

His gaze went to the dagger thrust into his mattress, and his eyebrows raised. But all he said was, "I thought you went to Aquilonia to live the life of a lady."

"I am no lady," she breathed. "I am a woman! And woman enough to put an end to you once and for all!" Her hand went to her shoulder, and suddenly she was rushing at him, brandishing three feet of curved razor-sharp steel.

Anger blazed in Conan's icy blue eyes, and he swung his sword to meet hers with a crash. Shock appeared on Karela's face, her mouth dropping open with incredulity as her blade was nearly wrenched from her grasp. She took a step back, and from that moment was ever defending from his flashing edge. He did not force her back, but every pace backwards she took, he followed. And she could not but move backwards, away from the force of those blows, panting, desperate to attack yet with no slightest opportunity. If he made certain that his sword struck only hers, he also made certain that every blow had his full strength behind it, rocking her to her heels. The cool smile on his face, calm even as he battled her, struck to her heart. It mocked her, wounding more deeply than ever steel could.

"Derketo take you, you over-muscled barbar," she rasped.

With a sharp ring her scimitar was hurled from her. For a breath she froze, then dove for the fallen blade.

Conan tossed his broadsword aside and seized the back of her tunic as she leaped. Fabric already strained by more than generous callimastian curves split down the front; her momentum carried her partly out of her tunic, stripping her half-way to the waist. In an instant Conan had twisted his fistful of cloth, trapping her arms at her sides. He found he had caught a spitting, kicking wildcat. But, he noted, a wildcat who still had the finest, roundest set of breasts he had seen in many a day.

"Coward!" she shouted. "Spawn of a diseased goat! Fight me blade to blade, and I'll spit you like the capon you are!"

Easily he pulled her over to the bed, seated himself, and jerked her across his knees. Easily he controlled her frenzied thrashings.

"Oh, no!" she gasped. "Not that! Cimmerian, I'll cut your heart out! I'll slice your manhood for—"

Her diatribe was cut off with a howl as his big hand landed forcefully on her taut-breeched buttocks.

A fist thumped against the heavy wooden door, and Machaon's voice sounded from the corridor. "What's happening in there, Conan? Are you all right?"

"All is well," Conan replied. "I'm tending to an unruly wench."

That provoked furious struggles from Karela,

futile against his iron grasp. "Release me, Cimmerian," she growled, "or I'll see you hanging by your heels over a slow fire. Unhand me, Derketo shrivel your manhood!"

Conan answered her with a smack that brought another howled curse. "You tried to kill me, wench," he said slowly, punctuating each word with his calloused palm. "You've been untrustworthy from the first day I laid eyes on you. In Shadizar you'd have let me be slain without a word of warning." Karela's shrieked imprecation became incoherent; she kicked frantically at the air, but he did not pause. "In the Kezankian Mountains you betrayed me to a sorcerer. I saved your life there, but in Nemedia you bribed my jailors with gold to torture me. Why? Why a knife for my heart while I lay sleeping? Have I ever harmed you? Is your soul filled with treachery, woman?"

A half-formed plea among her cries penetrated his rage, killing his anger and staying his hand. Karela pleading? Whatever she had done or tried to do, that was not right. As he could not kill her, neither could he bring himself to break her pride completely. He pushed her off his lap to fall with a thump to her knees.

Her tear-streaked face twisted with sobs, Karela's slender hands stole back gingerly to her buttocks. Then, as if suddenly remembering Conan's presence, she tore them away again; moist green eyes glared daggers at him. "May Derketo blast your eyes, Cimmerian," she said jerkily, "and Erlik take your soul for a plaything.

No man has ever treated me as you do and lived."

"And no one," he said quietly, "man or woman, has ever dealt with me as treacherously as you have without incurring my enmity. And yet I cannot find it in me to hate you. But this! Murder was never your way, Karela. Was it for gold? You've always loved gold above all else."

"It was for me!" she spat at him, pounding a small fist on her thigh. Her eyes squeezed shut, and her voice dropped to a whisper. "Your presence turns my muscles to wine. Your eyes on me sap my will. How can I not want you dead?"

Conan shook his head in wonderment. Never had he pretended to understand women, least of all this fierce female falcon. Once more he was convinced that whatever gods had created men had not been the gods who created women.

As she knelt there in disarray, naked to the waist, Conan felt other stirrings than amazement. She was a woman of marvelous curves to brighten the eye, a wonderful blend of softness and firmness to delight the touch. Always she had been able to rouse his desire, though she often attempted to use that to bend him to her will. Abruptly he decided that learning why and how she had come to Ophir could wait. Gently he drew her between his knees.

Her clear green eyes, still tremulous, fluttered open. "What are you doing?" she demanded unsteadily.

He lifted the tattered tunic from her and threw it aside.

Small white teeth bit into her full underlip, and

she shook her head. "No," she said breathlessly. "I will not. No. Please."

Easily he lifted her to the bed, disposed of her soft boots, peeled the tight breeches from her long legs.

"I hate you, Conan." But there was a curious note of pleading in her voice for such a statement. "I came to kill you. Do you not realize that?"

He plucked her dagger from his mattress and held it in two fingers before her gaze. "Take it, if you truly wish me dead."

For the space of three breaths his eyes held hers. Convulsively she turned her face aside. Conan smiled and, casually tossing the dagger to the floor, set about producing cries from her that had naught to do with pain.

6

Sunlight steaming through the windows woke Conan. He opened his eyes and found himself staring at Karela's dagger, once more driven to the hilt into his mattress. The blade held a fragment of parchment. Karela was gone.

"Blast the woman," he muttered, ripping the parchment free. It was covered with a bold, sprawling hand.

> Another debt added to those you already owe me. The next time you will die, Cimmerian. I will not run from another country

because of you. By the Teats of Derketo I swear, I will not.

Frowning, he crumpled the parchment in his fist. It was like the woman, leaving before he woke, with threats but without answers to any of his questions. He had thought she was done with threats altogether; she had enjoyed the night as well as he, of that she had left no doubt.

Hurriedly he dressed and headed into the bowels of the palace. He was still settling his swordbelt about his waist when he entered the long room where his company took their meals, near the kitchen Timeon had given over to them. The simple hearty provender Fabio prepared offended his own cooks, so the lord said. Some score and a half of the mercenary warriors, unarmored but weapons as always belted on, were scattered among crude trestle-tables that had been rooted out of storage in the stables. Machaon and Narus sat by themselves, their attention to the leather jacks of ale in their fists and the wooden bowls of stew before them not so great that they did not note his entrance.

"Ho, Cimmerian," Machaon called out loudly. "How was that, ah, unruly wench last night?" A sprinkling of rough laughter made it clear he had shared his story with the rest.

Could not the accursed fool keep his tongue behind his teeth, Conan thought. Aloud he said, "Double the guards on the roof, Machaon. And see they keep eyes and ears open. A parade of temple virgins would be undetected up there as it is."

Narus laughed dolefully into his ale as Conan straddled a bench across from them. "The wench was *too* unruly, was she? 'Tis the way of all women, to be least accomodating when you want them most."

"Do you have to beat all of them?" Taurianus called, a jealous edge to his bantering tone. "I thought her shrieks would bring the roof down."

"Food!" Conan bellowed. "Must I die of hunger?"

"There's a morsel in that kitchen," Machaon chuckled, "I could consume whole." He nudged Narus as Julia hurried from the kitchen, balancing with some difficulty a bowl of stew, a loaf of bread and a mug of ale.

She was much changed from the last time Conan had seen her. Her long auburn hair was tied with a green ribbon, and pulled back from a face bare of rouge or kohl but streaked with sweat from the heat of the kitchen fires. Her long robe of soft white wool, soot smudged and damp with soapy water, was meant to be modest, he assumed, but it clung to her curves in a way that drew the eye of every man in the room.

"You must speak to that man," she said as she set Conan's meal before him. He stared at her questioningly, and she flung out an arm dramatically toward the kitchen. "That man. Fabio. He threatened me . . . with a switch. Tell him who I am."

Conan scooped up a horn spoon full of stew. In one form or another it served the men of the company for both meals of the day, morning and night. "You work in the kitchens," he said. "That is Fabio's domain. Did a queen somehow come to scrub his pots he'd switch her an she did it badly. You'd best learn to do as he tells you."

Julia sputtered in indignation, the more so when Machaon laughed.

"You've too many airs, wench," the grizzled veteran chortled. "Besides, you're well padded for it." And he applied a full-fingered pinch to punctuate his claim.

Squealing, the auburn-haired girl leaped. To seize Conan's bowl and upend it over Machaon's head. Narus convulsed with laughter so hard that he began coughing.

"Fool girl," Conan growled. "I was eating that. Fetch me another, and quick about it."

"Fetch your own," she snapped back. "Or starve, if you wish to eat with the likes of him." Spinning on her heel, she stalked into the kitchen, her back rigid.

A stunned Machaon sat raking thick gobbets of stew from his face with his fingers. "I've a mind to take a switch to that conceited jade myself," he muttered.

"Go easy with her," Conan said. "She'll learn in time, whether she will or no. She is used to a gentler way of life than that which faces her now."

"I'd like to gentle her," Machaon replied. "But

I'll keep my hands from her as she's yours, Cimmerian."

Conan shook his head. "She's not mine. Nor yours either, till she says she is. There are bawds aplenty in the town, is that your need."

The two men stared at him perplexedly, but they nodded, and he was satisfied. They might think he was in truth laying claim to the girl—though doubtless wondering why he wished to make a secret of it—but they would not demand more of her than she was willing to give. And they would speak it among the company, giving her protection with the others as well. He was not sure why he did not, save for Karela. It was difficult for him to think too much of other women when that fiery wench was about.

In any case, she was likely to give him ten times the trouble Julia did, and without trying half so hard. Karela was a woman who kept her word. If he did not find a way to stop her she would put steel between his ribs yet. Worse, she had a mind for vengeance like a Stygian. It would be like her to destroy the Free-Company, if she could, before killing him.

"Have either of you heard rumors of a woman bandit?" he asked in a carefully casual tone.

"I'll have to bathe to get clean of this," Machaon growled, picking a lump of meat from his hair. He popped it into his mouth. "I've heard no such tales. Women are meant for other things than brigands."

"Nor I," Narus said. "Women are not suited to

the violent trades. Except perhaps that red-haired jade we encountered in Nemedia. She claimed to be a bandit, though I'd never heard of her. The buxom trull was offended I did not know her fame. Remember?"

"She's no trull," Conan said, "and she'll carve your liver does she hear you name her so." Immediately the words were gone he wished he had held his tongue.

"She's here!" Machaon exclaimed. "What was her name?"

"Karela," Narus said. "A temper like a thornbush, that one has."

Machaon laughed suddenly. "She was the wench last night." He shrugged at Conan's glare. "Well, there's no woman in the palace who'd need her bottom warmed to crawl into your blankets. It must have been her. I'd not bed her without my sword and armor, and mayhap a man to watch my back."

"It was her," the Cimmerian said, and added grudgingly, "She tried to put a dagger in me."

"That sounds like the woman I remember," Narus chortled. "From the yells, I'd say you taught her better manners."

"Twould be sport," Machaon crowed, "to stuff her and our Julia into a sack together."

Tears ran down Narus' face from his laughter. "I would pay coin to see that fight."

"Erlik take the pair of you," Conan snarled. "There's more danger in that woman than sport. She thinks she has a grievance against me, and she will cause trouble for the company if she can."

"What can a woman do?" Narus said. "Nothing."

"I would not like to wager my life on that," Conan told him. "Not when the woman is Karela. I want you to ask questions in the taverns and the brothels. 'Tis possible she's changed her name, but she cannot change the way she looks. A red-haired woman bandit with a body like one of Derketo's handmaidens will be known to someone. Tell the others to keep their eyes open as well."

"Why can you not manage her grievance as you did last night?" Machaon asked. "A smack on the bottom and to bed. Oh, very well—" he raised his hands in surrender as Conan opened his mouth for more angry words—"I will ask questions in the brothels. At least it gives me an excuse to spend more time at the House of the Doves."

"Forget not the House of the Honeyed Virgins," Narus added.

Conan scowled wordlessly. The fools did not know Karela as he did. He hoped for the sake of the company that they had time to learn before it was too late. Abruptly he became aware of the horn spoon of stew he still held, and put it in his mouth. "Fabio's cooking horse again," he said when he'd swallowed.

Narus froze with his own spoon half lifted. "Horse?" he gasped. Machaon stared at his bowl as if he expected it to leap from the table at him.

"Horse," Conan said, tossing his spoon to the rough planks. Narus gagged. Not until he was out of the room did the Cimmerian permit a smile to grow on his face. The meat tasted like beef to him, but those two deserved the worrying they were going to do over what Fabio was feeding them.

"Conan!" Julia ran out of the door he had just exited, bouncing off his chest as he turned. Her hands clutched her robe at the waist, twisting nervously. "Conan, you didn't . . . that is, last night . . . I mean. . . ." She stopped and took a deep breath. "Conan, you must speak to Fabio. He struck me. Look." Half-turning she lifted her robe to expose the alabastrine rounds of her buttocks.

Conan was barely able to make out a pink stripe across the undercurve. He raised his gaze to her face. Her eyes were closed; the tip of her tongue continually wetted her full lips.

"I'll speak to him," he said gravely. Her eyes shot open, and a smile blossomed on her face. "I'll tell him he must strike harder than that to make any impression on a stubborn pot-girl."

"Conan!" she wailed. Hastily she covered herself, smoothing the pale wool over her hips. Her eyes became as hard as sapphires. "You had a woman in your . . . your chamber last night. I . . . I was passing in the corridor, and I heard."

He smiled, and watched a blush spread over her cheeks. So she had had her ear pressed to his door, had she? "And what concern is that of yours?" he asked. "You are here to scrub pots and stir the stew, to fetch and carry for Fabio. Not to be wandering parts of the palace where you have no business."

"But you kissed me," she protested. "And the way you kissed me! You cannot make me feel like that, then calmly walk away. I'm a woman, curse you! I'm eighteen! I will not be dismissed like a plaything."

For the second time in the space of hours, he mused, a woman was protesting her womanhood to him. But what a contrast between them. Karela was bold and defiant even as she melted with passion; Julia frightened despite her bluff front. Karela knew well the ways of men and women; Julia was ravaged by a kiss. Karela knew who she was and what she wanted; Julia. . . .

"Do you want to come to my bed?" he said softly, taking her chin in his hand and tilting her face up. Scarlet suffused her face and neck, but she did not try to wrench free. "Say yes, and I'll carry you there this moment."

"The others," she whispered. "They'll know."

"Forget them. 'Tis you must chose."

"I cannot, Conan." She sobbed when he released her, and leaned toward him as if seeking his touch. "I want to say yes, but I fear to. Can you not just . . . take me? Men do such things, I know. Why must you put this burden I do not want on me?"

Barely four years seperated them, yet at that moment he felt it could as well be four hundred. "Because you are not a slave, Julia. You say you are a woman, but when you are truly a woman you will be able to say yes or no, and know it is what you mean to say. But till then . . . well, I take only women to my bed, not frightened girls."

"Erlik curse you," she said bitterly. Instantly she was contrite, one hand raised to touch his cheek. "No, I didn't mean that. You confuse me so. When you kissed me you made me want to be a woman. Kiss me again, and make me remember. Kiss me, and give me the courage I need."

Conan reached for her, and at that instant a bellow of pain and rage echoed down the halls. He spun, grabbing instead for the leather-wrapped hilt of his sword. The cry came again, from above he was certain.

"Timeon," he muttered. His blade came into his hand, and he was running, shouting as he ran. "Rouse yourselves, you poxed rouges! 'Tis the baron screaming like a woman in birth! To arms, curse you!"

Servants and slaves ran hysterically, shrieking and waving their arms at his shouts. Men of the company knocked them aside without compunction as they poured out of the corners where they had been taking their ease. Helmets were tugged on and swords waved as a growing knot of warriors followed the big Cimmerian up marble stairs.

In the corrider outside Timeon's chamber the two guards Conan had caused to be set there stood staring dumbfounded at the ornately carved door. Conan slammed into that door at a dead run, smashing it open.

Timeon lay in the middle of a multi-hued Iranistani carpet, his body wracked by convulsions, heels drumming, plump hands clawing at his throat. His head was thrown back, and every time he managed to fight a breath he loosed it again in a scream. Tivia, his leman, stood with her back to a wall, clutching a cloak about her tightly, her eyes, large and dark, fixed on the helplessly jerking man in an expression of horror. An overturned goblet lay near Timeon, and a puddle of wine soaking into the rug.

"Zandru's Hells!" Conan growled. His eye lit on Machaon, forcing his way through the men crowding the hall. "A physician, Machaon. Quickly! Timeon's poisoned!"

"Boros is in the kitchens," the tattoed man called back. Conan hesitated, and the other saw it. "Curse it, Cimmerian, it'll take half the day to get another."

Timeon's struggles were growing weaker; his screams had become moans of agony. Conan nodded. "Fetch him, then."

Machaon disappeared, and Conan turned back to the man on the floor. How had the fool gotten himself poisoned? The answer might mean life or death to him and the rest of the company. And he had to have the answer before the matter was turned over to the King's torturers. Valdric might ignore the great part of what was happening in his country, but he would not ignore the murder of a noble in the very shadow of his throne.

"Narus!" Conan shouted. The hollow-faced man stuck his head into the room. "Secure the palace. No one leaves, nor any message, till I say. Hurry, man!"

As Narus left Machaon hurried Boros into the room. The former mage's apprentice looked sober at least, Conan was glad to see.

"He's poisoned," the Cimmerian said.

Boros looked at him as he might at a child. "I can see that."

Fumbling in his pouch the gray-bearded man knelt beside Timeon. Quickly he produced a smooth white stone the size of a man's fist and a small knife. With difficulty he straightened one of the baron's arms, pushed up the sleeve of his robe, and made a deep cut. As blood welled up he pressed the white stone to the cut. When he took his hand away the stone remained, tendrils of black appearing in it.

"Bezoar-stone," Boros announced to the room. "Sovereign for poison. A physician's tool, strictly speaking, but I find it useful. Yes."

He tugged at his full beard and bent to study the stone. It was full black, now, and as they watched it became blacker, as a burned cinder, as a raven's wing, and blacker still. Suddenly the stone shattered. In the same moment a last breath rattled in Timeon's throat, and the fat baron was still.

"He's dead," Conan breathed. "I thought you said that accursed stone was sovereign for poison!"

"Look at it!" Boros wailed. "My stone is ruined. 'Twould take poison enough to kill ten men to do that. I could not have saved him with a sack full of bezoar-stones."

"It is murder, then," Narus breathed. A murmur of disquiet ripplied through the men in the corridor.

Conan's hand tightened on his sword. Most of the three-score who followed him now he had recruited in Ophir, a polyglot crew from half a dozen lands, and their allegiance to him was not as strong as that of the original few. They had faced battle with him often—such was the way of the life they led, and accepted by them—but unless he found the murderer quickly fear of being put to the question would do what no enemy had ever been able to. Send them scattering to the four winds.

"Do you want me to find who put the poison in the wine?" Boros asked.

For a moment Conan could only gape. "You can do that?" he demanded finally. "Erlik blast you, are you sober enough? An you make some drunkard's mistake, I'll shave your corpse."

"I'm as sober as a priest of Mitra," Boros replied. "More so than most. You, girl. The wine came from that?" He pointed to a crystal flagon, half-filled with ruby wine, on a table near the bed. Tivia's mouth opened, but no words came out. Boros shook his head. "No matter. I see no other, so the wine must have come from there." Climbing to his feet with a grunt, he delved into his pouch once more.

"Is he truly sober?" Conan said quietly to

Machaon.

The grizzled man tugged nervously at the three thin gold rings dangling from the lobe of his right ear. "I think so. Fabio likes his company, but doesn't let him drink. Usually."

The Cimmerian sighed. Avoiding the hot irons meant trusting a man who might give them all leprosy by mistake.

With a stick of charcoal Boros scribed figures on the tabletop around the flagon of wine. Slowly he began to chant, so softly that the words were inaudible to the others in the room. With his left hand he sprinkled powder from a twist of parchment over the flagon; his right traced obscure patterns in the air. A red glow grew in the crystal container.

"There," Boros said, dropping his hands. "A simple thing, really." He stared at the flagon and frowned. "Cimmerian, the poisoner is close by. The glow tells."

"Crom," Conan muttered. The men who had been in the doorway crowded back into the hall.

"The closer the wine is the one who poisoned it," Boros said, "the more strongly it will glow."

"Get on with it," Conan commanded.

Picking up the flask, Boros moved closer to Machaon. The glow remained unchanged. As he moved past the door, briefly thrusting the flask toward the men outside, it dimmed. Abruptly the bearded man pressed the wine-filled vessel against Narus' chest. The hollow-cheeked man started back; the glow did not brighten.

"A pity," Boros murmured. "You look the part. And that leaves only. . . ."

All eyes in the room went to Tivia, still standing with her back pressed against the wall. Under their gaze she started, then shook her head vigorously, but still said nothing. Boros padded toward her, holding the flagon of glowing wine before him. With each step the light from the wine became brighter until, as he stopped not a pace from the girl, the crystal he held seemed to contain red fire.

She avoided looking at the luminous vessel. "No," she cried. "Tis a trick of some sort. He who placed the poison in the wine put a spell on it."

"Sorcerer as well as poisoner?" Boros asked mildly.

With an oath Conan strode across the room. "The truth, girl! Who paid you?" She shook her head in denial. "I've no stomach for torturing woman," he continued, "but mayhap Boros has some spell to force the truth from you."

"Well, let me see," the old man mused. "Why, yes, I believe I have just the thing. Aging. The longer you take to tell the truth, the older you'll become. But it works rapidly, child. I should speak quickly, were I you, or you may well leave this room a toothless crone. Pity."

Tivia's eyes swiveled desperately from the grim-faced Cimmerian to the kindly-appearing man, calmly stroking his beard, who had voiced the awful threat. "I do not know his name," she said, sagging against the wall. "He wore a mask. I was given fifty pieces of gold and the powder, with fifty more to come when Timeon was dead. I can tell you no more." Sobbing, she slid to the floor. "Whatever you do to me, I can tell you no more."

"What do we do with her now?" Machaon asked. "Give her over to the judges?"

"They'll have her beheaded for slaying a noble," Narus said. "A shame, that. She's too pretty to die like that, and it should hardly count a crime to kill a fool like Timeon."

"Giving her to the judges won't help us," Conan said. He wished he could carry on this conversation with Machaon and Narus in privacy, but the door was open and most of the company had jammed themselves into the corridor. Shut them out now and there might not be a dozen left when the door was opened again. He took a deep breath and went on. "We've lost our patron to an assassin. Ordinarily that would be the death knell for a Free-Company." Uneasy mutters rose in the hall, and he lifted his voice to a roar. "Ordinarily, I said. But Timeon was a supporter of Count Antimides to succeed Valdric. Perhaps we can take service with Antimides, if I deliver the murderer to his hands." At least it was a chance, he thought. Antimides might well find them employment simply to keep secret his own ambitions.

"Antimides?" Machaon said doubtfully. "Cimmerian, 'tis said he's one of the few nobles who does *not* seek the throne at Valdric's death." There were murmured agreements from the hall.

"Timeon spoke too freely in his cups," Conan

said. "Of how Antimides was so clever he had fooled everyone. Of how he himself would be one of the most powerful lords of Ophir once Antimides took the throne."

"Well enough," Machaon said, "but will Antimides take us in service? If he pretends to be aloof from the struggle to succeed Valdric, how will he have need for a Free-Company?"

"He'll take us," Conan said with more confidence than he felt. "Or find us service. I'll take oath on it." Besides, he thought, it was the only course they had open.

"That aging spell," Narus said suddenly. "It seems a strange sort of spell, even for folk as strange as sorcerers are reputed to be. Why would you learn a thing like that?"

"Cheese," Boros replied with a chuckle. "I had a taste for well-aged cheese when I was young, and I created the spell for that. My master flogged me for wasting time. In truth, I doubt it would work on a human."

"You tricked me," Tivia gasped. "Whoreson dog!" she shrieked, launching herself at the bearded man with fingernails clawed. Conan caught her by the arms, but she still struggled to get to the old man, who stared at her in amazement. "I'll pluck your eyes, you old fraud! You dung beetle's offspring! I'll take your manhood off in slices! Your mother was a drunken trull, and your father a poxed goat!"

"Get me a cord to tie her wrists," Conan said, then added, "And a gag." Her tirade was becoming obscene to the point where Machaon was listening with interest. The Cimmerian glared at Narus, who looked abashed as he hurried to fetch what Conan required. It was all he needed, to have to carry a shrieking girl through the streets. Narus returned with strips of cloth, and, muttering to himself, Conan bound his writhing prisoner.

7

Conan drew few stares as he made his way through Ianthe, even with a wiggling, cloak-wrapped woman over his massive shoulder. Or because of the woman. In the streets of the capital, eaten by fear and riddled with suspicion, no one wanted to interfere in something that might even possibly involve them in the troubles beyond the walls of the city. They could see a kidnapping take place or murder done and walk by looking the other way. Who the young giant might be, or why he carried a woman like a sack of grain, no one wanted to know. It could be dangerous to know. It could be dangerous even to appear curious. Therefore none looked too closely at the big Cimmerian or his burden.

He had already been to Antimides' palace. With more than a little difficulty—for the well-fed chamberlain, as proud in his manner as any noble of the land, had seen no reason to give any information whatsoever to a stranger, and a barbarian at that—he learned that the count was a guest of the King. King Valdric liked Antimides' conversation, claiming it was better tonic than any of his physicians or sorcerers could compound. Lord Antimides would be remaining at the royal palace for several days. It was remarkable how free the chamberlain had become with his tongue once a big hand had lifted him until his velvet shoes dangled clear of the floor.

The royal palace of Ophir was a fortress rather than the marble and alabaster edifices erected in the city by nobles. It was not by chance that the King dwelt behind massive granite walls while his lords spent their days in the capital in manors more suited to pleasure than defense. More than once the throne of Ophir had only been held secure by a King taking refuge behind those walls, betimes even refuge from his own nobles. They, having no strong points within Ianthe, had always been forced to abandon the city to the King. And as control of Ianthe was the key to keeping the crown, it was said that whoever held the royal palace held Ophir.

The guards at the towering barbican gate before the royal palace stirred themselves at Conan's approach. A paunch-bellied sergeant, the small triangular beard that was in favor among the nobles waggling on his chins, stepped forward and raised a hand for the Cimmerian to halt.

"What's this, then? Do you mercenaries now think to give us your leftover women?" He chuckled over his shoulder to the pikemen behind him, enjoying his own wit. "Off with you. The royal palace is no place for your drunken carousing. And if you must bind your women, keep them from sight of the army or we will be forced to take cognizance of it."

"She's a gift for Count Antimides," Conan replied, and managed a conspiratorial wink. "A tasty pastry from my patron. Perhaps he wishes to curry favor with a great lord." Tivia redoubled her squirming; unintelligible noises came from behind the twist of rag gagging her.

"She seems not to like the idea," the sergeant chortled.

Conan grinned back at him. "I wager Lord Antimides will know what to do with her, whether she likes it or not."

"That he will. Wait you here." Belly shaking with mirth, the soldier disappeared through the gate. In a few moments he was back with a slender man, his black hair streaked with gray, in a tabard of gold and green, Antimides' colors.

The slender man turned a supercilious gaze on the big Cimmerian. "I am Ludovic," he said sharply, "Count Antimides' steward. You've come to see the count? Who are you?" He appeared to ignore Conan's burden.

"I am Conan of Cimmeria, Captain of the Free-Company in service to Baron Timeon."

Ludovic stroked his beard thoughtfully with a single finger, his eyes traveling to the wriggling girl over Conan's shoulder, then nodded. "Follow me," he commanded. "Perhaps the count will grant you a brief time."

Conan's mouth tightened. All this obsequiousness and play-acting was enough to turn his stomach. But he followed the slender man under the portcullis and into the royal palace.

If a fortress from the outside, the seat of the Kings of Ophir was still a palace within. Gleaming white marble walls, floors covered with a profusion of many-hued mosaicks, fluted alabaster columns. Golden lamps depending on silver chains from high vaulted ceilings, painted with scenes from Ophir's glorious history. Gardens, surrounded by shaded colonnades and filled with rare blossoms from the far corners of the world. Courtyards, tiled with greenstone, where ladies of the court in diaphanous gowns that concealed little of their curves dabbled pale fingers in the babbling waters of ornate fountains.

Their passage left a wake of giggles and murmurs, and stares at the towering Cimmerian and the burden across his broad shoulder. No fear was there here in noticing the unusual, and commenting on it. High-born, hot-eyed women speculated loudly on the pleasures to be found in being carried so—without the cords, of course.

The slender man scowled and increased his pace, muttering under his breath. Conan followed and wished the steward would go faster still.

Finally Ludovic stopped before a wide door carved with the ancient arms of Ophir. "Wait," he said. "I willl see if the count will give you audience."

Conan opened his mouth, but before he could speak, the slender man disappeared through the door, carefully closing it behind him. Audience, he thought disgustedly. Antimides already acted as if he wore the crown.

The door swung open, and Ludovic beckoned him. "Hurry, man. Count Antimides can spare you but a few moments."

Muttering to himself Conan bore his burden within. Immediately he saw the room, his eyebrows lifted in surprise. Perhaps to the casual observer the room would not seem odd, but to one who knew Antimides' ambitions it was clearly a small throne room. An arras depicting a famous battle scene, Moranthes the Great defeating the last army of Acheron in the passes of the Karpash Mountains, hung across one wall. On a dais before the great tapestry was a massive chair with a high back, its dark wood carved with a profusion of leopards and eagles, the ancient symbols of Ophirean Kings.

If the chair seemed not grand enough by itself for a throne, the man seated there made it so. Deep-seated, piercing black eyes flanked a strong, prominent nose. His mouth was hard above a firm chin with its precisely trimmed fashionable beard. Long fingers bearing swordsman's callouses played with a ruby chain hanging across the chest of a robe of cloth-of-gold, slashed to show emerald silk beneath.

"My lord count," Ludovic said, bowing to the man on the dais, "this is the man calling himself Conan of Cimmeria."

" 'Tis my name," Conan said. He lowered Tivia to the thick-carpeted floor, layered in costly multi-colored rugs from Vendhya and Iranistan. She crouched there silently, fright seeming at last to have stilled her rage.

"Count Antimides," Ludovic pronounced grandly, "wishes to know why you have come to him."

"The girl is Tivia," Conan replied, "late mistress of Baron Timeon. Until she did poison him this morn."

Antimides raised a finger, and Ludovic spoke again. "But why have you brought her to him? She should be given to the King's justices."

Conan wondered why the count did not speak for himself. But the ways of nobles were as strange as those of sorcerers. And there were more troublesome matters to concern him. Time for his gamble had come. "As Baron Timeon supported Count Antimides in his quest to succeed Valdric, it seemed proper to bring her before the count. My Free-Company is now without a patron. Perhaps the count can find—"

"My quest!" Antimides burst out, his face choleric with rage. "How dare you accuse me of. . . ." He broke off, grinding his teeth. Ludovic stared at him in obvious surprise. Tivia, her mouth working futilely at her gag, seemed transfixed by his gaze. "You, jade," he breathed. "So you poisoned your master, and were caught at it by this barbar mercenary. Pray that justice is mercifully swift for you. Take her away, Ludovic."

Desperately and futilely Tivia attempted to force words past the cloth gagging her. She flung herself against her bonds as the steward seized her, but the slender man bore her behind the arras with little effort. A door opened and closed behind the hanging, and her cries were cut off.

The Cimmerian reminded himself that Tivia was a self-confessed murderer, and for gold. Still, it pained him to have a hand in a woman's death. In his belief women were not meant to die violently; such was for men. He forced himself to stop thinking of her, and put his attention on the hawk-eyed man on the dais. "Count Antimides, there is still the matter of my Free-Company. Our reputation is well known, and—"

"Your reputation!" Antimides snarled. "Your patron assassinated, and you speak of your reputation. Worse, you come to me with vile accusations. I should have your tongue torn out!"

"Pray, Antimides, what accusations are these to put you in such a rage?"

Both men started at the question; so intent had they been on each other that neither had noticed the entrance of another. Now that Conan saw her, though, he drank her in appreciatively. Long of leg and full of breast, an exotic beauty blending the extraordinary combination of hair like fine, spun silver and large, dark eyes that spoke of deep wells of untapped passion, she moved with sinuous grace, her shimmering scarlet robe, barely opaque and slit up one thigh to a rounded hip, clinging to the curves of breast and thigh.

"Why do you come here, Synelle?" Antimides demanded. "I will not be bothered by your sharp tongue today."

"I have not seen this chamber since you came to the royal palace, Antimides," she said with a dangerous smile. "Seeing it, a suspicious mind might think you sought the crown after all, no matter your public pronouncements of disdain for those who strive beyond the city walls." Antimides' face darkened, and his knuckles grew white on the arms of the chair; Synelle's smile deepened. "But as to why I came. It is said in the palace that a giant northlander came to you bearing a woman wrapped like a package from a fishmonger. Surely I could not miss seeing that? But where is this gift? She is a gift, is she not?"

"This does not concern you, Synelle," Antimides grated. "Go back to your woman's concerns. Have you not needlework waiting?"

Synelle merely arched her eyebrows and moved closer to Conan. "And this is the barbarian? He is certainly as large as was reported. I have a liking for big men." Shivering ostentatiously, she fingered the small, overlapping steel plates on his hauberk. "Are you a mercenary, my handsome northlander?"

He smiled down at her, preening under her sultry look despite himself. "I am captain of a Free-Company, my lady. My name is Conan."

"Conan." Her lips caressed the name. "And why do you come to Antimides, Conan?"

"Enough, Synelle," Antimides barked. "That lies between me and this barbar." He had shot a hard look at the big Cimmerian, a warning to silence.

Conan bristled, and glared back. "I came seeking employment for my company, my lady, but the count has nothing for us." Did the fool think he had no sense? Speaking of Timeon, and the baron's connection to Antimides, would gain him naught and perhaps cost much.

"Nothing?" Pity dripped from Synelle's voice. "But why do you not enter my service?" She raised her eyes boldly to his, and he thought he read a promise in them. "Would you not like to. . . serve me?"

Antimides snorted derisively. "You outdo yourself, Synelle. Are you not satisfied with Taramenon? Do you need an entire company of rogues to satisfy you? Or do you think to contend for the throne yourself?" He roared with laughter at his own wit, but jealous anger colored his glare at Conan.

Synelle's face hardened, and Conan thought she bit back words. At last she spoke in icy tones. "My house is as ancient as yours, Antimides. And did the succession depend on blood alone, I would stand first after Valdric." She drew a deep, shuddering breath, and her smile returned. "I *will* take your company in service, Conan. At twice the gold Antimides would give."

"Done," Conan said. It was not the sort of service he had sought, but the men of his company would at least be pleased with the gold.

The stern-faced count seemed bewildered over what had happened. "Can you be serious, Synelle?" he asked incredulously. "What use have you for such men? You throw your gold away like a foolish girl, on a whim."

"Are not my holdings subject to bandit attacks as others are, now that the army keeps to the cities? Besides," she added with a smouldering look at the Cimmerian, "I like his shoulders." Her voice hardened. "Or do you try to deny me even the right to take men-at-arms in service?"

"Women who need men-at-arms," Antimides replied hotly, "should make alliance with a man who can provide them."

"Why, so I have," she said, her mercurial mood becoming all gaiety. "Come with me, Conan. We have done here."

Conan followed as she moved from the chamber, leaving a fuming Antimides on his wooden throne.

In the corridor she turned suddenly, her mouth open to speak. Conan, caught by surprise, almost walked into her. For a moment she stood, words forgotten and dark eyes wide, staring up at him. "Never have I seen such a man," she whispered then, as if to herself. "Could you be the one to. . . ." Her words trailed off, but she still stood gazing at him as if in a trance.

A woman-wise smile appeared on Conan's face. He had not been sure if her flirting in the other room had been for his benefit or Antimides, but of this he had no doubt. Lifting her into his arms, he kissed her. She returned his kiss with fiery lips, cupping his face with both hands, straining her body to him.

Abruptly she pulled back, horror filling her eyes; her hand cracked against his face. "Loose me!" she cried. "You forget yourself!"

Confused, he set her feet back on the floor. She took two quick steps back from him, one trembling hand to her lips.

"Your pardon, my lady," he said slowly. Did the woman play a game with him?

"I will not have it," she breathed unsteadily. "I will not." Slowly her composure returned, and when she went on her voice was as cold as it had ever been for Antimides. "I will forget what just happened, and I advise you to do the same. I have a house on the Street of Crowns where you may quarter your company. There are stables behind for your horses. Ask for it, and you will be directed. Go there, and await my instructions. And forgot, barbarian, as you value your life.

Did women ever know their own minds, Conan wondered as he watched her stiff back recede down the corridor. How then did they expect men to know them? His consternation could not last long, however. Once more he had managed to save his company. For a time, at least, and that was all a man could ask. All that was left was to convince them there was no disgrace in taking service with a woman. Thinking on that he set about finding his way out of the palace.

8

The massive walls and great outer towers of the royal palace had stood for centuries unchanged, but the interior had altered with every dynasty till it was a warren of corridors and gardens. Soon Conan felt he had visited all of them without making his way to the barbican gate.

Servants rushing through the halls on their duties would not even pause at question from the young barbarian in well-used armor. They were nearly as arrogant as the nobles who lounged in the fountained courts, and inquiries made to richly-clad folk got him little from the haughty men except gibes that brought him close to drawing his sword a time or two. The sleek, languorous women gave inviting smiles and even offers as open as those of any trull on the streets. Such might have appealed had he not been in haste to return to the Free-Company, but even they had only amusement for his ignorance of the palace, tinkling laughter and directions that, followed, sent him in circles.

Conan stepped into yet another courtyard, and found he was staring at King Valdric himself, trailing his retinue as he crossed the greenstone tiles. The King looked worse than Narus, the young Cimmerian thought. Valdric's gold-embroidered state robes hung loosely on a shrunken body that had once weighed half again as much as it did now, and he used the tall, gem-encrusted scepter of Ophir as a walking staff. His golden crown, thickly set with emeralds and rubies from the mines on the Nemedian border, sat low on his brow; and his eyes, sunken deep in a hollow-cheeked face, held a feverish light.

The retinue consisted mainly of men with the full beards of scholars, leavened with a sprinkling of nobles in colorful silks and soldiers of rank in gilded armor, crested helms beneath their arms. The bearded men held forth continuously, competing loudly for Valdric's ear as the procession made its slow way across the courtyard.

"The stars will be favorable this night for an invocation to Mitra," one cried.

"You must be bled, your majesty," another

shouted. "I have a new shipment of leeches from the marshes of Argos."

"This new spell will surely cast the last of the demons from you," a third contributed.

"'Tis time for your cupping, my King."

"This potion. . . ."

"The balance of fluxes and humors. . . ."

Conan made an awkward bow, though none of them seemed to notice him. Kings, he knew, were particular about such things.

When he straightened, King and retinue had gone; but one, a white-haired soldier, had stayed behind and was looking at him. Conan knew him immediately, though he had never met the man. Iskandrian, the White Eagle of Ophir, the general who kept the army aloof from the struggle to succeed Valdric. Despite his age and white hairs, the general's leathery face was as hard as the walls of the palace, his bushy-browed gray eyes clear and sharp. The calloused hand that rested on his sword hilt was strong and steady.

"You're the one who brought the girl to Antimides," the white-haired general said abruptly. "What is your name?"

"Conan of Cimmeria."

"Mercenary," Iskandrian said drily. His attitude toward mercenaries was well known. To his mind no foreign warrior should tread the soil of Ophir, not even if he *was* in service to an Ophirean. "I've heard of you. That fat fool Timeon's man, are you not?"

"I am no one's man but my own," Conan said hotly. "My company did follow Baron Timeon, but we have lately taken the Lady Synelle's colors." At least, they would once he drummed the fact into their heads.

Iskandrian whistled between his teeth. "Then, mercenary, you have gotten yourself a problem along with your lady patron. You've a set of shoulders like an ox, and I suppose women account you handsome. 'Twill light a fire in Taramenon's head to have a man like you near Synelle."

"Taramenon?" Conan remembered Antimides mentioning that name as well. The count had implied this Taramenon had some interest in Synelle, or she in him.

"He is the finest swordsman in Ophir," Iskandrian said. "Best sharpen your blade and pray to your gods for luck."

"A man makes his own luck," Conan said, "and my sword is always sharp."

"A good belief for a mercenary," Iskandrian laughed. "Or a soldier." A frown quickly replaced his mirth. "Why are you in this part of the palace, barbarian? You are far from the path from Antimides' chambers to the gate."

Conan hesitated, then shrugged ruefully. "I am lost," he admitted, and the general laughed again.

"That does not sound like what I've heard of you. But I'll get you a guide." With a wave of his hand he summoned a servant, who bowed low before Iskandrian and ignored Conan. "Take this man to the barbican gate," the general commanded.

"My thanks," the Cimmerian told him. "Yours

are the first words I have heard in some time that were neither mocking nor lies."

Iskandrian eyed him sharply. "Make no mistake, Conan of Cimmeria. You have a reputation for daring and tactical sense, and were you Ophirean, I'd make you one of my officers. But you are a mercenary, and an outlander. Do I have my way, the day will come when you'll leave Ophir with all the haste you can muster or have your ashes scattered here." With that he stalked away.

By the time Conan got back to Timeon's palace, he was uncertain if he had ever had so many opposed to him before. Iskandrian seemed to like him personally, and would see him dead given the chance. Antimides hated him to the bone, and without doubt would like to put him on his funeral fires whether he went to them alive or dead. Synelle he was unsure of; what she said she wanted and what her body said she wanted were opposites, and a man could be shaved at the shoulders for involving himself with such a one as that. Karela claimed that she desired him dead, for all she had not taken the opportunity granted her, and she had a knack of making her desires come true that would make a statue sweat in the circumstances. Then there was the thrice-accursed horned figure. *Had* the second group of attackers been after it, as those first two had been? If they were, he could wager good coin on future attempts, though he still had no clue as to why.

Of course, he could rid himself of the threat of attack by ridding himself of the bronze, but that smacked too much of fright to suit him. Let him but discover why it was worth killing and dying for, and he would willingly shed himself of it, but it was not his way to run from trouble. The Cimmerian almost laughed when he realized that the murder of Timeon was the only trouble to come his way of late that had been resolved.

The guards on the white-columned portico looked at him expectantly, and he put on a smile for their benefit. "All is well," he told them. "We have a patron, and gold to tempt the wenches."

He left them slapping each other's back in relieved laughter, but once he was inside his own smile disappeared. Did they know half of what faced them, they would likely throw down their bows on the spot and desert.

"Machaon!" he called, the name echoing in the high-ceilinged entry hall.

Narus, on the balcony above, shouted down. "He's in the garden. How went matters with Antimides?"

"Assemble the men here," Conan told him, hurrying on.

The tattooed veteran was in the garden as Narus had said, on a bench with a girl, his arms wrapped around her and hers around him. Trust Machaon, the Cimmerian thought with a chuckle, even when waiting to see if they must flee the country. It was about time he found something for merriment in the day.

"Leave her be," he said jovially. "There'll be time for wenches lat—" He broke off as the girl leaped to her feet. It was Julia, cheeks scarlet and breasts heaving.

Clutching her skirts with both hands she looked helplessly at him, turned suddenly tear-filled eyes on Machaon, then ran wailing past the Cimmerian into the palace.

Machaon flung up his hands as Conan rounded on him angrily. "Hear me out before you speak, Cimmerian. She came about me, teasing, and taunted me about kissing her. And she did not try to run when I did it, either."

Conan scowled. He had saved her from a life as a trull, given her honest employment, for this? "She's no camp-follower, Machaon. If you want her, then court her. Don't grab her like a doxy in a tavern."

"Mitra's mercies, man! Court her? You speak as if she were your sister. Zandru's Hells, I've never taken a woman against her will in my life."

The young Cimmerian opened his mouth for an angry retort, and found that none came. If Julia wanted to be a woman fully-fledged, who was he to say her nay? And Machaon was certainly experienced enough to make her enjoy her learning.

"I'm trying to protect someone who apparently doesn't want it any more, Machaon," he said slowly. His reason for seeking out the grizzled man returned to him. "Events have turned as I said they would. We have our patron." Machaon barked a laugh and shook a fist over his head in triumph. "Narus is bringing some of the men to the entry hall. You fetch the rest, and I'll tell the company."

The wide, tapestry-hung hall filled rapidly, threescore men—less the guards posted, for there was no reason to be foolish—crowding it from wall to wall. All looking expectantly to him, Conan thought as he watched them from a perch on the curving marble stair. Boros was among them, he saw, but after the gray-bearded man had ferreted out Tivia for him, he was willing to let him remain. So long as he remained sober and stayed away from magic, at least.

"The company has a new patron," he announced, and the hall exploded in cheers. He waited for the tumult to subside, then added, "Our payment is twice what we were getting." After all, he thought while they renewed their shouts of glee, Synelle had offered to double Antimides' best offer; why would she not do the same for Timeon's? "Listen to me," he called to them. "Quiet, and listen to me. We'll be quartering in a house on the Street of Crowns. We leave here within the hour."

"But whom do we serve?" Taurianus shouted. Others took up the cry.

Conan drew a deep breath. "The Lady Synelle." Flat silence greeted his words.

At last Taurianus muttered disgustedly, "You'd have us serve a woman?"

"Aye, a woman," the Cimmerian answered. "Will her gold buy less when you clink it on the table in a tavern? And how many of you have worried as to how we'd fare if, when someone does succeed Valdric, it turned out we followed the wrong side? We'll be out of that. A woman cannot succeed to the throne. There'll be naught to do but guard her holdings from bandits and spend her gold."

"Twice as much gold?" Taurianus said.

"Twice as much." He had them, now. He could see it in their faces. "Get your belongings together quickly. And no looting! Timeon has heirs somewhere. I want none of you rogues hauled before the justices for theft."

Laughing again, the company began to disperse, and Conan dropped to a seat on the stair. At times it seemed as much of a battle to hold the company together as to fight any of the foes they had been called on to face.

"You handled that as well as any king," Boros said, creakily climbing the stairs.

"Of kings I know little," Conan told him. "All I know are steel and battle."

The gray-bearded man chuckled drily. "How do you think kings get to be kings, my young friend?"

"I neither know nor care," the Cimmerian replied. "All I want is to keep my company together. That and no more."

Sweat glistened on the body of the naked woman stretched taut on the rack, reflecting the flames of charcoal-filled iron cressets of the damp-streaked stone walls of the royal palace dungeon. Nearby, the handles of irons thrust from a brazier of glowing coals, ready in case they were called for. From the way she babbled her tale, punctuating it periodically with screams as the shaven-headed torturer encouraged her with a scourge, they would not be needed.

She had taken money to poison Timeon, but she did not know the man who paid her. He was masked. She became frightened when the first dose of poison showed no effect on the baron, and had placed all she had been given in his wine at once. Before all the gods, she did not know who had paid her.

Antimides listened quietly as the torturer did his work. It amazed him how the struggle for even a chance at life could continue when the person involved had to know there was no hope of it. Time and again, with men and women alike, had he seen it. As soon as he had spoken and seen the expression on Tivia's face, he was aware that she recognized his voice, that she knew him for the man behind the black silk mask. Yet even with the rack and the whip she denied, praying that he would spare her if he thought his secret was safe.

It was odd, too, how dangers suddenly multiplied just when he was in sight of his goal. Had the girl administered the poison in daily doses as directed the finest physician would have said Timeon died of natural causes, and he would have been free of a fool who drank too much and talked too freely when drunk. Then there was the barbarian with the outlandish name, bringing her to him, drawing attention to him when he least wanted it. No doubt that could be laid to Timeon's tongue. But what were the chances the man would fail to tell Synelle what he knew or suspected?

He, Antimides, had been the first to learn of Valdric's illness, the first to prepare to take the throne at his death, and all, he was certain, without being suspected by anyone. While the others fought in the countryside, he remained in Ianthe. When Valdric finally died, they who thought to take the throne, those few who managed to survive his assassins, would find that he held the royal palace. And he who held the royal palace held the throne of Ophir. Now all of his careful plans were endangered, his secrecy threatened.

Something would have to be done about Synelle. He had always had plans for that sharp-tongued jade. Prating about her bloodlines. Of what use were bloodlines in a wench, except with regard to the children she could produce? He had planned to take great pleasure in breaking her to heel, and in using those bloodlines she boasted of to make heirs with an even stronger claim to the throne than himself. But now she had to be done away with, and quickly. And the barbarian as well.

He perked an ear toward Tivia. She was repeating herself. "Enough, Raga," he said, and the shaven-headed man desisted. Antimides pressed a gold coin into the fellow's thick-thingered hand. Raga was bought long since, but it never hurt to ensure loyalties. "She's yours," Antimides told the man. Raga beamed a gap-toothed smile.

"When you are done, dispose of her in the usual fashion."

As the count let himself out of the dungeon Tivia's shrieks were rising afresh. Lost in his planning for Synelle and the barbarian, Antimides did not hear.

9

The house on the Street of Crowns was a large square, two stories high, around a dusty central court, with the bottom floor of the two sides being given over to stables. A wooden-roofed balcony, reached by stairs weakened from long neglect, ran around the courtyard on the second level. Dirty red roof tiles gleamed dully in the late afternoon sun; flaking plaster on the stone walls combined with shadows to give the structure a leprous appearance. An arched gate, its hinges squealing with rust, led from the street to the courtyard, where a dusty fountain was filled with withered brown leaves.

"Complete with rats and fleas, no doubt," Narus said dolefully as he dismounted.

Taurianus sat his horse and glared about him. "For this we left a palace?" A flurry of doves burst from an upper window. "See! We're expected to sleep in a roost!"

"You've all grown too used to the soft life in a palace," Conan growled before the mutters could spread. "Stop complaining like a herd of old women, and remember the times you've slept in the mud."

"'Twas better than this, that mud," Taurianus muttered, but he climbed down from his saddle.

Grumbling men began carrying blanket rolls and bundles of personal belongings in search of places to settle themselves. Others led their horses into the stables; curses quickly floated out as to the number of rats and cobwebs. Rotund Fabio hurried in search of the kitchens, trailed by a half-running Julia, her arms full of soot-blackened pots and bundles of herbs, strings of garlic and peppers dangling from her shoulders. Boros stood at the gate staring about him in amazement, though he certainly slept in little better as a matter of course. Synelle, Conan thought, had much to learn about what was properly provided a Free-Company.

They had attracted entirely too much attention for Conan's taste during their search for the house. Three-score armored men on horseback, laden with sacks and cloak-wrapped bundles till they looked like a procession of country peddlers, could not help but draw eyes even in a city that assiduously attempted to avoid seeing anything that might be dangerous. The Cimmerian would just as soon they could all have become invisible till the matter of Timeon's death was forgotten. And he was none too eager to look into any of those bundles, many of which clinked and seemed heavier than they had a right to be. For all his injunction against looting he was sure they were filled with silver goblets and trinkets of gold. More of those following him than not, the Ophireans most certainly, were light-fingered at the best of times.

Giving his horse over to one of the men, the big Cimmerian went in search of a room for himself, his blanket roll over one shoulder and the sack containing the bronze under his arm. Save for weapons and armor, horse and change of clothes, they were all the possessions he had.

Soon he found a large, corner room on the second floor, with four windows to give it light. A wad of straw in one corner showed that a rat had been nesting there. Two benches and a table stood in the middle of the floor, covered with heavy dust. A bed, sagging but certainly large enough even for his height, was jammed against a wall. The mattress crackled with the sound of dried husks when he poked it, and he sighed, remembering the goose-down mattress in Timeon's palace. Think of the mud, he reminded himself sternly.

Machaon's voice drifted up from the courtyard. "Conan, where are you? There's news!"

Tossing his burdens on the bed, Conan hurried

out onto the balcony. "What word? Has Synelle summoned us?"

"Not yet, Cimmerian. The assassins were busy last night. Valentius fled his palace after three of his own guards turned their blades on him. 'Tis said others of his men cut them down, but the lordling now seems affrightened of his own shadow. He has taken refuge with Count Antimides."

Conan's eyebrows went up. Antimides. The young fool had unknowingly put himself in the hands of one of his rivals. Another lord removed from the race, this one by his own hand, in a manner of speaking. Who stood next in the bloodright after Valentius? But what occurred among the contending factions, he thought, no longer concerned him or his company.

"We're done with that, Machaon," he laughed. "Let them all kill each other."

The grizzled veteran joined his laughter. "An that happens, mayhap we can make you King. I will settle for count, myself."

Conan opened his mouth to reply, and suddenly realized a sound that should not be there had been impinging on his brain. Creaking boards from the room he had just left. No rat made boards creak. His blade whispered from its sheath, and he dove through the door, followed by Machaon's surprised shout.

Four startled men in cast-off finery, one just climbing in the window, stared in shock at the appearance of the young giant. Their surprise lasted but an instant; as he took his first full step into the room, swords appeared in their fists and they rushed to attack.

Conan beat aside the thrust of the first to reach him, and in the same movement planted a foot in the middle of his opponent's dirty gray silk tunic. Breath left the man in an explosive gasp, and he fell in a heap at the feet of a thick-mustached man behind him. The mustached man stumbled, and the tip of Conan's blade slashed his throat in a fountain of blood. As the dying man fell atop the first attacker, a man with a jagged scar down his left cheek leaped over him, sword hacking wildly. Conan dropped to a crouch—whistling steel ruffled the hair atop his head—and his own blade sliced across scar-face's stomach. With a shriek the man dropped in a heap, both hands clutching at thick ropes of entrails spilling from his body. A sword thrust from the floor slid under the metal scales of Conan's hauberk, slicing his side, but the Cimmerian's return blow struck through gray-tunic's skull at the eyes.

"Erlik curse you!" the last man screamed. Sly-faced and bony, he had been the last into the room, and had not joined in the wild melee. "Eight of my men you've slain! Erlik curse all your seed!" Shrieking, he dashed at Conan with frenzied slashes.

The Cimmerian wanted to take this man alive, in condition to answer questions, but the furious attack was too dangerous to withstand for long. A half-mad light of fear and rage gleamed in the man's sweaty face, and he screamed with every blow he made. Three times their blades crossed, then blood was spurting from the stump of sly-face's neck as his head rolled on the floor.

With a clatter of boots mercenaries crowded into the room, led by Machaon, all with swords in hand. "Mitra, Cimmerian," the tattooed man said, scanning the scene of carnage. "Couldn't you have saved just one for us?"

"I didn't think of it," Conan replied drily.

Julia forced her way through the men. When she saw the bodies her hands went to her face, and she screamed. Then her eyes lit on Conan, and her composure returned as quickly as it had gone. "You're wounded!" she said. "Sit on the bed, and I will tend it."

For the first time Conan became aware of a razor's edge of fire along his ribs, and the blood wetting the side of his hauberk. "'Tis but a scratch," he told her. "Get these out of here," he added to Machaon, gesturing to the corpses.

Machaon told off men to cart the dead away.

Julia, however, was not finished. "Scratch or not," she said firmly, "if it is not tended you may grow ill. Fetch me hot water and clean clothes," she flung over her shoulder, as she attempted to press Conan toward the bed. "Clean, mind you!" To everyone's surprise two of the mercenaries rushed off at her command.

Amused, Conan let her have her way. Muttering to herself she fussed over getting his metal-scaled leather tunic off. Gently she palped the flesh about the long, shallow gash, a thoughtful frown on her face. She seemed unconcerned about his blood on her fingers.

"It seems you are ahead once more," Machaon said ruefully, before leaving them alone.

"What did he mean by that?" she asked absently. "Don't talk. Let the wound lie still. There are no ribs broken, and I will not have to sew it, but after it is bandaged you must take care not to exert yourself. Perhaps if you lie—" She broke off with a gasp. "Mitra protect us, what is that evil thing?"

Conan followed her suddenly frightened gaze to the bronze figure, lying on the bed and now out of the sack. "Just something I bought as a gift for Machaon," he said, picking it up. She backed away from him. "What ails you, girl? The thing is but dead metal."

"She is right to be affrighted," Boros said from the door. His eyes were fixed on the bronze as on a living demon. "It is evil beyond knowing. I can feel the waves of it from here."

"And I," Julia said shakily. "It means me harm. I can feel it."

Boros nodded sagely. "Aye, a woman would be sensitive to such. The rites of Al'Kiir were heinous. Scores of men fighting to the death while the priestesses chanted, with the heart of the survivor to be ripped from his living body. Rites of torture, with the victim kept alive and screaming on the altar for days. But the most evil of all, and the most powerful, was the giving of women as sacrifices. Or as worse than sacrifices."

"What could be worse than being sacrificed?" Julia asked faintly.

"Being given to the living god whose image that is," Boros answered, "to be his plaything for all eternity. Such may well have been the fate of the women given to Al'Kiir."

Julia swayed, and Conan snapped, "Enough, old man! You frighten her. I remember now that you mentioned this Al'Kiir once before, when you were drunk. Are you drunk now? Have you dredged all this from wine fumes in your head?"

"I am deathly sober," the gray-bearded man replied, "and I wish I were pickled in wine like a corpse. For that is not only an image of Al'Kiir, Cimmerian. It is a necessary, a vital part of the worship of that horrible god. I thought all such had been destroyed centuries ago. Someone attempts to bring Al'Kiir again to this world, and did they have that unholy image they might well succeed. I, for one, would not care to be alive if they do."

Conan stared at the bronze gripped in his big hand. Two men had died attempting to take it from him in the shop. Three more perished in the second attack, and that that had been for the same thing he no longer doubted. Before he himself died, sly-face had accused Conan of slaying about eight of his men. The numbers were right. Those who wanted to bring back this god knew the Cimmerian had the image they needed. In a way he was relieved. He had had stray thoughts that some of these attacks, including the one just done, were Karela's work.

The men fetching the hot water and bandages entered the room; Conan thrust the image under his blanket roll and signed the others to silence until they were gone.

When the three were alone again, Julia spoke. "I'll tend your wound, but not if you again remove that evil thing from its hiding. Even there I can sense it."

"I'll leave it where it is," the young Cimmerian said, and she knelt beside him and busied herself with bathing and bandaging his wound. "Go on with your telling, Boros," he continued. "How is it this god cannot find his own way to the world of men? That seems like no god to fear greatly, for all his horns."

"You make jokes," Boros grumbled, "but there is no humor in this. To tell you of Al'Kiir I must speak of the distant past. You know that Ophir is the most ancient of all the kingdoms now existing in the world, yet few men know aught of its misty beginnings. I know a little. Before even Ophir was, this land was the center of the worship of Al'Kiir. The strongest and handsomest of men and the proudest and most beautiful of women were brought from afar for the rites of which I have spoken. But, as you might imagine, there were those who opposed the worship of Al'Kiir, and foremost of these were the men who called themselves the Circle of the Right-Hand Path."

"Can you not be shorter about it?" Conan said. "There's no need to dress the tale like a storyteller in the marketplace."

Boros snorted. "Do you wish brevity, or the facts? Listen. The Circle of the Right-Hand Path was led by a man named Avanrakash, perhaps the most powerful practitioner of white magic who has ever lived."

"I did not know there was such a thing as white magic," Conan said. "Never have I seen a sorcerer who did not reek of blackness and evil as a dunghill reeks of filth."

This time the old man ignored him. "These men made contact with the very gods, 'tis said, and concluded a pact. No god would stand against Al'Kiir openly, for they feared that in a war between gods all that is might be destroyed, even themselves. Some—Set, supposedly, was one—declared themselves apart from what was to happen. Others, though, granted those of the Right-Hand Path an increase in powers, enough so that they in concert could match a single god. You can understand that they would not give so much to a single man, for that would make him a demigod at the least, nor enough to all of them that they could not be vanquished easily by as few as two of the gods in concert."

Despite himself Conan found himself listening intently. Julia, her mouth hanging open in wonderment, held the ties of the Cimmerian's bandages forgotten as she followed Boros' words.

"In the battle that followed, the face of the land itself was changed, mountains raised, rivers altered in their courses, ancient seas made desert. All of those who marched against Al'Kiir, saving only Avanrakash, perished, and he was wounded to the death. Yet in his dying he managed with a staff of power to sever Al'Kiir from the body the god wore in the world of men, to seal the god from that world.

"Then came rebellion among the people against the temples of Al'Kiir, and the first King of Ophir was crowned. Whole cities were razed so that not even their memory remains. All that kept so much as the name of Al'Kiir in the minds of men was destroyed.

"The earthly body of the god? Men tried to destroy that as well, but the hottest fires made no mark, and the finest swords shattered against it. Finally it was entombed beneath a mountain, and the entrances sealed up, so that with time men should forget its very existence.

"They both succeeded and failed, they who would have destroyed the god's name and memory, for the name Tor Al'Kiir was given to the mountain, but for centuries gone only a scattered few have known the source of that name, though all men know it for a place of ill luck, a place to be avoided.

"I believed I was the last to have the knowledge I possess, that it would go to my funeral fires with me. But I have seen lights in the night atop Tor Al'Kiir. I have heard whispers of knowledge sought. Someone attempts to bring Al'Kiir back to this world again. I was sure they would find only failure, for the lack of that image or its like, but do they get their hands on it, blood and lust and slavery will be the portion of all men."

Conan let out a long breath when the old man at

last fell silent. "The answer is simple. I'll take the accursed thing to the nearest metalworker's shop and have it melted down."

"No!" Boros cried. A violent shudder wracked him, and he combed his long beard with his fingers in agitation. "Without the proper spells that would loose such power as would burn this city from the face of the earth, and perhaps half the country as well. Before you ask, I do not know the necessary spells, and those who do would be more likely to attempt use of the image than its destruction."

"That staff," Julia said suddenly. "The one Avanrakash used. Could it destroy the image?"

"A very perceptive question, child," the old man murmured. "The answer is, I do not know. It might very well have that power, though."

"Much good that does," Conan muttered. "The staff is no doubt rotted to dust long ago."

Boros shook his head. "Not at all. 'Tis a staff of power, after all, that Staff of Avanrakash. Those men of ancient times revered its power, and made it the scepter of Ophir, which it still is, though covered in gold and gems. It is said 'twas the presence of that scepter, carried as a standard before the armies of Ophir, that allowed Moranthes the Great to win his victories against Acheron. If you could acquire the scepter, Conan. . . ."

"I will not," Conan said flatly, "attempt to steal King Valdric's scepter on the off chance that it might have some power. Zandru's Nine Hells, the man uses the thing as a walking staff! It's with him constantly."

"You must understand, Cimmerian," Boros began, but Conan cut him off.

"No! I will put the thrice-accursed beneath the floor boards yonder until I can find a place to bury it where it will never be found. Crack not your teeth concerning any of this until I can do so, Boros. And stay away from the wine till then as well."

Boros put on a cloak of injured dignity. "I have been keeping this particular secret for nearly fifty years, Cimmerian. You've no need to instruct me."

Conan grunted, and let Julia lift his arm to finish her bandaging. It was yet another rotten turnip to add to the stew before him. How to destroy a thing that could not be destroyed, or as well as could not, given the lack of trustworthy sorcerer, and such were as rare as virgin whores. Still, he was worried more about Karela than any of the rest. What, he wondered, was that flame-haired wench plotting?

10

Karela reined in her bay mare at the edge of the tall trees, thick with the shadows of the setting sun, and studied the small peak-roofed hut in the forest clearing. A single horse was tethered outside, a tall black warmount colorfully caprisoned for a noble, though its scarlet and black bardings bore the sign of no house. A lone man was supposed to meet her there, but she would wait to make sure.

The snap of a fallen twig announced the arrival of a man in coarse woolen tunic and breeches of nondescript brown that blended well with the shadows. The sound was deliberate, she knew, that she, being warned, would not strike with the Turanian scimitar she wore on her belt at his sudden appearance; Agorio could move in the woods as silently as the fall of a feather, did he choose. Both the man's ears had been cropped for theft, and his narrow face bore a scar that pulled his right eye into a permanent expression of surprise. "He came alone, my lady, as you instructed," he said.

Karela nodded. They were not so good as her hounds of the Zamoran plains, the men who followed her now. Most had been poachers, and petty thieves if the opportunity presented itself, when she found them, and they had little liking for the discipline she forced on them, but given time, she would make them as good and as feared as any band of brigands that ever rode.

She rode slowly into the clearing, sitting her saddle as proudly as any queen. She disdained to show more caution than she had already. As she dismounted she drew her curved sword, and pushed open the crude plank door of the hut with the blade.

Within was a single room with the rough furnishings to be expected in such a place, dimly lit by a fire on the hearth. Dust covered everything, and old, dried cobwebs hung from the bare, shadowed rafters. A man with a plain scarlet surcoat over his armor stood in the center of the dirt floor, his thumbs hooked casually in the wide, low-slung belt that supported his scabbarded longsword. He was almost as tall as Conan, she noted, with shoulders nearly as broad. A handsome man, with an eye for women from the smile that came to his lips when she entered.

She kicked the door shut with her heel and waited for him to speak. She did not sheath her blade.

"You are not what I expected, girl," he said finally. His dark eyes caressed the curves beneath her snug-fitting jerkin and breeches. "You are quite beautiful."

"And you've made your first mistake." There was danger in her voice, though the man did not seem to realize it. "No man calls me girl. I'll have the answers to some questions before we go further. Your message came to me through ways I thought known only to a trusted few. How did you come to know of them? Who are you, and why would you send me fifty golds, not knowing if I'd come or not?" For that was the amount that had accompanied the message.

"Yet you did come," he said, radiating cool confidence. From beneath his surcoat he produced two bulging leather purses and tossed them to the table. They clinked as they landed. "And here are a hundred more pieces of gold, if you will undertake a commission for me, with as many to follow at its completion."

Her tone hardened. "My questions."

"Regrettably I cannot answer," he said smoothly. "You need have no fear of being seized, my inquisitive beauty. I came alone, as I said I would. There are no men in the trees about us."

"Except my own," she said, and was pleased to see surprise flicker across his face.

He recovered his aplomb quickly. "But that is to be expected. When I heard of a bandit band led by a . . . a woman, I knew they must be very good indeed to long survive. You see, you're becoming famous. Put up your blade. Eastern, is it not? Are you from the east, my pretty brigand? You have not the coloring of the eastern beauties I have known, though you are as lovely as all of them together."

His smile deepened, a smile she was sure sent he expected to send tingles through every woman favored with it. And likely had his expectations met, she admitted. She also knew that only her danger at his manner—girl, indeed! My pretty brigand. Ha!—armored her against it. She held hard to that anger, prodded at it. She did, however, sheathe her sword.

"I'll not tell you my history," she growled, "when I get not even your name in return. At least you can tell me what I am to do for these two hundred gold pieces."

His smoldering-eyed study of her did not end, but at least it abated. "Baron Inaros is withdrawing from his keep to his palace in Ianthe. He is not involved in the current struggles. Rather, he is afraid of them. 'Tis the reason for his move, seeking the safety of the capital. His guards will be few in number, not enough to trouble a bold band of brigands. For the two hundred you will bring me his library, which he brings with him in two carts. And of course you may keep anything else you take from his party."

"A library!" Karela burst out. "Why would you

pay two hundred pieces of gold, two hundred and fifty, in truth, for a collection of dusty scrolls?"

"Let us simply say I am a collector of rarities, and that there are works in Inaros' possession I am willing to pay that price for."

Karela almost laughed. This man as a collector of rare parchments was one thing she would not believe. But there was no profit in calling him liar. "Very well," she said, "but I will have two hundred gold pieces upon delivery of these, ah, rarities." It was her turn to smile. "Are you willing to pay *that* price?"

He nodded slowly, once more eyeing her up and down. "I could almost consider it cheap, though you'd best not try to press me too far, or I may take my commission to another who, if not so pretty, is also not so greedy. Now let us seal the bargain."

"What," she began, but before she could finish he took a quick step and seized her. Roughly he crushed her against him; she could not free an arm enough to draw her sword.

"I have a special way of sealing pacts with women," he chuckled. "Struggle if you wish, but you will enjoy it before 'tis done." Suddenly he froze at the sharp prick of her dagger point against his neck.

"I should slit your throat," she hissed, "like the pig you are. Back away from me. Slowly."

Obediently he stepped backwards, his face a frozen mask of rage. As soon as he was clear of her dagger stroke, his hand went to his sword.

She flipped the dagger, catching it by the point.

"Will you wager your life that I cannot put this in your eye?" His hand fell back to his side.

Desperately Karela fought her own desire to kill him. He deserved it clearly, to her thinking, but how could she keep it secret that she had slain a man come to hire her? Such things never remained buried long. All who heard the tale would think she had done it for the coins on the table, and there would be no more offers of gold.

"You codless spawn of a diseased camel!" she spat in frustration. "But recently I saw a figure that reminds me of you. An ugly thing to curdle any woman's blood, as you are. All horns and fangs, with twice as much manhood as any man, and like to think with that manhood, as you do, were it alive. If you have any manhood."

He had gone very still as she spoke, anger draining from his face, and there was barely contained excitement in his voice as he spoke. "This figure? How many horns did it have? How many eyes? Was it shaped otherwise like a man?"

Karela stared at him in amazement. Was this some attempt to draw her off guard, it was most surely a strange one. "What interest can you have in it?"

"More than you can possibly know. Speak, woman!"

"It was like a man," she said slowly, "except that it had too many fingers and toes, and claws on all of them. There were four horns, and three eyes. And a reek of evil as strong as yours."

His smile returned, but not for her this time. To her surprise it was a smile of triumph. "Forget Inaros," he said. "Bring me that figure, and I will give you *five* hundred pieces of gold."

"Think you I'd still take your gold," she said incredulously, "after this?"

"I think you'd take five hundred pieces of it if it came from Erlik himself. Think, woman. Five hundred!"

Karela hesitated. It was a tempting amount. And to think she could earn it at the Cimmerian's expense made it more so. But to deal with this one. "Done," she was surprised to hear herself say. "How shall we meet again, when I have the thing?"

He tugged off his brilliant red surcoat, revealing gilded armor beneath. "Have a man wearing this over his tunic stand before the main gate of the royal palace when the sun is at its zenith, and on that day at dusk I will come to this hut with the gold."

"Done," Karela said again. "I will leave you, now, and I advise you to wait the time it takes to count one thousand—an you can count—before following, else you will discover whether that pretty armor will avail you against crossbow bolts." With that she backed from the hut, and scrambled into her saddle.

As she rode into the forest she found that she almost felt like singing. Five hundred pieces of gold and another stroke against the Cimmerian, if a small one. But there would be greater, the first already under way. This time it would be Conan who was forced to flee, not her. He would flee, or he would die.

Synelle paced the floor of her sleeping chamber like a caged panther, hating her agitation yet unable to quell it. Silver lamps lit the room against the night at the windows, lending a sheen to the gossamer hangings about her bed. Her pale hair hung damp with sweat, though the night was cool. Normally she guarded her exotic beauty jealously, never allowing a curl to be out of place or the slightest smudging of rouge even when she was alone, but now turmoil filled her to the exclusion of all else.

For the hundreth time she stopped before a mirror and examined her full, sensuous lips. They looked no different than they always had, but they felt swollen. With a snarl of rage she resumed her pacing, her long robe of canescent silk clinging to every curve of her body. She was aware of every particle of the sleek gray material sliding on the smoothness of her skin.

Ever since that . . . that barbarian had kissed her she had been like this. She could not stop thinking about him. Tall, with shoulders like a bull and eyes like a winter lake. A crude, unmannered lout. Wild and untamed, like a lion, with arms that could crush a woman in his embrace. She felt like bubbling honey inside. She could not sleep; already this night she had tossed for hours in torment, filled to the brim with feelings she had never before experienced.

Why had she even taken the Free-Company in service? Only to spite Antimides, as had always given her pleasure in the past. There was no reason to keep it, except that Antimides would certainly think he had won in some fashion if she dismissed them. And there was the barbarian.

Desperately she tried to force her mind away from Conan. "I will not give myself to him!" she cried. "Not to any man! Never!"

There were other things to think about. There had to be. The women. Yes. Of the bronze image of Al'Kiir, she was certain now. The men Taramenon had sent after Galbro would bring it to her. But she needed a woman for the rite, and not any woman would do. This woman must be beautiful above all others about her, proud to the point of fierceness. Proud women there were, but plain or old or disqualified on a score of other points. Beautiful women abounded, and some had pride, but where was the fierceness? Without exception they would tremble at a man's anger, give way to his will eventually, for all they might resist a time.

Why did they have to be so? Yet she could understand a little now. What woman could resist a man like the barbarian. Him again! She pounded a small fist on her sleek thigh in frustration. Why did he continually invade her thoughts?

Suddenly her face firmed with determination. She strode to a marble-topped table against the tapestried wall, touched her fingers to a twist of parchment there. Within were three long, black, silky hairs, left on her robe when the barbarian. . . . Her hand trembled. She could not think of that now; her mind must be clear. It must be.

Why did it have to be him? Why not Taramenon? Because he had never affected her as Conan did? Because she had toyed with him so long that only the pleasure of toying remained?

"It will be Conan," she whispered. "But it will be as I wish." Her hand closed on the parchment, and she swept from the room.

Slaves, scrubbing floors in the hours when their mistress was not usually about, scrambled from her path, pressing their faces to the marble tiles in obeisance. She took no more notice of them than she did of the furnishings.

Straight to her secret chamber she went, closing the door behind her and hurriedly lighting lamps. Triumph sped her movements, the certainty of triumph soon to be realized.

At the table covered with beakers and flasks she carefully separated one hair from the packet. One would be enough, and that would leave two in case further magicks must be worked on the huge barbarian.

On a smooth silver plate she painted the sign of the horns, the sign of Al'Kiir, in virgin's blood, using a brush made from the hair of an unborn child and handled with a bone from its mother's finger. Next two candles were affixed to the plate, one on either side, and lit. Black, they were, made from the rendered tallow of murdered men, stolen from their graves in blessed ground.

Haste was of the essence, now, but care, too, lest disaster come in place of what she sought. Gripping her tongue between her teeth, she painted the final symbols about the edge of the plate. Desire. Lust. Need. Wanting. Passion. Longing.

Quickly she threw aside the brush, raised her hands above her head, then lowered them before her, palms up, in a gesture of pleading. In the arcane tongue she had learned so painfully, Synelle chanted, soft spoken words that rebounded from the pale walls like shouts, invoking powers linked to Al'Kiir yet not of him, powers of this world, not of the void where he was imprisoned. In the beginning she had attempted to use those powers to make contact with Al'Kiir. The result had been a fire that gutted a tower of her castle, lying halfway to the Aquilonian border, a burning with flames that no water could extinguish, flames that died only when there was not even a cinder left to burn. For long after that she had feared to try again, not least for the stares directed at her and the whispers of sorcery at the castle of Asmark. To cover herself she had brought charges of witchcraft against a woman of the castle, a crone of a scullery maid who looked the part of a witch, and had her burned at the stake. Synelle had learned care from that early mistake.

Slowly the candles guttered out in pools of their own black tallow, and Synelle lowered her hands, breathing easily for the first time in hours. The painted symbols on the plate, the hair, all were ash. A cruel smile touched her lips. No more was there need to fear her desires. The barbarian was hers, now, to do with as she would. Hers.

11

Conan's skin crawled as he walked across the dusty courtyard of the house where his company was quartered. The hairs on his body seemed to move by themselves. Bright sunlight streamed from the golden globe climbing into the mourning sky; chill air seemed to surround him. It had been so ever since he woke, this strangeness, and he had no understanding of why.

Fear the big Cimmerian dismissed as a cause. He knew his fears well, and had them well in hand. No fear could ever affect him so, who had, in his fear years, faced all manner of things that quelled the hearts of other men. As for the image, and even Al'Kiir, he had confronted demons and sorcerers before, as well as every sort of monster from huge flesh-eating worms to giant spiders dripping corrosive poison from manibles that could pierce the finest armor to a dragon of adamantine scales and fiery breath. Each he had conquered, and if he was wary of such, he did not fear them.

"Cimmerian," Narus called, "come get yourself a cloak."

"Later," Conan shouted back to the hollow-faced, who was rooting with others of the company in the great pile of bales and bundles that had been delivered by carts that morning.

Synelle had finally seen to the needs of the Free-Company she had taken in service. Bundles of long woolen cloaks of scarlet, the color of her house, had been tumbled into the courtyard, along with masses of fresh bedding and good wool blankets. There had been knee-high Aquilonian boots of good black leather, small mirrors of polished metal from Zingara, keen-bladed Corinthian razors, and a score of other things, from a dozen countries, that a soldier might need. Including a sack of gold coin for their first pay. The mercenaries had turned the morning into a holiday with it all. Fabio had kept Julia running all morning, staggering under sacks of turnips and peas, struggling with quarters of beef and whole lamb carcasses, rolling casks of wine and ale to the kitchens.

Fabio found Conan by the dry fountain. The fat,

round cook was mopping his face with a rag. "Conan, that lazy wench you saddled me with has run off and hidden somewhere. And look, she hasn't swept a quarter of the courtyard yet. Claims she's a lady. Erlik take her if she is! She has a mouth like a fishwife. Flung a broom at my head in my own kitchen, and swore at me as vilely as I've ever heard from any man in the company."

Conan shook his head irritably. He was in no mood to listen to the man's complaints, not when he felt as if ants were skittering over his body. "If you want the courtyard swept," he snapped, "see to it yourself."

Fabio stared after him, open-mouthed, as he stalked away.

Conan scrubbed is fingers through his hair. What was the matter with him? *Could* that accursed bronze, the evil of it that Julia claimed to sense, have affected him from beneath the floor while he slept?

"Cimmerian," Boros said, popping out of the house, "I've been seeking you everywhere."

"Why?" Conan growled, then attempted to get a hold of himself. "What do you want?" he asked in a slightly more reasonable tone.

"Why, that image, of course." The old man looked around, then lowered his voice. "Have you given any thought to destroying it? The more I think on it, the more it seems the Staff of Avanrakash is the only answer."

"I am not stealing the Erlik-accursed scepter," Conan grated. When he saw Machaon approaching, the Cimmerian felt ready to burst.

The grizzled mercenary eyed the bigger man's grim face quizzically, but said only, "We're being watched. This house, that is."

Conan gripped his swordbelt tightly with both hands. This was business of the company, perhaps important business, and he had worked too long and too hard for that to allow even his own temper to damage it.

"Karela's men?" he asked in what was almost his normal voice. It took a great effort to maintain it.

"Not unless she's begun taking fopling youths into her band," Machaon replied. "There are two of them, garbed and jeweled for a lady's garden, with pomanders stuck to their nostrils, wandering up and down the street outside. They show an especial interest in this house."

Young nobles, Conan thought. They could be Antimides' men, if the count was concerned as to how much Conan was talking of what he knew. Or they could be seeking the image, though nobles hardly meshed with the sort who had tried for it thus far. They might even be this Taramenon, Synelle's jealous suitor, and a friend, come to see for themselves what manner of man the silvery-haired beauty had taken in service. Too many possibilities to reason out, certainly not in his present state of mind.

"If we seize them when next they pass," he began, and the two listening to him recoiled.

"You must be mad," Boros gasped. "'Tis the image, Cimmerian. It affects you ill. It must be destroyed quickly."

"I know not what this old magpie is chattering about," Machaon said, "but seizing nobles . . . in broad daylight from a street in the middle of Ianthe . . . Cimmerian, it would take more luck than ten Brythunian sages to get out of the city with our heads still on our shoulders."

Conan squeezed his eyes shut. His brain whirled and spun, skittering through fogs that veiled reason. This was deadly dangerous; he *must* be able to think clearly, or he could lead them all to disaster.

"My Lord Conan?" a diffident voice said.

Conan opened his eyes to find a barefoot man in the short white tunic of a slave, edged in scarlet, had joined them. "I'm no lord," he said gruffly.

"Yes, my lor . . . uh, noble sir. I am bid tell you the Lady Synelle wishes your presence at her house immediately."

Images of the sleek, full-breasted noblewoman flickered into Conan's mind, clearing aside all else. His unease was washed away by a warm flow of desire. Sternly he reminded himself that she no doubt wanted to consult with him about the company's duties, but the reminder could as well have been whispered into a great storm of the Vilayet Sea. When first he kissed her, she had responded. Whatever her words said, her body had told the truth of her feelings. It *must* have.

"Lead on," Conan commanded, then strode through the gate and into the street without waiting. The slave had to scurry after him.

Conan gave little heed to the man half-running

beside him to keep up as he moved swiftly through throng-filled streets. With every stride his visions of Synelle grew stronger, more compelling, and his breath came faster. Each line of her became clear in his mind, the swell of round breasts above a tiny waist his big hands could almost span, the curve of sleek thighs and sensuously swaying hips. She filled his mind, clouded his eyes so that he saw none of the teeming crowds nor remembered anything of his journey.

Once within Synelle's great house the man in the short tunic rushed ahead to guide Conan up stairs and through corridors, but the Cimmerian was certain he could have found the way by himself. His palms sweated for the smooth satin of her skin.

The slave bowed him into Synelle's private chamber. The pale-skinned beauty stood with one small hand at her alabaster throat, dark eyes seeming to fill a face surrounded by silken waves of spun-platinum hair. Diaphanous silk covered her ivory lushness, but concealed nothing.

"Leave us, Scipio," she said unsteadily.

Conan was unaware of the slave leaving, closing the door behind him. His breath was thick in his throat; his nails dug into calloused palms. Never had he taken a woman who did not want him, yet he knew he was at the brink. One gesture from her, one word that he might take as invitation; it would be enough. Battle raged within the giant Cimmerian, ravening lust warring with his will. And for the first time in his life he felt his will begin to bend.

"I called you here, barbarian," she began, then swallowed and began again. "I summoned you to me. . . ."

Her words faded away as he covered the floor between them. His hands took her shoulders gently; how great the struggle not to rip that transparently mocking garment from her. As he gazed down at her upturned face, he read fear there, and longing. Her melting eyes were bottomless pools into which he could fall forever; his were azure flames.

"Do not fear me," he said hoarsely. "I will never harm you."

She pressed her cheek to his chest, crushing her full breasts against him. Unseen by him a small smile curved her lips, softening, though not supplanting, the fear in her eyes. "You are mine," she whispered.

"When first I kissed you," Conan panted, "you wanted me. As I want you. I knew I had not imagined it."

"Come," she said, taking his hand as she backed from him. "My bed lies beyond that archway. I will have wine brought, and fruits packed in snow from the mountains."

"No," he growled. "I can wait no longer." His hand closed on sheer silk; the robe shredded from her ripe nakedness. Careless of her protests of servants who might enter, he pulled her to the floor. Soon she protested no more.

12

The sun was rising toward its height once more as Conan left Synelle's house, and he wondered wearily at the passing of unnoticed hours. But she had so occupied him with herself that there had been no room for time. Had she not been gone from her bed at his waking, he might not be leaving yet. For all of a day and a night together, and little sleeping in it, a knot of desire still burned in his belly, flaring whenever he thought of her. Only the need to see to his Free-Company, and her absence, had stirred him to dress and go.

Bemused he strode through the crowded streets

as if they were empty of all but him, seeing only the woman who still held his mind in thrall with her body. Merchants in voluminous hooded robes and tarts in little save gilded bangles scurried from his way lest they be trampled; satin-clad nobles and long-bearded scholars abandoned dignity to leap aside when they incredulously saw he would not alter his path. He heard the curses that followed him, but the stream of abuse from scores of throats did not register. It was so much meaningless babble that had naught to do with him.

Suddenly a man who had not stepped aside bounced off Conan's chest, and the Cimmerian found himself staring into an indignant face as the memory of Synelle's silken thighs dimmed, but did not fade. The man was young, no older than he himself, but his tunic of blue brocade slashed with yellow, the golden chain across his chest, his small, fashionable beard, the pomander clutched in his hand, all named him nobly born.

"You there, thief," the youthful lord sneered. "I have you now."

"Get out of my way, fool," Conan growled. "I've no time or desire to play lordlings' games." The man wore a sword strapped around his waist, the Cimmerian noted, unusual with the garb he wore.

Conan tried to step around the brocaded youth, but another young noble, with thin mustachios in addition to his beard, stepped in front of him with a swagger. Jeweled rings bedecked all his fingers, and he, too, wore a sword. "This outlander," he said loudly, "has robbed my friend."

Conan wondered for whose benefit he was speaking so; no one in the teeming street paid the three any mind. In fact, a large space had opened about them as passersby studiously avoided their vicinity. Whatever sport these two sought, he wanted none of it. He wished only to see that all was well with his company and return as quickly as possible to Synelle. Synelle of the alabaster skin as soft as satin.

"Leave be," he said, doubling a massive fist, "or I'll set your ears to ringing. I've stolen nothing."

"He attacks," the mustachioed lordling cried, and his sword swept from its sheath as his fellow flung his rose-scented pomander at Conan's face.

Even with his brain fogged by a woman's memory the big Cimmerian had survived far too many battles to be taken so easily by surprise. The blade that was meant to take his head from his shoulders passed through empty air as he leaped aside. Anger washed his mind clean of all but battle rage. The sport these fops sought was his death, a killing for which, with the times as they were and the fact that he was an outlander, they would not be brought to book. But they had chosen no easy meat. Even as Conan's own steel was coming into his fist, he booted the first young noble who had accosted him squarely in the crotch; the youth shrieked like a girl and crumpled, clutching himself.

Whirling, Conan beat aside the thrust the mustachioed lordling had meant for his back. "Crom!" he bellowed. "Crom and steel!" And he waded ferociously into the combat, his sword a flashing engine of destruction.

Step by step his opponent was forced back, splashes of blood appearing on his tunic as his desperate defenses failed to turn aside the Cimmerian's blade quickly enough. Disbelief grew on his face, as if he could not understand that he faced a man better with the sword than he. Recklessly he attempted to go over to attack. Only once more did Conan's steel strike, but this time it split the lordling's skull to his black mustachios.

As the body fell the grate of the boot on pavement gave Conan warning, and he turned to block the first noble's slash. Chest to straining chest they stood, blades locked.

"I am better than ever Demetrios was," his youthful attacker sneered. "In this hour you will meet your gods, barbar."

With a heave of his mighty shoulders Conan sent the other staggering back. "Run to your mother's breast, youngling," he told him, "and live to do your boasting to women. If you know their use."

With a cry of fury the man rushed at Conan, a blur of steel before him. Eight times their blades met, striking sparks with the force of the blows, filling the street with a ringing as of a blacksmith's hammer and anvil. Then the Cimmerian's broadsword was slicing through ribs and flesh to the heart beneath.

Once more, for a moment, Conan stared into

those dark eyes. "You were better," he said, "but not by enough."

The young lord opened his mouth, but blood spilled out instead of words, and death dulled his eyes.

Hastily Conan freed his blade and cleaned it on the tunic of blue brocade. The space about them still was clear, and as if an invisible wall separated him and the two dead from those hurrying by, no one so much as glanced toward them. Given the mood of the city, it was more likely than not that no one of them would admit to what he had seen, short of being put to the question by the King's torturers, but there was no point in standing there until a score of Iskandrian's warriors appeared. Sheathing his sword, Conan melded into the crowd. Within a few paces they had closed around him, cloaking him in their number.

No more did thoughts of Synelle clog his mind. With the death of the second of his attackers he had remembered Machaon telling him of two young nobles watching the house where the Free-Company was quartered. That two different lordlings should attack him on the very next day was beyond his belief. The one had called loudly that Conan had robbed the other, as if inviting witnesses. Hardly the act of one intending murder, but perhaps slaying him had been but part of their plan.

Had they succeeded, who in Ianthe would have taken the part of a dead barbarian over that of two from noble houses? The people rushing by had done their best to ignore what happened, but if collared by a noble and pressed, which of them would not remember that Conan had been accused of theft and had then attacked the two, proving his guilt? With a King's Justice and a column of Ophirean infantry, Demetrios and his friend could have descended on the Free-Company, demanded the object they claimed had been stolen—and which they could no doubt describe as well as Conan—and have the house torn apart to find it. The bronze would have been in the hands of those who sought to use it. Boros might try to speak of evil gods and rites beneath Tor Al'Kiir, or Julia, but no ear would pay heed to the pratings of a drunken former apprentice mage, nor the babblings of a pot-girl.

Conan quickened his pace, brimming with an urgent need to assure himself that the image still lay beneath the floorboards of his sleeping chamber. He had become convinced of one thing. He would not have another night of rest in Ophir until that malevolent figure was beyond the reach of men.

The black candles guttered out, and Synelle lowered her hands with a satisfied sigh. The spell binding the barbarian had been altered. He was still held, but with more subtle desires than before.

With a weary groan she sagged to a low stool, wincing with the movement, and brushed spun silver hair back from her face. She pulled her cloak—that unadorned covering of scarlet wool had been all she had taken time to snatch in her flight, and it *had* been flight—about her nakedness. Her breasts were swollen and tender, her thighs and bottom bruised by Conan's fierce desires.

"How could I have known what would be unleashed in him?" she whispered. "Who could have thought a man could be so. . . ." She shivered uncontrollably.

In the barbarian's arms she had felt gripped by a force of nature as irresistable as an avalanche. Fires he had built in her, feeding them till they raged out of control. And when the leaping flames had consumed all before them, when he had quenched and slaked what he had aroused, he stoked still new fires. She had tried to bring that endless cycle to a halt, more than once she had tried—memories flooded her, memories of incoherent cries when words could not be formed and reason clung by the slenderest of threads to but a single corner of her passion-drugged mind—but her sorcery had not only wakened lust in him, it had magnified that lust, made it insatiable, overwhelming. His powerful hands had handled her like a doll. His hands, so strong, so knowing and sure of her.

"No," she muttered angrily.

She would not think of his hands. That way led to weakness. She would remember instead the humiliation of crawling weakly from her own bed when the barbarian fell at last to slumber, slinking like a thief for fear of waking him, of waking the desire that would bloom in him when his eyes touched her. On the floor of her secret chamber she had slept, curled on the hard marble with only the cloak for covering and lacking even the mat the meanest of her slaves would have, too exhausted to think or dream. Remember that, she told herself, and not the pleasures that sent tendrils of heat through her belly even in remembrance.

A ragged cry broke from her throat, and she staggered to her feet to pace the room. Her eye fell on the silver plate, black tallow hardening at its edges, the ash of blood and hair lying on its surface. The spell *was* altered. Not again would she have to face a night where she was a mote caught in the stormwind of the giant barbarian's desires. Her breathing slowed, grew more normal. He was still hers, he would still bring her to rapture, but his lusts would be more controllable. Controllable by her, that is.

"Why did I fear it so long?" she laughed softly. Taken altogether, this thing of men was quite wonderful. "They must simply be controlled, and then their vaunted strength and power can avail them nothing."

That was the lesson women had not learned, that she had only just come to. If women would not be controlled by men, then they must rather control men. She had always coveted power. How strange and beautiful that power should be the key to safety in this as well!

A knock at the door shattered her musings. Who would dare disturb her there? The rapping came again, more insistent this time. Gathering her cloak across her breasts with one hand, she flung open the door, tongue ready to flay whoever had violated her sanctorum.

A surprised, "You!" slipped out instead.

"Yes, me," Taramenon said. His face was tight with barely controlled anger. "I came to speak to you last night, but you were . . . occupied."

Laying a hand gently on his chest, she pushed him back—how easily he moved, even in his rage—and closed the door firmly behind her. No man, not even he, would ever enter that chamber.

"It is well you are here," she said as if he had had no accusation in his words. "There are matters of which we must speak. A woman must be found—"

"You were with him," the tall nobleman grated. "You gave that barbarian swine what was promised to me."

Synelle drew herself to her full height, and flung cold fury at him like a dagger. "Whatever I gave was *mine* to give. Whatever I did was *mine* to do, and none with right to gainsay me."

"I will slay him," Taramenon moaned in anguish, "like a dog in the dirt."

"You will slay whom I tell you to slay, when I tell you to slay them." Synelle softened her voice; shock had driven anger from Taramenon's face. There was still uses for the man, and she had long since learned means of controlling him that had naught to do with sorcery. "The barber will be useful for a time. Later you may kill him if you wish."

The last had been a sudden thought. Conan was a wonderful lover, but why limit herself to one? Men did not limit themselves to one woman. Yet the young giant would always hold a place in her affections for the vistas of pleasure he opened to her; when she was Queen of Ophir she would have a magnificent tomb erected for him.

"I found the brigand you wanted," Taramenon muttered sullenly. "A woman."

Synelle's eyebrows arched. "A *woman* bandit? A hardened trull, no doubt, with greasy hair and gimlet eye."

"She is," he replied, "the most beautiful woman I have ever seen."

Synelle flinched, and her jaw tightened. Why had the fool forced his presence on her before her tire-maids could see to her toilet? "So long as she brings me the scrolls from Inaros' library, I care not what she looks like." He chuckled, and she stared at him. Suddenly he was more relaxed, as if he thought he was in command. "If you think to make sport of me," she began dangerously.

"I did not send her after Inaros' scrolls," Taramenon said.

Words froze in her throat. When she found speech again she hissed at him. "And pray tell me why not?"

"Because I sent her after the image of Al'Kiir that you speak. She knows where it is. She described it to me. It will be I who provide you with what you so desperately need. Did you think you could hide your impatience, your eagerness beyond that you've ever shown for all the parchments and artifacts you have gathered placed together? I bring it to you, Synelle, not that barbar animal, and I expect at least the reward that he got."

Her pale, dark-eyed beauty became icy still. She let her cloak gap open to the floor; Taramenon gasped, and sweat beaded his forehead. "You will come to my bed," she began softly, but abruptly her words became lashes of a whip tipped with steel, "when I summon you there. You will come, yes, perhaps sooner than you dream, certainly sooner than you deserve, but at *my* command." Slowly and calmly she covered herself once more. "Now when will the image be delivered to your hand?"

"The signal that she has it," he mumbled sulkily, "will be a man in my red surcoat standing before the main gate of the royal palace at noon. That night at dusk I will meet her at a hut in the forest."

Synelle nodded thoughtfully. "You say this woman is beautiful? A beautiful woman who does what men do, who leads men rather than belonging to them. She must have great pride. I shall be at that meeting with you, Taramenon." From the corner of her eye she saw a slave creeping down the corridor toward them, and rounded on him, furious at the interruption. "Yes?" she snapped.

Falling to his knees, the man pressed his face to the marble tiles. "A message, my gracious lady, from the noble Aelfric." Without lifting his head he held up a folded parchment.

Synelle frowned and snatched the message.

Aelfric was Seneschal of Asmark, her ancestral castle, a man who served her well, but who liked as well the fact that she seldom visited or troubled him. It was not his way to invite her attention. Hastily she broke the lump of wax sealed with Aelfric's ring.

> To My Most Gracious Lady Synelle,
> With pain I send these tidings. In the day past have vile brigands most cowardly struck at my Lady's manor-farms, burning fields, touching barns, driving oxen and cattle into the forests. Even as your humble servant writes these dire words, the night sky glows red with new fires. I beseech my Lady to send aid, else there will be no crops left, and starvation will be the lot of her people.
>
> I remain obediently,
> your faithful servitor,
> Aelfric

Angrily she crumpled the letter in her fist. Bandits attacking *her* holdings? When she held the throne she would see every brigand in the country impaled on the walls of Ianthe. For now Aelfric would have to fend for himself.

But wait, she thought. With the power of Al'Kiir she could seize the throne, overawe both lords and peasants, yet would it not be even better had she some incident to point to that showed she was more than other women? Did she take Conan's warriors into the countryside and quell these bandits herself. . . .

She prodded the slave with her foot. "I am leaving for the country. Tell the others to prepare. Go."

"Yes, my lady," the slave said, backing away on his knees. "At once, my lady." Rising, he bowed deeply and darted down the hall.

"And you, Taramenon," she went on. "Set a man to watch for this woman's signal and bring me word, then ride you for Castle Asmark. Await me there, and this night your waiting will be ended." She almost laughed at the lascivious anticipation that painted his visage. "Go," she said, in the same tone she had used with the slave, and Taramenon ran as quickly as the other had.

It was all a matter of maintaining proper control she told herself. Then she went in search of writing materials, to send a summons to the barbarian.

13

Conan straightened from checking his saddle girth and glared about him at the assemblage pausing for yet another rest at Synelle's command. Three and twenty high-wheeled carts, each drawn by two span of yoked oxen, were piled high with what the Countess of Asmark considered necessary for removing to her castle in the country, rolled feather mattresses and colorful embroidered silk cushions, casks of the rarest wines from Aquilonia and Corinthia and even Khauran, packages of delicate viands that might not be readily available away from the capital, chests upon chests of satins and velvets and laces.

Synelle herself traveled in a gilded litter, borne by eight muscular slaves and curtained with fine silken net to admit the breeze yet keep the sun from her alabastrine skin. Her four blonde tire-women crouched in the shade of a cart, fanning themselves against the midday heat. Their lithe sleekness drew many eyes among the thirty mercenaries surrounding the carts, but the women were attuned only to listening for the next command from the litter. Nearly three score other servants and slaves hunkered out of the sun or tended to errands, drivers for the oxen, maids, seamstresses, even two cooks who were at that moment arguing vociferously over the proper method of preparing hummingbirds' tongues.

"Watch the trees, Erlik take you!" Conan shouted. Abashedly the mercenaries tore their eyes from the blondes to scan the forest that ran along two sides of the broad, grassy meadow where they had halted.

The Cimmerian had opposed halting; he had opposed each stop they had made thus far. Slowed by the oxcarts, they would not arrive at Synelle's castle until the following afternoon did they make the best speed the lumbering animals were capable of. Even one night in the forests with this strange cortege was more than he might wish for, much less risking a second such camp. A pavillion would have to be erected for Synelle to sleep in, another in which she would bathe, and yet a third for her tire-women's mats. There would be a fire to warm Synelle, fires for the cooks, fires to keep the maids from becoming affrighted of the night, and all no doubt large enough to announce their presence and location to anyone with eyes.

Machaon led his horse over to Conan. "I've word of Karela, Cimmerian," he said. "I crossed paths last night at the *Blue Bull* with a weedy scoundrel, a panderer who lost his women, and thus his income, to another, and whose tongue was free after his third pitcher of ale. I meant to speak of it earlier, but what with our patron's summons arriving hard on your heels this morn I forgot."

"What did you hear?" Conan asked eagerly.

"She uses her own name again, for one thing. She has not been long in Ophir, but already some twenty rogues follow her, and she is making reputation enough that Iskandrian has put twenty pieces of gold on her head."

"Such a small price must anger her," Conan laughed. "I fear not it will remain so low for long. But what of getting a message to her, or finding her? What did he say of that?"

"After a time the fellow seemed to realize he was babbling, and shut his teeth." At the Cimmerian's look of disappointment Machaon smiled. "But he let fall enough for me to question others. North of Ianthe, an hour's ride on a good horse, part of an ancient keep still stands, overgrown by the Sarelian Forest. There Karela camps her band on most nights. I am sure of it."

Conan grinned broadly. "I'll make her admit

she has no grievance against me if I have to paddle her rump until she does."

"A treatment I could recommend for others," the tattooed man said with a significant look at the litter.

Conan followed his look and sighed. "We have been halted long enough," was all he said.

As the young Cimmerian walked toward the net-curtained palanquin he tried to make some slight sense of these last two days, not for the first time that morning. The previous day and night seemed like a dream, but a fever-born dream of madness, with lust burning all else from his mind. Had what he remembered—Synelle's sweat-slicked thighs and wanton moans flashed in his mind—actually happened? It all seemed distant and dim.

When he answered her summons this morn, he had felt no such all-consuming desire. He wanted her, wanted her more than he had ever wanted any woman, more than he had wanted all the many women of his life together, but there had been a sense of restraint within him, strictures unnatural to his nature holding him in check. He did not lose control of himself with women—were his memories of the day before true?—but neither did he face them feeling bound with stout ropes.

And he had deferred to her! When, as haughty and regal as any queen, she commanded him as to how to order his men on the march, his urge had been to snort and tell her brusquely that such matters were his province. Instead he had found himself almost pleading with her, painfully convincing her that she should leave the command of his company to him. He had met kings and potentates and not acted so. How did this woman affect him in this manner? This time, he vowed, it would be different.

He stopped before Synelle's curtained litter and bowed. "If it pleases my lady, we should be moving on." Inwardly he snarled at himself. He was no man to break vows, and this had gone as swiftly as if it had never been made. What was the matter with him? Yet he could change nothing. "It is dangerous, my lady, to stay still so long with bandits and worse about."

A delicate hand parted the mesh curtain, and Synelle looked out at him calmly, a small smile curling her full lips. Her traveling garb of cool linen clung to her, revealing the curves and shadows of her. Conan's mouth went dry, and his palms dampened, at the sight.

"It would not be so dangerous," she said, "had you obeyed me and brought your entire company."

Conan gritted his teeth. Half of him wanted to tell this fool woman that she should leave the trade of arms to those who knew it; the other half wanted to stammer an apology. "We must be moving, my lady," he said finally. It had been an effort to say only that, and he feared he did not want to know what else he might have said.

"Very well. You may see to it," she said, letting the curtain fall.

Conan bowed again before turning away.

His stomach roiled as he strode back to his horse. Perhaps he *was* going mad. "To horse!" he roared, swinging into his saddle. "Mount and prepare to move! Oxdrivers to your animals!" Chattering men and giggling women darted along the row of carts. "Keep those maids off the carts!" he shouted. "We need what speed we can manage, and no extra weight for the animals! Move you!"

Harness creaked as massive beasts took up the strain; mercenaries scrambled to their mounts in a rattle of armor.

Conan raised his arm to signal the advance, and at that instant a mass of horsemen in chain-mail charged from the trees. Shrieks rose from terrified women, and the oxen, sensing the humans' fear, bellowed mournfully. This was what the Cimmerian had feared since leaving Ianthe, but for that reason he was ready for it.

"Bows!" he commanded, and short, curved horse-bows came into thirty hands beside his own.

Those powerful bows, unknown in the west except for Conan's Free-Company, could not be drawn as ordinary bows were. Nocking an arrow with a three-fingered grip on the bowstring, the huge Cimmerian placed those fingers against his cheek and thrust the bow out from him.

There were close to a hundred of them, he estimated as he drew, wearing the sign of no house and carrying no banners or pennons, yet armored too well for bandits. He loosed, and thirty more shafts flew after his. They were still too distant to pick individual targets, but the mass of them made target enough. Saddles emptied, but the onrushing men-at-arms, their wordless battle cries rising, came on. By the time Conan let his third arrow fly—the feathered shaft lanced through the eye-slit of the foremost horseman's white-plumed helmet; the man threw his hands to his face and rolled backwards over the rump of his still racing horse—the enemy had closed too much for bows to be of further use.

"Out swords!" he called, thrusting his bow back into its lacquered wooden scabbard behind his saddle. As he drew sword and thrust his left arm through the leather straps of his round shield with its spiked boss, he realized his helm still hung from his pommel. Battle rage was on him; let them see who killed them, he thought. "Crom!" he shouted. "Crom and steel!"

At the pressure of his knees, the big Aquilonian black burst forward into a gallop. Conan caught sight of Synelle, standing by her litter with her mouth open in a scream he could not hear for the blood pounding in his ears, then his mount was smashing into another horse, riding the lighter animal down, trampling its armored rider beneath steel-shod hooves.

The huge Cimmerian caught a blade on his shield, and his answering stroke severed the arm wielding it at the shoulder. Immediately he reversed to a backslash that cut deep into the neck of another foe.

Dimly he was aware of others of his men about him in the frenzied melee, but such were of necessity a series of individual combats; only when the vagaries of battle drew two comrades together did men of one side or the other stand together against their enemy.

A chain-mailed man rode close with broadsword raised high to chop, and Conan drove the spike on his shield into the man's chest, ripping him from the saddle with one jerk of a massive arm. War-trained, his big black lashed out with flashing fore-hooves at foemen's horses as he hacked deeper into the press with his murderous steel.

From beyond the swirling frenzy of slashing, shouting, dying men came a cry. "Conan! For the Cimmerian!"

About time, a cool corner of Conan's brain thought, and Narus, with twenty more mercenaries following, charged into the rear of the enemy. There was no time for more thought, for he was trading furious sword-strokes with a man whose chain-mail was splashed with blood not his own. He saw one of his men go down, head half-severed. The killer came galloping past, waving his gory blade and screaming a warcry. Conan kicked a foot free of its stirrup and booted the shouting man from his horse. The Cimmerian's blade freed itself from his opponent's and thrust under the other's chin, shattering the steel links of his mail coif and bringing a scarlet gout from his ruined throat. The man Conan had kicked from his saddle scrambled to his feet as his fellow fell, but the young giant's broadsword struck once, battering down his upraised steel, twice, and his headless corpse dropped across his comrade's body.

"Crom and steel!"

"Conan! Conan!"

"For the Cimmerian!"

It was too much for the mailed attackers, embattled before and behind, a huge northland beserker in their midst and no knowing in the fog of battle how many it was they faced. First a single man fled the combat, then another. Panic rippled through them, and cohesion was gone. By twos and threes they fought to get away. As they scattered some of the mercenaries set out in pursuit, echoing the halloing cry of hunters riding down deer.

"Back, you fools!" Conan bellowed. "Back, Black Erlik rot you!"

Reluctantly the mercenaries gave over the chase, and in moments the last of the mailed men still able to flee had melted into the forest. The men of the company who had pursued trotted back, waving gory swords and rasing shouts of victory.

"A most excellent plan, Cimmerian," Narus laughed as he galloped up, "having us trail behind as a surprise for unwelcome guests." His jazeraint hauberk was splattered with blood, no drop of which was his. The gaunt-faced man, disease-riddled though he appeared, was equal to Machaon with a blade, and none but Conan was their master. "Ten to one in gold they never knew how many hit them."

"A difficult wager to settle," Conan said, but

half his mind on the other. "Machaon," he called, "what's the butcher's price?"

"I'm taking a count, Cimmerian." Quickly the tattooed veteran finished and rode to join them. "Two dead," he retorted, "and a dozen who'll need the carts to get back to Ianthe."

Conan nodded grimly. Well over a score of the enemy lay on the hoof-churned ground, meadow grass and soil now seeming plowed, and only a few moved weakly. As many more were scattered back to the trees, sprouting feathered shafts. In the grim world of the mercenary it was little better than an even trade, for enemies were always there and easily found, but new companions were hard to come by.

"See if one of them lives enough to answer questions," the Cimmerian commanded. "I would know who sent them against us, and why."

Hurriedly Machaon and Narus dismounted. Moving among the bodies, stopping occasionally to heave one over, they returned supporting between them a bloodstreaked man with a wicked gash down the side of his face and neck.

"Mercy," he gasped faintly. "I cry mercy."

"Then name he who sent you," Conan demanded. "Were you to kill us all, or one in particular?"

The Cimmerian had no intention of slaying a wounded and helpless man, but the prisoner clearly feared the worst. Almost eagerly he said, "Count Antimides. He bid us slay you and seize the Lady Synelle. Her we were to bring to him naked and in chains."

"Antimides!" Synelle hissed. The men shifted

uneasily to see her picking her way across the bloody ground; such sights as lay about them, men hacked and torn by the savagery of battle, were not for women's eyes. Synelle did not seem to notice. "He dares so much against me?" she continued. "I will have his eyes and his manhood! I will—"

"My lady," Conan said, "those who attacked us may rejoin and seek you again." And he also, he added to himself, though that did not concern him as much as the other. "You must return to Ianthe, and quickly. You must ride one of the horses."

"Back to the city?" Synelle nodded vigorously. "Yes. And when I get there Antimides will learn the price of an attack on my person!" Her eyes were bright with eagerness for that teaching.

Conan began seeing to preparations, ordering men who hurried to obey. The warriors, at least, knew their vulnerability should the enemy return, perhaps with reinforcements. "Machaon, tell off ten men to ride with the carts. Unload everything except the Lady Synelle's jewelry and clothes to lighten the oxen's loads. Leave the litter here, so they can see she's no longer with the carts. Crom, of course we bring in our dead! Spread the wounded among the carts so they're not crowded, and have the maids tend them. Yes, their wounded as well."

"No!" Synelle snapped. "Leave Antimides' men! Fetch me naked and chained, will they? Let them die!"

Conan's hands tightened on his reins until his

knuckles were white. His temples throbbed like drums. "Load their wounded, too," he said, and drew a shuddering breath. Almost he had not been able to get the words out.

Synelle looked at him strangely. "A strong will," she said musingly. "And yet there could be pleasure in—" Abruptly she stopped, as if she thought she had said too much, but the Cimmerian could understand nothing of it.

"My lady," he said, "you must ride astride. We have no side-saddle."

She held out a hand to him. "Your dagger, barbarian."

When she took it from him it felt as though sparks jumped from her hand to his. Deftly she slit the front of her robe. Narus led forward a horse, and she mounted with flashing limbs, exposed to the tops of her pale thighs, nor did she do anything to cover them once in the saddle. Conan could feel her eyes on him as solidly as a touch, but of which sort he could not tell. He tore his gaze from her long legs, and heard a laugh softly, the sound burning in his brain.

"We ride!" he commanded hoarsely, and galloped toward Ianthe, the rest streaming behind.

14

Karela kept the hood of her dark blue woolen cloak pulled well forward; there were those about her in the crowd-filled streets of Ianthe who would put aside their habit of ignoring what occurred around them for a chance at Iskandrian's reward.

She snorted at the thought. Twenty pieces of gold! A thousand times so much had been placed on her head by the Kings of Zamora and Turan. The merchants of those countries had offered more, and would have considered it cheap to rid their caravans of her depredations at the price. High Councils had had debated methods of dealing with her, armies had pursued her, and no man took passage from one city to another without offering prayers that she would spare his purse, all with equal futility. Now, she found herself reduced to an amount of coin that spoke of petty irritation. The humiliation of it was so great that barely could she keep her mind on her purpose for entering the city.

The house where Conan's company of rogues was gathered lay just ahead. That morning she had watched him ride out with half his company. A short time later another large contingent of his men had departed by another gate and trailed after the first. Wily Cimmerian! She had long since gotten over the foolishness of failing to respect his abilities. He would be taken in no ordinary trap. But then she was no ordinary woman.

Unbidden, her thoughts went back to that woman of the nobility he had been escorting. Did she know him, he had already visited the wench's bed. He had always had an eye for willing wenches, and few were those who were not willing did he once smile at them. The red-haired woman wished she could get her hands on this Synelle. Lady, indeed. She would not soil her hands with the like of those who called themselves ladies. Karela would show her what a real woman looked like, then send her back to Conan as a present, stuffed naked into a sack. When someone had offered her gold to burn the jade's farms, she had not stopped to ask why or query who the man with the deep-set, commanding eyes was behind his mask of black silk. It had been a chance to strike at Conan, and his precious Synelle, and she leaped at it. She would prick him and prick him until he was forced to flee, and if he would not. . . .

Angrily she pulled her mind back to the matter at hand. She no longer cared what women he took, she told herself. Such interest in the man had brought her naught but grief. With the men he had taken to protect his new trull, he could not have left many behind. She looked through the arched gateway as she passed. Yes. There were only a handful to be seen, playing at dice against the side of the fountain in the courtyard. He who had made the cast cursed, and the others laughed as they scooped up his losings.

Karela raised a hand to her face as if brushing away a fly, and two men pushing a handcart toward her, its flat bed piled high with wooden boxes held in place by ropes, suddenly turned it into the alley beside the house. Karela followed them. The men glanced at her questioningly; she nodded, and they turned to watch the street.

One, a dark-faced Zamoran with drooping mustaches, whom she had taken on out of memory of better days, said softly, "No one looks."

In the space of two breaths Karela scrambled up the carefully arranged boxes and into a window on the second floor. It was Conan's room. Her sources of information had discovered that for her easily enough.

Her lip curled contemptuously as she looked around the bare chamber. So this was what he had come to since forsaking a palace in Nemedia. She had never heard the straight of his departing that land when he had been offered honors and wealth by the King, but it brought a measure of continuing satisfaction that he had not profited from the adventures which ended in her flight. It did her good to think of him brought low. Yet the blankets were folded neatly on the bed. There were no cobwebs on the ceiling, no dust in the corners, and the floor had been freshly swept. A woman, she thought, and not likely it was his fine Synelle. The Cimmerian gathered a zenana about him like an easterner.

Sternly she reminded herself of her lack of interest in Conan's women. She had come for that obscene bronze figure, and nothing more. But where to begin searching? There did not look to be many places for hiding. Beneath the bed, perhaps.

Before she could take a step, the door opened and a girl wearing plain white robes walked in. There was something oddly familiar about her face and hair, though Karela could swear she had never seen the girl before.

"Keep your silence, wench," Karela commanded. "Close the door and answer my questions quickly, and you'll come to no harm."

"Wench!" the girl said, her eyes flashing indignantly. "What are you doing here . . . wench? I think I'll let you see if you like Fabio's switch. Then you can answer questions for me."

"I told you," Karela began, but the girl was already turning back to the door. With a curse the woman bandit jumped across the room and grappled with her, managing to kick the door shut as she did.

She expected the girl to surrender, or try to scream for help at most, but with a sqawl of rage the other woman buried her hands in Karela's red hair. The two women fell to the floor in a kicking, nail-clawing heap.

Derketo, Karela thought, she did not want to kill the jade, but she had defended herself too long with a sword to remember well this woman-fighting. She almost screamed as the other sank teeth into her shoulder; handfuls of her hair were at the point of being ripped from her head. Desperately she slammed a knee into the girl's belly. Breath left the other woman in a gasp, and Karela wriggled forward to kneel on her arms. Her dagger slipped into her hand, and she held it before the girl's face.

"Now be silent, Derketo take you!" she panted. The girl glared up at her defiantly, but held her tongue.

Abruptly Karela realized what was familiar about the girl. The eyes were different, but the color of her hair, the shape of her face. Conan had found himself an imitation of herself. She could not think whether to laugh, or cry, or slit the wench's throat. Or wait for the Cimmerian and slit his. No interest, she told herself again. No interest at all.

"What is your name?" she grated. That would never do. She made an effort to sound more friendly, if that was possible while brandishing a dagger in the wench's face. "What's your name, girl? I like to know who I'm talking to."

The woman beneath her hesitated, then said, "Julia. And that is all you will get from me."

Karela dressed her face with a smile. "Julia, Conan has a bronze figure that I must have, a filthy thing with horns. An you've seen it, you'll not have forgotten. No woman could. Tell me where it is, and I'll leave you unharmed when I go."

"I'll tell you nothing!" Julia spat. But her eyes had flickered to a corner of the room.

There was nothing there at all that Karela could see. Still. . . . "Very well, Julia, I must search without your help then. But I'll have to bind you. Now hear my warning well. Do you try to fight or flee, either one, this," she gestured with her blade, "will find a home in your heart. Do you understand?"

Julia's face was still filled with fury, but she nodded, albeit with obvious reluctance.

Carefully Karela cut away Julia's robe. The girl flinched, but otherwise did not change her hate-filled expression. As Karela was slicing strips from the robe with her dagger she could not help noticing her naked prisoner's body. The Cimmerian always had had a liking for full-breasted women, she thought sourly. But hers were better. That was, if she had still been interested in him in that way, which she was not.

"Roll over," she commanded, nudging Julia with her foot. When the girl obeyed, Karela swiftly tied her hands and feet. The wench groaned through clenched teeth as she pulled the bindings together in the small of the naked woman's back, but the threat of the dagger was enough to keep the protest muted. Not comfortable, Karela thought savagely, but then the girl had not truly answered her question. A wadding of cloth fastened with another strip of cloth did her a gag, but before Karela left she lifted Julia's face by a handful of hair. "Conan likes round bottoms," she said with a biting smile. "You have a bottom like a boy."

Julia jerked wildly at her bonds and made angry sounds behind her gag, but Karela was already studying the corner the girl's eyes had indicated. There *was* nothing there. Neither crack in the plaster nor new work gave sign that anything had been hidden behind the wall, and no opening in the fly-specked ceiling. . . . A board sagged beneath her foot, and she smiled.

Swiftly she knelt and levered up the floorboard with her dagger. The malevolent bronze lay beneath, nestled in decades of dirt and rat droppings. Fitting, she thought. She reached for the horned figure, but her fingers stopped, quivering, a handsbreadth away. She could not bring herself to touch it. The evil she had felt before still radiated from it, twisting her stomach. Contact with it would surely have her wretching. Hastily she fetched a blanket from the bed, folded it around the bronze, and gathered it up like a sack, holding the weighty burden well away from her.

Even so she could sense the abomination of the thing, but so long as she did not have to look at it she could stand carrying it.

At the window she paused. "Thank Conan for me," she told the struggling girl. "Tell him I thank him for five hundred pieces of gold."

With that she dropped through the window and scampered down the boxes. In the alley she hid the blanket-wrapped figure inside a box on the cart. And the relief it was to get rid of it, she thought, even after so brief a contact.

"We'll meet in one turn of the glass," she told the mustached Zamoran, "at the Carellan Stables."

As she slipped back into the crowded street, the hood of her cloak once more shielding her face, she glanced regretfully at the sun. Too late today to post a man before the royal palace. On the morrow, though, the signal would be sent, and by nightfall she would have her five hundred pieces of gold. She wished fervently that she could see the Cimmerian's face when he learned how much he had lost.

15

Silvery hair and slit robe alike flowing behind her, Synelle raced through the wide corridors of her great house, heedless of the horrified cries of servants and slaves at her dusty dishevelment, unhearing of their pleas after her welfare and concern for her precipitate return. Conan had left ten of his archers, now standing watch at the entrances, to protect her, then rode off before she could stop him. To deal with Count Antimides, one of those left behind had told her. But she would not wait for him to deal with the Mitra-accursed wretch. Antimides had struck at her—at her!—and his destruction, utter and complete, was her right and hers alone. The means of it must be exquisite, so that when the truth of it could at last be proclaimed to the world the expunging of that excresence would be told and retold for centuries. His desire for the crown and and chains he had meant to emprison her in, that was it.

From a wall she snatched a mirror of silvered glass. With that under her arm, she swept into her secret chamber. From amidst the scintillant flasks and seething beakers of vile substances she took a vial of Antimides' blood. He had been a useful, if unknowing, tool until now, adding to the confusion and weakening those she would eventually have to cow, but always had she been aware that he might become dangerous to her. That blood had been obtained from an ensorceled serving girl, one who often shared Antimides' bed and passed on to Synelle, for the bewitchment that held her, all she learned of the great lord's plans, and kept against just such a day as this. Necromantic spells that could hold a corpse incorruptible for a thousand years kept it liquid.

With great care she sketched the crown of Ophir on the mirror in the count's blood. Below that she drew a sanguine chain.

"See yourself with the crown you seek upon your head, Antimides," she whispered. "But only for a time. A brief, painful time." Laughing cruelly, she bent back to her dark work.

"We attract attention," Machaon announced to no one in particular.

The file of nineteen armored horsemen in spiked helms with round shields slung on the arms, led by Conan, made its way slowly through the streets of Ianthe, and the crowds who parted before them did indeed stare. Deadly intensity hung about them like a cloud, stunning even those who would have looked away, numbing their reticence to see.

"There will be trouble for this," Narus said dolefully. He rode next in line behind Machaon. "Even can we slay Antimides—and the gods alone know how many guards he has—Iskandrian will not look the other way for our killing of a noble within the very walls of the capital. We shall have to flee Ophir, if we can."

"And if we do not slay him," Conan said grimly, "then still we must flee. Or would you ever be sitting with your back to a wall for protection, ever looking across your shoulder for his next attack?"

And more attacks there would be, the Cimmerian was sure. Whatever Antimides' reason for wanting to seize Synelle, he could only be seeking Conan's death to still his tongue. The attacks would continue until Conan was dead, or Antimides was.

"I didn't say we should not kill him," Narus sighed. "I simply said we must flee afterwards."

"If we must flee in any case," Taurianus demanded, "why should we then take this risk? Let the lord live, and let us be gone from Ianthe with all our blood in us." The lanky man looked more glum even than Narus, and the dark hair that straggled from under his helm was damp with anxious sweat.

"You'll never make a captain, Ophirean," the gaunt-faced mercenary replied. "A Free-Company lives by its name, and dies by it, as well. Can we be attacked with impunity, then the company is as dead as if we have all had our weazands slit, and we are no better than vagabonds and beggars."

Taurianus muttered under his breath, but spoke no more complaints aloud.

"There is Antimides' palace," Machaon said abuptly. He frowned suspiciously at the sprawling, golden-domed edifice of marble and alabaster. "I see no guards. I do not like this, Cimmerian."

Antimides' palace was second in size within Ianthe only to the royal palace itself, a massive structure of columns and terraces and spired towers, with broad, deep steps leading up from the street. There were no guards in sight on those steps, and one of the great bronze doors stood ajar.

A trap perhaps, Conan thought. Had Antimides learned of his failure already? Was he inside with his guards gathered close about him for protection? Such would be a foolish move, sure to have been protested by any competent captain. Yet a lord with Antimides' arrogance might well have bludgeoned his guard commander into complacent compliance long since.

He turned in his saddle, studying the men behind. The seven besides Machaon and Narus who had crossed the border from Nemedia with him were there. They had followed him far, and loyally.

Long and hard had he labored to build this company, and to keep it, yet fairness made him say, "What numbers we face inside I do not know. Does any man wish to leave, now is the time."

"Speak not foolishness," Machaon said. Taurianus opened his mouth, then closed it again without speaking.

Conan nodded. "Four men to hold the horses," he ordered as he dismounted.

With steady, purposeful tread they climbed the white marble steps, drawing swords as they did. Conan stepped through the open door, its broad bronze face scribed hugely with the arms of Antimides' house, and found himself in a long, domeceilinged hall, with grand, alabaster stairs sweeping up to a columned balcony that encircled the hall.

A buxom serving girl in plain green robes that left her pretty legs bare to the tops of her thighs dashed out of a door to one side of the hall, a large, weighty bag over her shoulders. A scream bubbled out of her when she saw the armed and armored men invading the palace. Dropping the bag, she sped wailing back the way she had come.

Narus thoughtfully eyed the array of golden goblets and silver plate that had spilled out of the bag. "A guess as to what happens here?"

"Antimides fleeing our righteous wrath?" Machaon hazarded hopefully.

"We cannot afford let him escape us," Conan

said. He did not believe the count would flee, but there was strangeness here that worried him. "Spread out. Find him."

They scattered in all directions, but warily, swords at the ready. Too many battles had they faced, too many traps had been sprung around them, for complacency. The continued survival of a mercenary lay in his readiness to give battle on an instant. Any instant.

A lord's chambers would be above, the Cimmerian thought. He took the curving stairs upward.

Room by room he searched, finding no one, living or dead. Everywhere there were signs of hasty flight, and of a desire to carry away everything of value. Marks where tapestries had been pulled from the walls and carpets taken up. Tables overturned, whatever they had borne gone. Golden lamps wrenched halfway from brackets that had resisted being pried from the walls. Oddly, every mirror he saw was starred with long cracks.

Then he pushed open a door with his sword, and looked into a room that seemed untouched. Furniture stood upright, golden bowls and silver vases in place, and tapestries depicting heroic scenes of Ophir's past hung from the walls. The one mirror in the room was cracked, however, as the others were. An intricately carved chair was set before it, the high back to the door, but the voluminous, gold-embroidered green silk sleeve of a man's robe hung over one gilded wooden arm.

With the strides of a great hunting cat the giant Cimmerian crossed the room, presented his sword to the throat of the man seated there. "Now, Antimides—" Conan's words died abruptly, and the hairs on the back of his neck stirred.

Count Antimides sat with eyes bulging from an empurpled face and blackened tongue protruding between teeth clenched and bared in a rictus of agony. The links of a golden chain were buried in the swollen flesh of his neck, and his own hands clutched the ends of that chain, seeming even in the iron grip of death to strain at drawing it tighter.

"Crom!" Conan muttered. He would not believe that fear of his vengeance had been enough to make Antimides sit before a mirror and watch as he strangled himself. The Cimmerian had met sorcery often enough before to know the smell of it.

"Conan! Where are you?"

"In here!" he replied to the shout from the hall.

Machaon and Narus entered with a slender, frightened youth in filthy rags that had been fine satin robes not long past. His wrists bore the bloody marks of manacles; the palor of his skin and the thinness of his face spoke of long days in darkness and missed meals.

"Look what we found chained below," the tattooed man said.

Not so much of a youth, Conan saw at second glance; there was that in the man's manner—a petulant thrust of a too-full lower lip; a sulkiness of eye and stance—that gave an air of boyishness.

"Well, who is he?" the Cimmerian asked. "You speak as if I should know him."

The youthful appearing man lifted his chin with almost feminine hauteur. "I am Valentius," he said in a high voice that strained for steadiness, "count now, but King to be. I give you my thanks for this rescue." His dark eyes flickered uncertainly to Narus and Machaon. "If rescue it indeed is."

Narus shrugged. "We told him why we are here," he said to Conan, "but he does not believe. Or not fully."

"There are two guards below with their gullets slit," Machaon said, "but we've seen no one living. There is madness in this place, Cimmerian. Has Antimides truly fled?"

For an answer Conan jerked his head toward the high-backed chair. The other three hesitated, then moved quickly to look.

Shockingly, Valentius giggled. "However did you make him do this? No matter. 'Tis fitting for his betrayal of my trust." His fine-featured face darkened quickly. "I came to him for aid and shelter, and he laughed at me. At me! Then he clapped me in irons and left me to rot and fight rats for my daily bowl of swill. So pious, he was. So unctuous. He would not have my blood on his hands, he said, and laughed. He would leave that to the rats."

"I've seen death on many fields, Conan," Machaon said, "but this is an ugly way to slay a man, for all he deserved killing." His knuckles were white on his sword hilt as he gazed on the corpse. Narus formed his fingers into a sign to ward off evil.

"I did not kill him," Conan told them. "Look at his hands on the chain. Antimides slew himself."

Valentius laughed again, shrilly. "However 'twas done, it was done well." Moods shifting like quicksilver, his face screwed up viciously, and he spat in the corpse's bloated face. "I but regret I could not see the doing."

Conan exchanged glances with his two friends. This was the man with the best blood claim to succeed Valdric on the throne of Ophir. The young Cimmerian shook his head in disgust. The urge to be rid of the youth quickly was strong, but did he simply leave him the fool would have his throat cut in short order. Perhaps that would be the better for Ophir, but such was not his decision to make.

To Valentius he said, "We will take you to the royal palace. Valdric will give you protection."

The slender young man stared at him, wild-eyed and trembling. "No! No, you cannot! Valdric will kill me. I am next in line for the throne. He will kill me!"

"You speak foolishness," Conan growled. "Valdric has no care for aught but saving his own life. 'Tis likely in a day he'll not even remember you are in the palace."

"You do not understand," Valentius whined, wringing his hands. "Valdric will look at me, knowing that he is dying, knowing that I will be

King after. He will think of the long years I have before me, and he will hate me. He will have me slain!" He looked desperately from one face to the next, and finished with a sullenly muttered, "'Tis what I would do, and so will he."

Machaon spat on the costly Turanian carpet. "What of blood kin?" he asked gruffly. "What of friends, or allies?"

The cringing man shook his head. "How can I know who among them to trust? My own guards turned on me, men who have served my house faithfully for years." Suddenly his voice quickened, and his dark eyes took on a sly light. "You protect me! When I am King, I will give you wealth, titles. You shall have Antimides' palace, and be count in his stead. You and your men shall be the King's personal bodyguard. Riches beyond imagining I shall grant you, and power. Choose a woman, noble or common, and she will be yours. Two, do you wish them, or three! Name the honor you desire! Give it name, and I shall grant it!"

Conan grimaced. It was true that there could be no better service for a Free-Company than what Valentius offered, but he would sooner serve a viper. "What of Iskandrian?" he said. "The general takes no part in these struggles, follows no faction."

Valentius nodded reluctantly. "If you will not serve me," he said sulkily.

"Then let us leave this place," Conan said, "and quickly. It would be ill to be found standing over Antimides' corpse." As the others hurried from the room, though, he paused for one last look at the dead man. Whatever sorcery Antimides had enmeshed himself in, the Cimmerian was glad it did not touch him. With a shiver he followed the others.

16

Dusk was falling as Conan returned to the house where his company was quartered, and the gray thickening of the air, the coming blackness, fitted his mood well. Iskandrian had taken Valentius under his protection at the army's barracks readily enough, but the old general had listened to their story with a suspicious eye on the Cimmerian. Only for Valentius' agreement that Antimides appeared to have strangled himself had the mercenaries left those long, stone buildings unchained, and the petulant glare the young lord gave Conan as he said the words was as clear as a statement that he would have spoken differently could he but be sure he would not himself be implicated.

And then there had been Synelle. Conan had found her in a strange mixture of fury and satisfaction. She already knew of Antimides' death, though he was not aware the word had spread so quickly; that accounted for her contentment. But she had upbraided him savagely for riding away without her permission, and for taking the time to bring Valentius to Iskandrian's care.

The last seemed to infuriate her more than the first. He was in her service, not that of the fopling Valentius, and he would do well to remember it. To his own amazement he had listened meekly, and worst of all had had to fight with himself to stop from begging her forgiveness. He had never begged anything from man or woman, god or demon, and it made his stomach turn to think how close he had come.

He slammed open the door of his room, and stopped dead. In the dimness Julia, naked and bound hand and foot, frowned up at him with her mouth working frantically at a gag.

"Machaon!" he shouted. "Narus!" Hastily he untied her gag. Her bonds had been tightly tied, and she had pulled them tighter with her struggles. He had to wield his dagger carefully to cut only the strips of cloth and not her flesh. "Who did this?" he demanded as he labored to free her.

With a groan she expelled a damp wad of cloth from her mouth, and worked her jaw before speaking. "Do not let him see me like this," she pleaded. "Hurry! Hurry!"

Machaon, Narus and Boros tumbled through the door, all shouting questions at once, and Julia screamed. As Conan severed the last binding, she jerked free of him and scrambled to the bed, snatching a blanket to cover herself.

"Go away, Machaon!" she cried, cowering back. Rubiate color suffused her cheeks. "I will not have you see me so. Go away!"

"'Tis gone," Boros said drunkenly, pointing to the corner where Conan had hidden the bronze figure.

For the first time the Cimmerian realized the board was lifted aside, and the space beneath it empty. A chill as of death oozed through him. It seemed meet that this day should end so, with disaster peering at him like the vacant eye-sockets of a skull.

"Mayhap," Boros muttered, "do we ride hard, we can be across the border before it's used. I've always wished to see Vendhya, or perhaps Khitai. Does anyone know a land more distant?"

"Be quiet, you old fool," Conan growled. "Julia, who took the bronze? Crom, woman, stop worrying about that accursed blanket and answer me!"

Not ceasing her efforts to make the blanket cover all of her bountiful curves, and less precariously, Julia glared at him and sniffed. "'Twas a trull in men's breeches and wearing a sword." She glanced at Machaon out of the corner of her eye. "She said I have a boy's bottom. My bottom is as round as hers, only not so big."

Conan ground his teeth. "Her eyes," he asked impatiently. "They were green? Her hair red?

Did she say anything else?"

"Karela?" Machaon said. "I thought she meant to kill you, not steal from you. But why is Boros so affrighted by this thing she took? You've not got us meddling with sorcerers again, Cimmerian?"

"You know her," Julia said accusingly. "I thought so from what she said about my. . . ." She cleared her throat and began again. "All I remember of what she said is that she swore by Derketo and thanked you for five hundred pieces of gold. Have you truly given her so much? I remember my father's lemans, and I'd not think this Karela was worth a silver."

Conan pounded a huge fist on his thigh. "I must find her, Machaon, without delay. She has stolen a bronze figure that came to me by happenstance, a thing of evil power that will wreak destruction undreamed of, does she sell it to those I fear she will. Give me precise directions to find that ruined keep."

Julia moaned. "That is what she meant about gold? She takes the hellish thing to those Boros spoke of? Mitra protect us all, and the land!"

"I understand not a word of all this," Machaon said, "but one thing I do know. An you enter the Sarelain Forest in the night, you'll break your neck. That tangle is bad enough to travel in daylight. 'Twould take a man born there to find his way in the dark."

"I can find her," Boros said, swaying, "so long as she has the bronze. Its eyil is in truth a beacon." He pushed his sleeves up bony arms. "A simple matter of—"

"An you attempt magic in your condition," Conan cut him off, "I'll put your head on a spike over the River Gate with my own hands." The gray-bearded man looked hurt, but subsided, muttering under his breath. Conan turned to Machaon. "There is no time to waste. Daylight may be too late."

Machaon nodded reluctantly, but Narus said, "Then take a score of us with you. Her band—"

"—would hear so many coming and melt away," the Cimmerian finished for him. "I go alone. Machaon?"

Slowly the tattooed veteran spoke.

Machaon was right, Conan thought as an unseen branch whipped across his face for what seemed the hundredth time. A man could easily break his neck in that blackness. He forced his horse on through the heavy thicket of vines and undergrowth, hoping he moved in the right direction. As a boy he had learned to guide himself by the stars, but the sky was seldom visible, for the forest was ancient, filled with huge oaks whose thick interwoven branches formed a canopy with few openings above his head.

"You've come far enough," a voice called from the dark, "unless you want a quarrel in your ribs!"

Conan put a hand to his sword.

"None of that!" another man said, then

chuckled. "Me and Tenio grew up in this forest, big man, poaching the King's deer by night. He sees better than I do, and you might as well be standing under a full moon for all of me."

"I seek Karela," Conan began, but got no further.

"Enough talk," thc first voice said. "Take him!"

Suddenly rough hands were pulling the big Cimmerian from his horse, into the midst of a knot of men. He could not even see well enough to count how many, but he seized an arm and broke it, producing a scream. There was no room to draw his sword, nor light to see where to strike; he snatched his dagger instead and laid about him, bringing yells and curses when he slashed flesh. In the end their numbers were too great, and he was pressed to the dirt by the weight of them, his wrists bound behind him and a cord tied between his ankles for a hobble.

"Anybody hurt bad?" panted the man who had chuckled earlier.

"My arm," someone moaned, and another voice said, "Bugger your arm! He near as cut my ear off!"

Cursing the dark—not all had cat's eyes—they pulled Conan to his feet and pulled him through the trees, dragging him, when the hobble caught roots and tripped him, until he managed to get his feet under him again.

Abruptly a blanket was pulled aside before him, and he was thrust into a stone-walled room lit by rush torches in rusted iron sconces on the walls. A huge hearth with a roaring fire of logs as big as a man's leg, a great iron pot suspended on pivoting arm above it, filled one wall. Blankets at the windows—narrow arrow-slits, in fact—kept the light from spilling into the surrounding forest. A dozen men, as motley a collection of ruffians as Conan had ever seen, sprawled on benches at crude trestle tables, swilling wine from rough clay mugs and wolfing down stew from wooden bowls.

Karcla got to her feet as Conan's captors crowded in after him, complaining loudly about their wounds and bruises. Her dark leather jerkin, worn over tight breeches of pale gray silk tucked into red boots, was laced snugly, yet gaped enough at the top to reveal the creamy upper slopes of her full, heavy breasts. A belt worn low on her well-rounded hips supported her scimitar.

"So," she said, "you're more fool than I thought you, Cimmerian. You'll force me to kill you yet."

"The bronze, Karela," he said urgently. "You must not sell it. They're trying—"

"Silence him!" she snapped.

"—to raise Al'Kiir," he managed to get out, then a club smashed against the back of his head, and darkness claimed him.

17

The fool, Karela thought as she stared at Conan's huge prostrate form. Was his masculine arrogance so great that he could believe all he must needs do to retrieve the figure was ride up and take it? She knew him for a priceful man, and knew as well that the pride was justified. By himself, with naught but his broadsword, he was more than a match for. . . .

Abruptly she cursed to herself. The Cimmerian was no longer the same man who had emprisoned a part of her and carried it away with him. She had been thinking of him as he was when she first knew him, a thief and a loner with naught but his wits and the strength of his sword arm. Now he commanded men, and men who, she reluctantly admitted, were a more dangerous pack than the hounds she led.

"Was he alone?" she demanded. "An you've led his Free-Company here, I'll have your hides for boots!"

"Didn't see nobody else," Tenio muttered. "That means there weren't nobody else." A small, ferrety man with a narrow face and sharp nose, he spat a tooth into his palm and glared at it. "I say kill him." Some of those nursing broken ribs and knife gashes growled assent.

Marusas, her Zamoran, produced a dagger in his long, calloused fingers. "Let us wake him, instead. He looks strong. He would scream a long time before he died."

Instantly all of the men were shouting, arguing for one course or the other.

"Kill him now! He's too dangerous!"

"He's just a man. Flay him, and he'll scream like any other."

"You didn't fight him out there! You don't know!"

"He cut me to the bone with ten of us on him, and broke Agorio's arm!"

"Silence, you dogs!" Karela roared, and the bickering ceased as they turned to stare at her. "I say who dies, and I say he doesn't. Not yet, at least! Do any of you mangy curs care to dispute me? To your kennels!"

She put a hand to her scimitar hilt, and a dangerous light glowed in her green eyes. One by one they dropped their eyes from hers, muttered, and shuffled back to their drinking or to tend their wounds. Jamaran, a huge, shaven-headed Kushite with shoulders broader than Conan's and the thick fingers of a wrestler, was the last to remain glowering at her, his dark face twisted with anger. A split of his cheek showed where Conan's fist had landed in the struggle.

"Well, Jamaran?" she said. She knew he wanted to replace her, and take her to his bed as well, though he did not know she was aware of his desires. He had thoughts about the proper place for women; sooner or later she would have to show him the error of his ways or slay him. "Are you ready to dispute my rule?"

Surprise glimmered on his face, and was quickly supplanted by a sneering smile. "Not yet," he growled. "I will tell you when, my red-haired pretty." His black eyes ran over her body like a caress, then with incredible lightness on his feet for a man of his size he stalked to the nearest table and snatched up a mug, tossing back his head to drink deeply.

Karela quivered in shocked outrage as she glared at his broad back. Never before had he been so open. She would have to kill him, she thought, after this. But it could not be done now. The temper of her band was too delicately balanced. As much as she hated admitting it, a wrong move now could wreck all she had labored for. With a snarl she released her sword.

It was not like the days in Zamora, she thought grimly. Then none of her band dared to challenge her word, or to think of her as a woman. It was all Conan's fault. He had changed her in some way she did not understand, some way she did not want to be changed. He had woven a thread of weakness into her fabric, and other men could sense it.

As if her thoughts of him had been a call the Cimmerian groaned and stirred.

"Gag him," she ordered. "Move, Derketo curse you! I'll not be bothered by his babblings!"

Conan shook himself as Tenio and Jamaran knelt beside him. "Karela," he said desperately, "listen to me. These men are dangerous. They mean to bring an evil—"

Tenio tried to shove a rag into his mouth, and screamed as the Cimmerian sank teeth into his hand. Jamaran smashed a fist into Conan's jaw; the ferret-faced man jerked his hand free, sprinkling drops of blood as he shook it. Before Conan could speak again Jamaran had thrust the wadding home and bound it. As he got to his feet the shaven-headed man kicked Conan in the ribs and pulled back his booted foot for another. Tenio drew his dagger with his undamaged hand, a murderous gleam in his eyes.

"Stop that," Karela commanded. "Did you hear me? Leave him!"

Slowly, reluctantly, the two drew away from the Cimmerian.

She could feel those sapphire eyes on her. He shook his head furiously, fighting the gag, making angry noises behind it. Shivering, she turned her back to stare into the fire.

Karela knew she could not afford to let herself listen to the young giant. He had always been able to talk her into anything. Did he put his hands on her, her will melted. This time, she told herself, this time it would be different.

The night went slowly for her, and she was aware that it was because of Conan's eyes on her back. The rest of the bandits took themselves off to sleep, most simply pulling blankets about them on the stone floor, but sleep would not come near Karela. Like a leopard in a cage she paced, and the goad that made her pace was an unblinking icy blue gaze. She would have had him blindfolded, except that she would not admit even to herself that simply his eyes on her could affect her so greatly.

Finally the titian-haired beauty settled before the great hearth and studied the leaping flames as if they were the most important thing in the world. Yet even then she could not escape the Cimmerian, imagining him writhing in the fire, imagining him suffering all the tortures of the damned, all the tortures he so richly deserved. She could not understand why that seemed to make her feel even worse, or why from time to time she had to surreptitiously wipe tears from her cheeks.

At first light she sent Tenio riding for Ianthe with the scarlet surcoat. The rest of the day she spent in ignoring Conan. Food and drink she denied him.

"Let him eat and drink when I have gone," she commanded.

The men scattered about the room, most devoting their energies to dice or cards, gave her muttered assent and strange looks. She did not care. Not for the briefest moment would she allow the Cimmerian to be ungagged in her presence. Not until she had the five hundred pieces of gold in her hands to taunt him with. Not until she managed to settle herself, and that seemed strangely difficult to do.

Then the sun was making its downward journey. Time for Karela to leave for the hut. The bronze she had left, still wrapped in the blanket from Conan's bed, outside beneath a tree. There was no one about to steal it, and she would not have it under the same roof with her could she avoid it.

As she was tying the blanket-swathed bundle behind her saddle—and muttering to herself for the sickness it made her feel in the pit of her stomach—Jamaran came out of the lone tower that remained of thc ancient keep.

"That thing is valuable," he said challengingly. "Five hundred gold pieces, you say."

Karela did not answer him. This morning was no better time to kill him than last night had been.

"I should go with you," the huge man went on when she remained silent. "To make certain you return safely with the gold. This noble you go to may prove treacherous. Or perhaps something else might delay you, a woman alone with so much gold."

Karela's face tightened. Did the fool think she

planned to run off with the coin? Or did he think to take the gold and her both? "No!" she snapped as she swung into the saddle. "You are needed here to help guard the prisoner."

"There are a score to watch him. So much gold—"

"Fool!" She made the word a sneering whip-lash. "You must learn to think if you would lead men. That one inside, bound as he is, is more dangerous than any man you've ever seen. I but hope there are enough of you to keep him till I return."

Before Jamaran could speak the furious words she could read plainly on his face, Karela put spurs to her fleet eastern bay, and darted down a narrow path that was little more than a deer track. Many such crossed and criss-crossed in the thick forest, and she was soon gone beyond following.

In truth, she did not think all of her followers were necessary to keep Conan imprisoned. What she had told the big Kushite was true. The Cimmerian giant was dangerous enough to make even her wary, and she prided herself on walking carefully about no man. She had seen him struggle when defeat was inevitable, slay when his own death was certain, win when only doom lay ahead. Bound hand and foot, however, and guarded by twenty men, she did not doubt Conan would be waiting as she had left him when she returned.

Nor did she think Jamaran could take the gold —or what else he wanted from her—without her steel drinking his life in the attempt. But her pride would not allow the nameless noble to see the open disrespect the shaven-headed man now showed her. Besides, this noble would certainly have other commissions—he had already offered one, though changing it to acquiring the bronze—but he would not likely offer them if he thought she could not keep discipline in her own band.

When Karela reached the clearing where the rude hut stood, the sun was a bloody ball half-obscured by the treetops, and long shadows stretched toward the east. The scarlet-and-black caprisoned warhorse stood alone as before. Slowly she made a circuit of the clearing, within the shaded shelter of the trees. It was a desultory search, she was well aware, but she was also aware of the bronze tied behind her. More than once had she found herself riding forward on her saddle to avoid the brush against her buttocks of the rough wool that contained it. She knew a desperate urgency to be rid of the figure.

With a snorted laugh for her own sensitivity, Karela galloped into the clearing and dismounted. She carried the blanket gripped like a sack, and kicked open the rough door of planks. "Well, Lord Nameless, do you have my. . . ." Her words trailed away in surprise.

The tall nobleman stood as he had at the first meeting, but this time he was not alone. A woman with a scarlet cloak pulled around her, the hood pulled well forward, stood beside him, cool dark eyes studying Karela over a veil of opaque silk.

Karela stared back boldly, tossing the blanket

to the dirt floor at their feet. "Here is your accursed image. Now where is my gold?"

The veiled woman knelt, hastily pulling aside the folds of coarse wool. A reverent sigh came from her as the horned figure was revealed. With delicate hands she lifted it to the crude table. Karela wondered how she could bear to touch it.

"It is Al'Kiir," the veiled woman breathed. "It is what I sought, Taramenon."

Karela blinked. *Lord Taramenon?* If half what she had heard of his swordplay were true, he would be no easy opponent. She let her hand drift to the hilt of her scimitar. "There are five hundred pieces of gold to be handed over before it is yours."

The other woman's eyes swiveled to her.

"Is she what you seek also?" Taramenon asked.

The veiled woman nodded thoughtfully. "She seems so. How are you called, wench?"

"I am Karela, wench!" the red-haired bandit snapped, emphasizing the last word. "Now let me tell your fates, if you have not brought the coin agreed on. You, my fine lordling, I will sell into Koth, where your pretty face may please a mistress." Taramenon's face darkened, but the veiled woman laughed. Karela turned her attention to her. "And you I will sell into Argos, where you may dance naked in a tavern in Messantia, and please the patrons one by one for the price of a mug of ale."

"I am a princess of Ophir," the veiled woman said coldly, "who can have you impaled on the walls of the royal palace. Do you dare speak so to one before whom you should tremble?"

Karela sneered. "I not only dare speak so, by Derketo's Teats, if my gold is not forthcoming I'll strip you on the spot to see if an Argossean tavern will have you. Most Ophirean noblewomen are bony wenches who could not please a man did they try with all their might." Steel whispered across leather as her blade left its scabbard. "I'll have my gold now!"

"She will indeed do," the scarlet-cloaked woman said. "Take her."

Karela spun toward Taramenon, had an instant to see him watching with a bemused smile on his face, making no move toward her or his sword, then two men in the leather armor of light cavalry dropped from the dark rafters atop her. In a struggling heap she was borne to the packed-earth floor.

"Derketo blast you!" she howled, writhing futilely in their grip. "I'll spit you like capons! Codless jackals!"

Taramenon plucked her sword from her hand and tossed it into a corner. "You'll not be needing that any longer, girl."

Despite her frenzied striving, the cavalrymen dragged Karela to her feet. Fool! she berated herself. Taken like a virgin in a kidnapper's nets! Why had she not wondered why there was no horse for the woman?

"I suppose it's too much to hope for that she's a maiden," the woman said.

Taramenon laughed. "Much too much, I should say."

"Treacherous trull!" Karela snarled. "Catamite fopling! I'll peel your hides in strips! Release me, or my men will stake you out for the vultures! Are you fool enough to think I came alone?"

"Perhaps you did not," Taramenon said calmly, "thought I saw no one the last time you claimed to have men about this hut. In any case, my shout will bring fifty men-at-arms. Shall we see what your miserable brigands can do against them?"

"Enough, Taramenon," the veiled woman said. "Do not bandy words with the baggage. There was talk of stripping." She eyed Karela's tight breeches and snug-laced leather jerkin, and a note of malicious amusement entered her voice. "I would see that she is not . . . too bony for my purpose."

Taramenon laughed, and the three men set to with a will. Karela fought furiously, and when they were done there was blood on her nails and teeth, but she stood naked, heavy round breasts heaving with her effort. Lecherous male eyes probed her beauty, slid along the curves of lush thighs and narrow waist. Dark feminine eyes regarded her more coldly, and with a touch of jealousy lighting them. Pridefully the green-eyed woman stood as erect as the twisting of her arms behind her back would allow. She would not cringe like a shrinking girl on her wedding night for these of any others.

The tall nobleman touched his cheek, now decorated by four parallel sanquinary streaks, and examined the blood on his fingertips. Suddenly his hand flashed out; the force of his slap was such that Karela and the two men holding her all staggered.

"Do not damage her!" the veiled woman said sharply. "Your beauty is not ruined, Taramenon. Now bind her for transport."

"A taste of the strap will do her no damage, Synelle," the darkly handsome lord growled, "and I would teach her her proper place."

The name so shocked Karela that she missed the veiled woman's retort. Conan's patroness! Could the woman have learned of her own connection with the Cimmerian and be thinking to dispose of a rival? Well, she had the Cimmerian to bargain for her release, and if Derketo favored her she would have this treacherous noblewoman to hang by her heels beside him.

Karela opened her mouth to make her offer—Conan's freedom in return for her own—and a wadded rag pushed the words back into her throat. Like a starving panther she stuggled, but three men were too much for her. With ease that seemed to mock her they corded her into a neat package, wrists strapped to ankles, knees beneath her chin, thin straps laced around and around her, digging deep into her flesh. When one of the cavalrymen produced a large leather sack the memory of her plans for Synelle, including her method of returning her to Conan, flooded her face with scarlet.

"At least she can still blush," Synelle laughed as Karela was stuffed into the sack. "From her language, I thought she was lost to all decency.

Carry her to the horses. We must hurry. Events procede more quickly than I would like, and we must meet them."

"I must return to the palace to pay my respects," Taramenon said. "I will join you as quickly as I can."

"Do so quickly," Synelle said smoothly, "or I may put Conan in your place."

As Karela's dark prison was heaved swaying into the air, she felt tears running down her cheeks. Derketo curse the Cimmerian! Once again he had brought her humilation. She hoped Jamaran would slit his throat. Slowly.

18

Conan lay on the dirt-strewn stone floor as he had for a day and a night now, bound and biding his time with the patience of a jungle predator, all of his mind and energies given over to waiting and watching. Karela's injunction to give him food and water had been ignored, and he was dimly aware of hunger and thirst, but they affected him little. He had gone longer without either, and he knew he would have both once the men who guarded him were dealt with. Soon or late a mistake would be made, and he would take advantage. Soon or late, it would come.

Brass lamps had been lit against the deepening

night, but with Karela gone no one had rehung blankets to cover the tall, narrow arrow slits. Rough clay jars of wine had been passed more freely with the red-haired woman's departure, and the four brigands who had not already staggered to one of the upper rooms of the tower for drunken sleep were engrossed in drinking more and gaming with dice. The fire on the long hearth burned low; the last of the thick logs that had been stacked against the wall had long since gone into the flames, and no more had been brought from outside. None of them had thought to tend the iron kettle suspended over the flames, and the smell of burning stew blended with the unwashed stench of bandits.

Abruptly Tenio hurled dice and leather dice-cup aside. "She should have returned by now," he muttered. "What keeps her?"

"Perhaps she keeps herself," Jamaran growled. His black eyes went to Conan, and he bared large, yellow teeth in a snarl. "Leaving us with this one she seems so affrighted of."

Marusas paused in the act of scooping up the dice. "You think she has run away with the gold? It sounds a tidy sum, but her share of our raids has been as much in the last month alone."

"Erlik take you, play!" snapped a man with a slitted leather patch tied over where his nose had been cut off. His pale eyes had a permanent look of suspicious anger, as if he knew and hated what men thought when they saw his disfigurement. "I'm twenty silvers down with coin on the table. Play, curse you!" The three ignored him.

Jamaran slammed a fist the size of a small ham on the table top. "And that's another thing. Why should a woman receive ten times the share that the rest of us do? Let her try our work alone and see what sport the men she tries to rob will have with her. Without us, she'd be no more than a cut-purse, bargaining when she was caught to escape having her cheek branded for a grant of the favors she is so stingy with now."

"Without her," Tenio rebutted, "what are we? How much did we get on our own? Now you moan about only fifty golds in a month, but you didn't never get ten before her."

"She's a woman!" the huge Kushite said. "A woman's place is in a man's bed, or cooking for him, not giving orders."

Marusas laughed and tugged at his drooping black mustaches. "I would like riding her myself. Much fun in breaking that one to bridle, eh?"

"'Tis more than the pair of you could do together," Tenio sneered. "I don't like taking orders from a woman no better than you, but she puts gold in my purse, more than *I've* seen before. And I know I'd have to keep her tied hand and foot or risk waking with my own dagger in my throat. Or worse."

"No cods at all on you," Jamaran snorted. He nudged the Zamoran with a huge elbow. "I always knew there was more woman than man in him. Likely spends all his hours in Ianthe at the House of the Yearling Lambs." The two of them roared with laughter, and patch-nose joined in as if despite himself.

All the blood left Tenio's face, and his narrow-bladed dagger flickered into his hand. "I don't take that from nobody," he snarled.

"From me you take what I give," Jamaran said, all mirth gonc from his voice, "or I'll use that blade of yours to make *sure* you've no cods."

"Curse the lot of you for chattering old women!" patch-nose shouted. "Am I suddenly not good enough to dice with?"

Conan made a sound behind his gag; had his throat not been parched it would have been a chuckle. A while longer and they would kill each other, leaving him only his bonds to worry about.

Flinging his mug across the room in a spray of wine, Jamaran heaved himself from his bench and strode on legs as big around as a normal man's waist to stand over the Cimmerian. Conan's icy azure gaze calmly met the dark glower directed at him.

"Big man," Jamaran said contemptuously, and his foot thudding into Conan's ribs lifted the Cimmerian from the stone floor. "You seem not so big to me." Again his foot drove Conan back. "Why does Karela want you kept safe? Is she afraid of you? Or maybe she loves you, huh? Perhaps I'll let you watch while I enjoy her, if she comes back." Each sentence he punctuated with a massive booted foot, until Conan lay struggling for breath on the very edge of the hearth. The Cimmerian glared at Jamaran as the shaven-headed man squatted beside him, doubling a heavy fist. "Ten men have I beaten to their death with this. You will be number eleven. I do not think Karela will return—she's been gone too long already—but I'll wait a bit longer. I want her to see it. Watching a man killed that way does something to a woman." Laughing, the huge Kushite straightened. With a last kick he turned back to the table. "Where's my mug?" he roared. "I want wine!"

Cursing behind his gag Conan jerked himself out of the coals he had landed in, but his mind was not on his burns. So intent had he been on awaiting his chance for escape that their talk of Karela's lateness had barely impinged on his thoughts. He knew her well enough to be sure she had not fled with the gold. Boros' words came back to him. The most beautiful and proudest women of the land were sacrificed to Al'Kiir. Few were the women more beautiful than Karela, and to her pride he could well attest. The fool wench had not only taken those who wanted to raise the god the means to do so, she had delivered herself as a sacrifice. He was sure of it. Now he must rescue her from her own folly. But how? How even to free himself?

He shifted to ease his weight on a burn on his arm, and suddenly his lips curled in a smile around his gag. Careless of searing flame he thrust his bound wrists into the fire. Gritting his teeth on his gag against fiery agony, he strained mighty arms against the ropes, massive muscles knotting and writhing. Sweat beaded his face.

The reek of burning hemp came to him; he wondered how the others could fail to be aware of it, but none of the four so much as looked in his direction. They were immersed in their mugs of wine, and patch-nose kept up his arguing for a chance to win back his loses. Abruptly, the ropes parted, and Conan pulled his half-cooked wrists from the flames, careful to keep them yet behind his back. His gaze sought his ancient broad-sword, leaning against the wall behind the drinking men. There would be no chance to grasp it before he came to grips with the men between him and his steel.

With a crash patch-nose kicked over his bench. Conan froze. Snarling the man snatched up his mug and began to stalk back and forth across the room, muttering angrily about men who won and then would not gamble, and shooting dark glances at the other three, still intent on their drink. His eyes did not stray to the Cimmerian, lying rigid on the hearth-stone.

Slowly, so as to draw no attention, Conan slid his booted feet back until he could feel the heat of flames licking about them. To the smell of burning rope was added that of scorching leather, but the latter was no more noticed than the first. Then those cords were burned through as well. There was no time to waste on the gag. Rolling to his feet the big Cimmerian snatched a long, black fire-iron from the hearth.

Patch-nose was the first to see Conan free of his bonds, but the man had only time to goggle before wine sprayed out of his mouth and his skull was crushed by the fire-iron. Shouting, the others scrambled to their feet. Tenio produced his dagger, but Conan drove the fire-iron point-first through the ferret-faced man's chest and caught the blade as it dropped from the transfixed man's nerveless fingers. Marusas' sword leaped into his hand, then the Zamoran was staggering back, trying to scream around the dagger that had blossomed in fountains of scarlet in his throat.

Roaring, Jamaran leaped to grapple with the Cimmerian, throwing bearlike arms about his waist, heaving him into the air. Conan felt the man's huge fists locked in the small of his back, felt his spine begin to creak. Conan smashed his linked hands down on the nape of the huge man's bull neck, once, twice, thrice, to no effect. Jamaran's grip tightened inexorably. In moments, the Cimmerian knew, his back would snap. Desperately he slammed his palms against the other's ears.

With a scream Jamaran let him drop. Even as his heels hit the stone floor, Conan's bladed hand struck the huge Kushite's throat. Jamaran gagged, yet lashed out with a massive fist in the same instant. Conan blocked the blow, winding his arm around the shaven-headed man's to pull him close. With hammer-like blows the Cimmerian pounded the big man's body, feeling ribs splinter beneath his fist.

In the night a trumpet sounded the Ophirean army call for the attack. "Company one, ready torches!" a voice called. "Company two, attack! Take no prisoners!" Feet pounded on the floors above; frantic yells rose.

In his desperate struggle Conan had no time to

worry about the new danger. Jamaran smashed his head against the Cimmerian's; Conan staggered, clinging to consciousness. The huge Kushite tried to enfold Conan once more in his crushing embrace, but Conan rammed a knee into his crotch, lifting the man to his toes with bulging eyes. Like thunderbolts the heels of Conan's hands struck Jamaran's chin. The shaven head went back with a loud crack as the Kushite's neck broke, and he fell in a boneless heap.

Conan ripped the gag from his mouth and threw it atop the body of the man who had threatened to beat him to death. A torch was thrust through one of the arrow slits, then another. Putting a hand on the table top Conan vaulted across it to grab his sword hilt, baring the blade by slinging the worn shagreen scabbard away. When soldiers spoke of taking no prisoners they generally slew whatever moved, without questioning whether it was enemy or captive. Conan did not mean to die easily.

A man darted in at the door, sword ready; Conan swung his steel . . . and stopped a handsbreadth away from splitting Machaon's skull. Narus rushed in behind the grizzled veteran, and two more of the company.

"You!" Conan exclaimed. "You are the Ophirean army?"

Narus shrugged and held up a battered brass trumpet. "An odd talent of mine, but useful from time to time." He looked around at the bodies on the stone floor. "Once more you leave nothing for the rest of us."

"There are more above," Conan said, but Narus shook his head.

"They lept from breaks in the walls, thinking we were who we claimed, and fled into the night."

"We've still bloody work to do," Conan told him. "Karela has been taken prisoner, and I mean to rescue her." Atop Tor Al'Kiir, he thought. Boros said he had seen lights there, and he had no other clue. "We must move quickly, if you will come with me."

"Mitra, Conan," Machaon growled, "will you let me say a word? There's no time for wenches, not even her. We came after you because Zandru's Hells have come to sup in Ophir."

"Al'Kiir." Conan's heart sank. "They've raised the god already."

"I know naught of gods," Machaon muttered, "but Valdric lies dead of the sickness that consumed him, and Iskandrian has seized the royal palace."

Conan started in surprise. "Iskandrian!"

"The old general has declared for Valentius," Narus explained. "And that young coxcomb has taken the name Maranthes II, as if a name could make him a great king. I hear he didn't wait for funeral rites or even a priest, but took the crown from Valdric's corpse before it was cold and put it on his own head."

"Will you stop your nattering, Narus!" Machaon barked. "Most of the nobles think as you did, Cimmerian. They gather their forces, but Iskandrian moves to put them down before they can. He marched with most of the Ianthe garrison an hour after he put Valentius on the throne. If that isn't enough, Taurianus is talking loudly that the company should join the nobles. He's telling everyone if Iskandrian wins it means the end of Free-Companies in Ophir." His tattooed face grew grim. "I'll tell you, Conan, he's right on that. Iskandrian will give short shrift to mercenaries."

"We'll worry about Iskandrian later," Conan said. "Karela comes first, and matters even more important than her. How many of the company did you bring, Machaon?"

"Seven, including Narus and myself, all of whom crossed the Nemedian border with us. Two I left to guard Julia. The mood of the others is bad, Cimmerian. You must return now if you mean to hold them together. Karela can take care of herself for a time if any woman can."

"We found your black picketed with this lot's mounts," Narus added.

"Crom!" Conan muttered. The numbers were not enough if they faced what he feared atop Tor Al'Kiir. "We ride for Ianthe, to gather the company and ride out again. No, not to join the nobles. To Tor Al'Kiir. There'll be time for questions later. To horse, Erlik blast your hides. To horse, and pray to whatever gods you can think of that we are in time."

19

Iron-shod hooves struck sparks from paving stones as Conan galloped through the dark and empty streets of Ianthe, seven men trailing behind with their cloaks standing out in the wind of their charge. Atop the malevolent granite hump of Tor Al'Kiir torches flickered, distant points of light in the moonless sky mocking his efforts at haste. He cursed to himself, regretting even the time it had taken to bribe the gate-watch for entry.

He wanted to shout at the sleepers who felt a momentary safety behind their walls of brick and stone. Mourning cloths draped from shuttered windows and shrouded public fountains; sprigs of sa'karian, black and white berries intermixed as symbol of death and rebirth, adorned every door. The capital of Ophir mourned its dead King in fear and uncertainty, yet none in that city knew that what they felt was as a flickering lamp flame to the storm-lashed fire-death of a great forest beside the terror that awaited their wakening.

As he galloped through the archway of the house where his company was quartered, Conan bellowed. "To me! Out with you, and to horse! Move, damn you to Zandru's Hells!" Stillness lay heavily on the blackened building; his words echoed hollowly from the courtyard walls as the others clattered in behind him. "Taurianus!" he called. "Boros!"

A door open with the protest of rusty hinges, showing a tiny light, and four figures moved into the court. Slowly the shadowy shapes resolved into Boros, Julia, and two of his company holding shielded lanterns. The armored men were the two remaining besides those behind him who had come with him from Nemedia.

"Where are the others?" Conan demanded.

"Gone," Boros answered hollowly. "Taurianus—Erlik roast his soul for eternity—convinced most of them you were dead, since you didn't return. Half followed him to join the nobles againt Iskandrian. The rest?" His thin shoulders shrugged. "Faded away to hide as best they can. Without you, fear corroded their hearts."

Conan fought the urge to rain curses upon Taurianus' head. There was no time; the torches still burned atop the mountain. What must be done, must be done with the men he had. But he would lead no man blind to face sorcerers, and perhaps a god.

"Boros," he said grimly, "tell of Al'Kiir. But briefly, old man. The time of his coming is near, perhaps before first light, if we do not stop it."

Boros gasped and, tugging at his beard, spoke in a quavering voice, filled with all his years, of days before even ancient Ophir existed and the rites of Al'Kiir, of the Circle of the Right-Hand Path and the imprisonment of the demonic god, of those who would bring the abominable worship again into the world and the god whose horror they celebrated. When he was done there was silence, broken only by the call of an owl. Each man's breath was audible, and they all spoke of fear.

"If we go to Iskandrian with this tale," Conan said finally, "he will think it a ruse of the nobles and slay us, or emprison us for madmen until it is too late. But every word is as true and as dire as a spear thrust to the heart. Boros has told you what comes, what fate may lie in store for your sister, or wife or daughter, because she is comely and spirited. I ride to Tor Al'Kiir to stop it. Who rides with me?"

For a long moment only silence answered him, then Julia stepped forward, her chin held high. "If there is no courage among these who call themselves men, at least I will go with you."

"You will go to your sleeping mat," Machaon growled, "or I'll bind you in such a package as

Karela made of you, to keep you safe against my return." The girl moved hurriedly behind Boros, eyeing the grizzled mercenary warily as if unsure how much of his threat he meant. Machaon nodded with satisfaction, then turned in his saddle to Conan. "I've seen more of wizards following you, Cimmerian, than one man has a right to expect in a lifetime. But I cannot see that once more will make any difference."

"An owl calling on a moonless night means death," Narus said glumly, "but I've never seen a god. I, too, ride with you, Cimmerian."

One by one, then, the other seven mercenaries pledged to follow also, voices cold with humiliation at being surpassed in courage by a girl, with anger and determination to protect some particular woman from the bloody rites. And still with fear. Yet they would come.

Conan eyed their scant number in the pale light of the lanterns and sighed. "We will be enough," he said, as much to convince himself as anything else, "because we must. We must. Claran, Memtes, get your horses." The two men named set their lanterns on the ground and ran for the stables. "We ride as soon as they return," he went on. "We must needs scale the mountain afoot, for our horses cannot climb those slopes, but—"

"Wait, Conan," Boros broke in. "Make haste slowly, or you but hasten to your death. You must acquire the Staff of Avanrakash."

"There is no time, old man," Conan said grimly. He twisted impatiently in his saddle to peer through the night toward the deeper blackness of

Tor Al'Kiir. The torch lights still were there, beckoning him, taunting him to his core. What befell Karela while he sat his horse like a statue?

"Do you go forth to confront a lion," the bearded man chided, "would you then say there was no time to fetch spear or bow? That you must face it with bare hands? You go to face Al'Kiir. Think your courage and steel will avail you against a god? As well slit your own throat right here."

Conan's massive hands tightened on the reins in frustration until his knuckles cracked. He did not fear death, though he sought it no more than any other man, but his death would be of no use if Karela were still sacrificed, if Al'Kiir was freed again. Decision came swiftly, spurred by necessity. He tossed his reins to Machaon and dismounted.

"Take my horse with you to the mountain," he commanded as he tugged his hauberk off over his head. Such work as he had now to do was not best done in armor. He dropped to the gound to pull off his boots. "I will meet you at the crossroads at the foot of the mountain."

"Do you know where this staff the old man speaks of is to be found?" Machaon asked.

"In the throne room," Boros said. "By ancient law, at the death of a King the scepter and crown must be left on the throne for nine days and nine nights. Valentius has usurped custom by donning the crown so quickly, but he will not dare flout it altogether."

"The royal palace!" Machaon exclaimed. "Cimmerian, you are mad to think you can enter there.

Come! We will do the best we can with honest steel."

"I was a thief once," Conan replied. "Twill not be the first palace I've entered by ways other than the door." Stripped now to his breechcloth, he slung his swordbelt across his massive chest so that his sword hung down his back, dagger and pouch beneath his left arm. Claran and Memtes trotted their horses from the stable, hooves ringing on the thick slates of the court. "I will be at the crossroads, with the staff," the Cimmerian said, "without fail. Be you there also."

With ground-eating pantherish strides, Conan loped into the night. Behind him Machaon and the others clattered out of the courtyard and turned their mounts in the other direction, toward the North Gate, but he was already one with the darkness, a deadly ghost racing through unlit streets that were empty of other human forms. Every door was barred, every window shuttered, as the inhabitants of the city cowered in fear of what might come; only occasional scavenging dogs, gaunt-ribbed and half-wild, prowled the moonless streets, and they shied away from the huge shape that shared the way with them. Beneath his leathery-soled feet the paving stones felt like the rocks of his native Cimmeria, and the feel gave wings to his stride as when he raced up mountains as a boy. His great lungs pumped with the effort of his running, for this time he raced not for the pride of winning, but for Karela, and for every woman who would lose life or more if he failed.

Again an owl cried, and Conan's mind went to Narus' words. Perhaps the cry did mean death, his or someone else's. Crom, the fierce god of the harsh and icy land where he was born, gave a man life and will, but the grim Lord of the Mound never promised that life would be long, nor that will would always prevail. A man could but fight, and keep fighting so long as breath or life remained.

The Cimmerian did not slow until the massive walls of the royal palace loomed before him, crenelations and towertops only shadows against the ebon sky. The thick, iron-sheathed gates were closed and barred, the portcullis down, but he spared not a glance in that direction. Such was not his means of entry this night.

His fingers felt across the surface of the wall, featureless in the blackness. Long centuries past had the great wall been built, of stones each weighing more than twenty times as much as a big man. Only the largest trebuchet could hurl boulders weighty enough to trouble its solidity, but Conan did not mean to batter a way through. Those years had leeched at the mortar between the great stones, leaving gaps that made an easy path for one mountain-born.

With agile sureness Conan climbed, fingers and toes searching out the grooves where wind and rain and time had worn away the mortar, mighty muscles straining to pull him up where there was but room for fingernails to grip. Below was only the long, bone-shattering drop to pavement now swathed in the night, yet he did not slow in his swift ascent of that sheer wall. Time pressed on him too greatly to allow room for caution.

At the top of the wall he paused between two tall merlons topped with stone leopards, ears straining for the scuff of boots on the rampart, the creak of leather and armor. A combat there with guards would surely doom his quest before it had truly begun. There was no sound. Conan drew himself through the crennel. No guards were atop the wall. The palace was silent as a tomb. It seemed Iskandrian had left only men for the gates; the White Eagle would strike hard, as was his wont.

From the rampart a curving ramp led down toward the outer bailey. There, however, he would surely be seen, no matter how few guards had been left behind or how many servants hid in fear that too-ardent service to him who now wore the crown might be punished if he lost it. Rooftops must be his path. The nearest, a wing of the palace, lay but an easy jump from the ramp for a vigorous man. Easy if the approaching run could be made on level ground rather than down a steep ramp, and if a three-story drop to the granite paving of the bailey were ignored.

Conan measured distances and angles, then took a deep breath and sprinted down the ramp. At the sixth great stride he flung himself across the chasm. Fingertips caught at the edge of the roof. One tile broke free, spiraling into the dark to shatter on the stones below; for an instant the Cimmerian hung by one hand. Slowly he hauled himself up, swung to hook a leg over the edge. The tile he held to shifted under his hand. Then he was flat on the roof, carefully setting aside the loose tile and quieting his breath as he waited to see if the noise of the first tile's fall drew attention. Still nothing stirred.

Like a jungle beast Conan was up and running, feet sure on the slanting tiles, climbing granite gargoyles to a higher level, leaping from a balcony tiled in black and white marble to clutch at a high peaked gable, edging with chest pressed flat against smooth granite along a ledge wide enough only for the balls of his feet, then climbing again, past mullioned windows and trefoils, until at last he scrambled through a narrow ventilation arch and looked down from great height on the vast throne room of the royal palace.

Great golden lamps hung on thick chains of the same metal from the vaulted ceiling, their bright flames lighting well the floor far below, a floor mosaicked in huge representations of the leopards and eagles that were the royal symbols of Ophir. In the middle of that floor was a black-shrouded bier on which Valdric's body lay in state, clothed in ornate robes of gold embroidered purple set with pearls. No living man was there to keep vigil over the dead King.

Conan's eyes sought the throne. Like unto the great chair in which Antimides had sat it was, covered in leopards and eagles, but larger still and of solid gold. The beasts' eyes were rubies, and claws and talons clutched emeralds as large as the joint of a man's thumb. Of the crown there was no sign. Ancient law or no, the Cimmerian thought, Valentius had not found it in himself to part with the royal diadem for even nine days once he had gained it. Yet what he sought was there. Across the arms of the throne lay the scepter of Ophir, its golden length glittering with an encrustation of all manner of gems.

Carefully Conan let himself down inside the throne room, using the scrolls and arabesques carved in the marble walls to climb down until he reached their end, some twenty feet above the floor. Here great tapestries hung. He ripped loose a corner of one—a scene of a crowned King hunting deer from horseback—and let himself drop, swinging on it as at the end of a rope. His feet brushed the floor, and he released the tapestry to run to the throne.

Almost hesitantly he hefted the long scepter. So much had he risked on the word of a drunk, and so much depended on it. Hastily he produced his dagger and began prying away soft gold and sparkling jewels, letting them fall to the purple velvet cushion of the throne. At the sight of wood beneath he grunted in satisfaction, but continued until he had stripped away all the outer sheath. He was left with a plain wooden staff as long as his outstretched arms and as thick as his two thumbs together.

Yet could it be in truth the Staff of Avanrakash, he wondered. He felt no magical qualities in it, and it showed no signs of its supposed great age. In fact, had it been a walking staff he would have thought it cut no more than a few days previous.

"But it *was* within the scepter," he breathed, "and it is all I have." For luck he scooped a handful of gems from the cushion, not bothering to see what they were, and stuffed them into his pouch.

"A common thief," Taramenon said from the door to the throne room. "Will not Synelle be surprised when she returns to find your head on a spike atop the River Gate?"

Conan reached over his shoulder; his sword slid easily into his grasp. The staff clutched in his left hand, he strode toward the tall noble. He had no words to say, no time for words. Even so in a corner of his mind lust flared at the mention of the woman's name. Synelle. He could he have gone so long without thinking of her? How could he have gone so long without touching her? The frozen rage of battles forced the thoughts down, smothered them.

Taramenon threw aside his fur-trimmed scarlet cape and drew his own blade. "I but stepped in here a moment to spit in Valdric's face. To offer obeisance to a corpse that was half-rotted before even it died turned my stomach. Finding you is a pleasant surprise I did not expect." Abruptly rage contorted his face into an ugly mask. "I will tell her of your death when I see her this night. Your filthy hands will never touch her again, you barbarian swine!" Snarling he rushed forward, swinging his blade in a mighty chop at Conan's head.

The Cimmerian's broadsword met Taramenon's with a tremendous clash. The Ophirean's eyes widened at the force of the blow. but on the instant he struck again. Again Conan's blade met his in a shower of sparks. Taramenon fought with all the deadly finesse of one who was the finest swordsman in Ophir, his longsword as agile and swift and deadly as a Kothian viper; Conan fought with the cold ferocity of a northland beserker, his steel the lightning of the Cimmerian crags. Conan had no time to waste in defense—he must conquer, and quickly, or the noise of the fight would draw others, and he might well be overwhelmed by sheer numbers—but his contant attack left no room to Taramenon for aught *but* defense.

Sweat rolled down the face of the finest blade in Ophir as he found himself forced back, ever back, by an implacable demon with a face of stone and icy blue eyes, eyes in which depths he could read his own death. Panic clouded Taramenon's face, and for the first time in his life he knew fear. "Guards!" he screamed. "A thief! Guards!"

In that brief instant of divided attention Conan's blade engaged that of the tall Ophirean, brought it down, around, thrust under it. Chain mail links snapped, razor steel sliced through muscle and bone, and the Cimmerian's sword hilt slammed against Taramenon's chest.

Conan stared into dark incredulous eyes. "Synelle is mine," he grated. "Mine!"

Blood bubbled from Taramenon's mouth, and he fell. Conan stared at the body in wonder before remembering to pull his sword free. Why had he said such a thing? Synelle was of no import in this. Karela was important, Al'Kiir and the staff and getting to the crossroads quickly. Yet images suppressed by events rose unbidden, sleek thighs and satin skin and swelling breasts and. . . . Shaking his head wozzily he half-staggered to Taramenon's discarded cape to clean his bloody blade and cut strips to bind the staff across his back. Was he going mad, he wondered. Visions of Synelle kept crowding his brain, as if time spent not thinking of her had to be made up. Desperately he forced them back. The crossroads, he thought. The crossroads, and no time.

Running to the half-torn-down tapestry, he began to climb. Synelle. The crossroads, and no time.

20

Karela grunted as the sack in which she was carricd was upended, dumping her, still bound and naked, onto cold stone. After the darkness light blinded her, filling her eyes with tears. The tears infuriated her; she would not have those who had taken her prisoner think they had reduced her to crying. Blinking, she was at last able to make out the roughly cut stone walls of what seemed to be a small cave, lit by rush torches in black iron sconces.

She was not alone, she realized. Synelle was there, and four other women, alabastrine-skinned blondes who seemed to wear variations of one face. The noblewoman was not dressed as when last Karela had seen her. Now she wore bracelets of black iron chain on each wrist, and two narrow strips of ebon silk, before and behind, leaving the outer curvcs of hips and breasts bare, were all her garb save for a belt of golden links. Karela stared when she saw the buckle. It was the head of the malevolent bronze she had sold—tried to sell, she thought ruefully—but rendered in gold. A chaplet of gold chain encircled Synelle's silvery tresses, severely braided into a coronet, and on that golden band, too, were the four horns of that demonic figure.

The other women were dressed as was Synelle, but the narrow belts cinching their waists were of black iron, and dark metal enclosed their ankles and necks as well. Their hair, neatly coiled about their heads, bore no headdress. With bowed heads their humbly alert eyes watched the exotically beautiful noblewoman.

Karela swallowed hard, and was reminded again how dry was her throat. Had she the use of her mouth she would tell this Synelle she could have Conan. It would be a lie—she would not be driven from her business with the Cimmerian by this pale-haired trull who called herself a lady—but lying seemed much the better part of valor at the moment.

Synelle nodded, and the four women in iron belts produced leather straps. Karela jerked futilely at her bonds despite herself. If only she had a dagger, or but a single hand free, or even her tongue to shout her defiance at them.

"Listen to me, wench," Synelle said. "These women will prepare you. If you fight, they will beat you, but in any event they will carry out my orders. I would have you as little marked as possible, so if you will submit, nod your head."

Karela tried to shout through her gag. Submit! Did this fool woman think she was some milksop maiden to be frightened by threats? Her green eyes hurled all her silent fury at Synelle.

Abruptly Synelle moved, placing a foot on Karela's knees, bound beneath her chin, to roll her onto her back and hold her there. "A taste, then. Cut well in."

The other women darted forward, their leather straps slicing beneath Karela's corded heels, raining blows on her helpless buttocks, drawn taut by her tying.

Her green eyes bulged in her head, and she had an instant to be grateful for the gag that held back her cries, then her head was nodding frantically. Derketo! There was no use in being beaten while lying trussed like a pig for market.

Synelle motioned the women back. "I was sure you would be reasonable."

Karela tried to meet the dark eyes staring down at her, then closed her own in humiliation. It was clear from the look on Synelle's face that she had never doubted that the red-haired woman could be brought to heel. Let them free her, Karela prayed, and she would show them the worth of pledge wrung from whips. She would. . .

Suddenly the cords binding her were severed. Karela caught a flash of a dagger. She moved to grab it . . . and sprawled in boneless agony on the stone floor, muscles stiff from long confinement barely able to do more than twitch. Slowly, painfully, she brought a hand up to drag the gag from her mouth. She wanted to weep. The dagger was gone from sight, and she had neither seen who had held it nor where it was hidden.

Even as she dropped the wadded cloth two of the women pulled her to her feet. She gasped with the pain; had they not supported her she could not have stood. One of the others began drawing an ivory comb through her tangled locks, while the last wiped her sweat away with soft, damp clothes.

Karela worked her mouth for the moisture to speak. "I'll not sell you to a tavern," she managed. "I'll tear your heart out with my bare hands."

"Good," Synelle said. "I feared your spirit might have been broken. Often the journey here, bound, is enough for that. It is well that it was not in your case."

Karela sneered. "You want the pleasure of breaking me yourself, then? You will not have it, because you cannot do it. And if you want Conan back—"

"Conan!" the noblewoman cut her off, dark eyes widening in surprise. "How do you come to know of the barbarian?"

"We were once," Karela began, then spluttered to a halt. She was tired, and spoke of things of which she had no wish to speak. "No matter how

I know of him. If you want him, you'll cease your threats and bargain."

Synelle trilled with laughter. "So you think I merely attempt to dispose of a rival. I should be furious that such as you could think of yourself as my rival, but I find it merely amusing. I expect he is a man who has known many women in his time, and if you are one of that number I see he has little discrimination in his choosing. That is at an end, now." She held out a slender palm. "I hold the barbarian there, wench. He will crawl to me on his belly when I call him, dance like a bear for a tin whistle at my command. And you think to be my rival?" She threw back her head and laughed even harder.

"No woman could treat Conan so," Karela snapped. "I know, for I have tried, and by Derketo, I am ten times the woman you are."

"You are suitable for the rites," the silver-haired woman said coolly, "but I am High Priestess of Al'Kiir. Yet were I not, you would still not be woman enough to serve as my bowermaid. My tirewomen were nobly born in Corinthia, and she who draws my bath and rubs me with oils was a princess in far Vendhya, yet to obey my slightest wish is now the whole of their lives. What can a jade of a bandit be beside such as they, who are but my slaves?"

Karela opened her mouth for another retort, and gasped when a black-armored man in a horned helmet appeared in the entrance to the cavern. For an instant she had thought it was the creature the bronze represented. Foolishness, she berated herself. Such a creature could not exist.

"Has Taramenon come yet?" Synelle demanded of the man.

"No, my lady. Nor any message of him."

"He will suffer for this," Synelle said heatedly. "He defies me, and I will see him suffer for it!" Drawing a deep breath, she smoothed the already taut black silk over her rounded breasts. "We will proceed without him. When he comes, he is to be seized and bound. There are rites other than the gift of women."

"Taramenon, my lady?" the man said in shocked tones.

"You heard my command!" Synelle made a brusque gesture, and the armored figure bowed himself from her presence.

Karela had been listening intently, hoping for some fragment of information that might help her escape, but now she became aware of how the four women were dressing her, the tiny white tarla blossoms woven into her hair, the diaphanous layers of blue silk meant to be removed one by one for the titillation of a groom.

"What travesty is there?" she growled. "You *do* think me a rival, but if you mean to rid yourself of me in this way, you are mad! I'll marry no man! Do you hear me, you pasty-faced trull?"

A cruel smile curled Synelle's lips, and the look on her face sent a chill through Karela's blood. "You will marry no *man*," the haughty noblewoman said softly. "Tonight you will wed a god, and I will become ruler of Ophir."

The tall white marker at the crossroads, a square marble pillar inscribed with the distances to the borders of Nemedia and Aquilonia, loomed out of the night ahead of Conan. No sound broke the silence save his labored breath and the steady slap of his running feet on the paving stones. Beyond the marker reared the dark mass of Tor Al'Kiir, a huge granite outcropping dominating the flat country about it.

The big Cimmerian crouched beside the marble plinth, eyes straining at the blackness. There was so sign of his men. Softly he imitated the cry of a Nemedian nighthawk.

The muted jingle of tight-strapped harness announced the sudden appearance of Machaon and the rest, leading their horses. Memtes, bringing up the rear, gripped the reins of Conan's big Aquilonian black as well as those of his own mount. Bows and quivers were slung on their backs.

"I thought it best to keep from sight," the tattooed veteran told Conan quietly. "As we arrived, two score men-at-arms passed, chasing another band as large, and twice parties of light cavalry have gone by at the gallop. Scouts, the last, no doubt."

"Unless I miss my guess," Narus added in a low voice that would not travel far, "Iskandrian seeks action this night, and the nobles seek to avoid him until their strength is gathered. Never did I think that when the final battle for Ophir occurred, I would be scaling a mountain."

"Go to Taurianus, then," Conan growled, "if you seek glory!" Irritably he shook his black maned head. Such edginess was not his usual manner, but his thoughts scarcely seemed his own. With a desperation foreign to him he fought to cling to his purpose of mind, struggled against images of Synelle and lust that threatened to overwhelm him.

"Is that the famous staff?" Machaon asked. "It has no look of magic to me."

"It is," the Cimmerian replied, "and it has." He hoped he did not lie. Unfastening the strips of cloth that held the length of wood, he clutched it in one hand and drew his sword with the other. "This is the last chance to change your minds. Let any man unsure of what he does step aside." The soft and deadly susuration of steel sliding from scabbards was his answer. Conan nodded grimly. "Then hide the horses in yon copse of trees and follow me."

"Your armor," Machaon said. "'Tis on your saddle."

"There is no time," Conan said, and without waiting for the others he started up the stony slope.

Crom was not a god men prayed to; he gave nothing beyond his first gift. But now Conan offered a prayer to any god that would listen. If he died for it, let him be in time.

A silent file of purposeful men fell in behind

him in his climb, on their way to beard a god in his den.

The lash struck across her shoulders again, and Karela gritted her teeth against the howl she wanted to let pass. Bound between posts topped with the obscene head of Al'Kiir, she knelt, all but the last layer of thin blue silk torn away from her sweat-slick body. It was not the pain from the incessant bite of leather that made her want to cry out, or not alone; she would have died before giving her tormentors the satisfaction of acknowledging that. But the burning stripes that made scarlet lattices on her body were as pin-pricks beside the flaming desire the ointment with which Synelle had anointed her brought unbidden. Uncontrollably Karela writhed, and wept for the humilation of it.

The silvery-haired noble-woman danced before her, spinning and dipping, chanting words that defied hearing in rhythm to haunting flutes and the pounding of scabbarded swords on the stone floor of the vaulting cavern. Between Synelle and Karela stood the bronze she had stolen from Conan, but its evil was overpowered by the waves of horror that radiated from the huge sanguinary image that dominated the chamber. Three ebon eyes that seemed to drink in light held her own. She tried to tear her eyes from that hellborn gaze, she prayed for the strength to pull away, but like a bird hypnotized by a serpent she had no will left.

The lashes struck, again and again. Her hands

quivered in her bonds with the effort of not shrieking, for that demonic scarlet figure had begun to vibrate, giving off a hum that blended with the flutes and wrenched at the core of her that made her a woman. Conan, she cried silently, where are you?

Stirring where neither time nor space existed, where endless nihility was all. Awakening, almost full, as pleasure overwhelming lanced through the impenetrable shield. Irritation, vaster than the minds of all men together could encompass, flared. Would these torments never cease, these returnings of ancient memories near gone and better forgotten? Would not. . . . Full awareness for the first time in eons, awareness cold enough to freeze suns and stay worlds in their motion. There was direction. A single pristine strand of crystalline desire and pain stretching into the infinite. Slowly, with a wariness born of long centuries of disappointment, from the midst of nothingness the gleaming thread of worship was followed.

Conan peered around the edge of a huge, moss-covered block of marble which had once been intended for construction. Crickets chirped in the dark, and a nightbird gave a haunting cry. All else was still.

Roofless walls of niveous stone and truncated alabaster columns, never completed and now wreathed by thick vines, covered the leveled top of the mountain. Among the columns were more than a score of men in black armor and horned helms, the torches a third of them carried casting flickering shadows over the weather-beaten ruins. He wanted to sigh with relief at the symbol picked out in scarlet on their chests. It was clearly the head of the image Karela had stolen, the head of Al'Kiir. Not until that moment had he allowed himself to fear he might be coming to the wrong place.

The black-armored man had to be guarding an entrance to chambers below, Conan thought, where the horrible rite was to take place. Boros had said the tomb lay buried in the heart of the mountain. At least, they were supposed to be standing guard. The sinister reputation of Tor Al'Kiir made it unlikely anyone would come there, most especially in the night, and that made them careless. Some leaned against pale fluted marble. Others sat and talked among themselves. No eye was directed outward to watch for intruders.

Conan signaled with his hands; long practiced, the nine men behind him slid soundlessly away. The Cimmerian counted silently, knowing how long it would take each man to reach his place.

"Now!" he shouted, and burst from concealment to hurl himself at the guards. As he had known it would, his shout and the appearance of a lone man charging froze them for an instant, long enough for nine bowstrings to twang, for nine feathered shafts to drink life.

The guards of Al'Kiir had been chosen for their skill, though, and even as their comrades were falling the survivors darted for cover behind the columns. But then Conan was among them. Thrusting the staff like a lance he took a man under the chin; throat cartiledge snapped loudly, and blood spilled from a mouth that could no longer scream.

"For Conan!" he heard behind him. "Conan!"

A blade thrust at him, and his ancient steel severed the arm that held it. He ducked beneath a decapitating cut and, wielding his broadsword like an axe, chopped through his attacker's mid-section almost to the spine. Kicking the body away, he straightened to find no black-armored man standing. His mercenaries stood among the bodies, gripping bloody swords and warily watching for more of the enemy.

"Are they all dead?" Conan demanded.

Machaon shook his head. "Two managed to run down there." He pointed to a dark opening where steps had led down into the mountain.

"Crom!" the Cimmerian muttered. With quick strides he moved to the opening and started down. Wordlessly the others followed.

Sweat trickling down her sleek form, Synelle moved in the ancient forms and patterns, her body swaying and bending in an exaltation of lust and pain. Time-forgotten words spilled from her mouth, echoed against the walls, supplicating and glorifying her dire god. The monstrous horned malevolence before which she danced pulsated like the string of a harp. The drone that came from it now drowned out the flutes and the pounding scabbards and even the slap of leather on flesh, yet seemed to merge with and amplify her voice.

A part of her mind noted that the auburn-haired woman, naked now to the lash, sagged in her bonds, but struggled still against surrender. Not once had a cry passed her lips. That was well, Synelle thought, not pausing an instant in either movements or incantation. She was certain that the success she seemed to be having was as much due to the stubborn pride of this Karela as to the bronze image. Much better than any of the haughty noblewomen, who in the end always wept and begged and offered their bodies to the men whipping them in exchange for even a moment's surcease.

One of her guards, his chain-mail rent and bloodied, burst into the chamber. "We are attacked, my lady!" he gasped. "Hundreds of them! They cry, for Conan!"

Synelle faltered, then desperately continued with dance and invocation. To stop now would mean disaster, doom better undreamed of. Yet her mind spun. Conan? It was impossible. But then it was impossible that any should dare brave the night slopes of Tor Al'Kiir. Then who. . . .

Thoughts and words and movement died as one. All sound stopped as the great horned head turned toward her and three lidless eyes, black as death, regarded her like dark flames of unholy life.

Men in black chain-mail, their horned helmets making them seem more demons than men in the dim light of fires burned low in iron cressets, appeared as if from the walls to defend the rough-cut stone passage. Demons they might appear, yet they died like men. Into the midst of them Conan waded, his ancient broadsword tirelessly rising and falling in furious butchery, till its length was stained crimson and blood fell from it as if the steel itself had wounds. A charnel house he made, and those who dared confront him died. Many could not face that gory blade nor the deathly cold eyes of he who wielded it, and darted past the one man to face instead the nine behind.

The Cimmerian spared no thought for those who refused him combat. What they guarded and what he sought lay ahead, and he did not cease his slaying until he had hacked his way into a huge cavern. The blood chilled in his veins at what he saw.

Twenty more of the black-armored men stood there, but they were as frozen as he, and seemed as insignificant as ants beside what else the chamber contained. Karela, her lush nakedness welted, hanging by her wrists from two wooden pillars. Synelle, oddly garbed in black silk that clung damply to her, a horned chaplet on her brow. And beyond her a shape out of madmen's nightmares, its skin the color of dead men's blood. Al'Kiir awakened threw back his head, and from a broad fanged gash of a mouth came laughter to curdle the heart of heroes.

Even as the evil god's laughter stunned Conan's mind, Synelle's presence filled it. The staff fell from his fingers, and he took a step toward her.

The dark-eyed noblewoman pointed a slender finger at the young giant. As if commanding more wine she said, "Kill him."

The strange lethargy that had affected him of late when he was about her slowed Conan's hand, but his sword took the head of the first man to turn toward him before that man had his blade half-drawn. Nobles could prate while they lounged at their ease of chivalry in battle, though they rarely practiced it; a son of the bleak northland knew only how to fight to win.

The others came at him then, but he retreated to the entrance, wide enough for only three at a time to get near. With a frenzy approaching madness he fought, and his steel did murderous work among them. Synelle filled his brain. He would get to Synelle if he must wade to his waist in blood.

A scream drew his eye beyond the men struggling to slay him. Al'Kiir had seized Synelle in a clawed hand that almost encircled her narrow waist, lifting her before that triad of ebon eyes for inspection.

Conan redoubled his efforts, and the fury of his attack, seeming reckless of death, forced the mail-clad men to fall back before him.

"Not me!" Synelle screamed, her face contorted in terror. "I am thy faithful slave, o mighty Al'Kiir! Thy priestess! She is the one brought for thy delight!"

Al'Kiir turned his horned head to Karela, and his lipless mouth curled in a fanged smile. He took a step toward her, reaching out.

"No!" Conan roared, desperation clawing at him. "Not Karela!" His foot struck something that rolled with the sound of wood on stone. The Staff of Avanrakash.

Ignoring the men who still faced him, Conan seized the staff from the floor and hurled it like a javelin. Straight to the chest of the monstrous figure the plain wooden staff flew, struck, and pierced. Al'Kiir's free hand tugged at the length of wood, but it could as well have been anchored with barbs. Black ichor poured out around it, and the horned god shrieked, a piercing cry that went on without end, shattering thought and turning muscles to water.

Steel clattered to the stone floor as black-mailed men dropped their swords and fled, pushing past Conan as if he held no weapon at all. And he, in turn, paid them no heed, for the scream that would not stop allowed room for awareness of nothing else.

Around the staff drops of ichor hardened like beads of obsidian, and the hardening widened, spreading steadily through the malevolent shape.

Synelle plucked frantically at the claw-tipped fingers that held her; her long legs kicked wildly. "Release me," she pleaded. "Release thy faithful priestess, o mighty Al'Kiir." Now she struggled with fingers of stone. Slowly, as if it moved with difficulty, the horned head turned to look at her. "Release me!" she screamed. "Release me! No! Mitra, save me!" Her kicking slowed, then her legs were frozen, her cries stilled. Her pale skin gleamed like polished marble in the light from the torches. There was silence.

Flight. Flight from pain great enough to slay a thousand worlds. Flight back to the hated prison of nothingness. Yet something had been brought along. It was clothed in the flesh it had once worn, and a beautiful, naked woman, dark of eye and silvery of hair, floated in the void, mouth working with screams that were not worth hearing. Evil joy, black as the depths of the pit. Long centuries of delight would come from this one before the pitiful spark that was human essence faded and was gone. But the pain did not end. It grew instead. The crystalline thread that linked this place of nonexistence with that other world was still intact, unseverable. Yet it must be ended, least endless eons of agony follow. It must be ended.

Conan shook his head as if waking from a fever dream, and ran to Karela. Quickly he severed her bonds, caught her as she would have fallen.

The beautiful red-haired bandit turned her sweat-streaked face up to him. "I knew you would come," she whispered hoarsely. "I prayed for you to rescue me, and I hate you for it."

The Cimmerian could not help smiling. Whatever had happened to her, Karela was unchanged. Sheathing his sword, he picked her up in his arms. Sighing weakly, she put her arms around his neck and pressed her face to his chest. He thought he felt the wetness of tears.

His gaze went to the stone shape pierced by the wooden staff, the sanguinary horned monstrosity clutching the alabaster figure of a struggling woman, her face frozen in horror for eternity. All the raging feelings and confusions that had filled him were gone as if they had never been. Bewitched, he thought angrily. Synelle had ensorceled him. He hoped that wherever she was she had time for regret.

Machaon and Narus ran into the chamber, bloody swords in hand, and skidded to a halt, staring in awe. "I'll not ask what happened here," the gaunt-faced man said, "for I misdoubt I'd believe it."

"They flee from us, Cimmerian," Machaon said. "Ten of them together, and they ran down a side passage at the sight of us. Whatever you did took all the heart right out of them."

"The others?" Conan asked, and the tattooed mercenary shook his head grimly.

"Dead. But they collected their ferryman's fees and more."

Suddenly Narus pointed at the huge stone figure. "It's—it's—" He stammered, unable to get any more words out.

Conan spun. The petrified body of the god was quivering. A hum came from it, a hum that quickly rose in pitch until it pierced the ears like driven nails.

"Run!" the Cimmerian shouted, but could not hear his own words through the burning pain that clawed at his skull.

The other two men needed no urging, though.

The three of them sped through the rough-hewn stone passages, Conan keeping up easily despite carrying Karela. In their headlong flight they leaped over the bodies of the dead, but saw no one living. And the mind-killing vibration followed them up sloping tunnels, level after level, up the stone steps to the ruins.

As the Cimmerian dashed out among the overgrown columns, the skull-piercing sound ceased. Birds and crickets had fled; the loudest noise to be heard was their own blood thrumming in their ears. Before a breath could be drawn in the silence, the mountain shook. Half-built columns toppled and mossy walls collapsed, blocks of marble large enough to crush a man splashing dirt like water, but the sound of their fall was swallowed by the rumbling that rose from the granite bowels of Tor Al'Kiir.

Dodging through clouds of dust and flying chips of shattered rock, Conan hurtled down the slope, Karela's naked form clutched to his chest. The side of a mountain in the night was no place to be during an earthquake, but neither was the midst of crumbling marble walls. He had a feeling the only safe place to be in *this* earthquake was as far from Tor Al'Kiir as it was possible to run. And run he did, over ground that danced like the deck of a ship in a storm, fighting to keep his balance for rocks bouncing beneath his feet and stones flying through the air like hail. He no longer knew if Machaon and Narus ran with him, nor could he spare a thought for them. They were men, and must take their risks. Conan had to get

Karela to safety, for some primal instinct warned him that worse was to come.

With a sound like the splitting of the earth, the peak of Tor Al'Kiir erupted in fire, mountaintop and alabaster columns and marble walls alike flung high into a sky now lit by a fiery glow. The blast threw Conan into the air; he twisted so that his own huge frame took the bone-jarring impact of landing. It was no longer possible to gain his feet. He put his body over that of Karela, sheltering her from the stones that filled the air. As he did one image remained burned into his brain, a single flame towering a thousand paces from the destroyed top of Tor Al'Kiir, a single flame that took the form of the Staff of Avanrakash.

Epilogue

In the paleness before full dawn Conan peered toward Ianthe, towers thrusting into the early morning mist, glazed red roof tiles beginning to gleam with the light of a sun not yet risen. An army approached the city, men-at-arms with gaily colored pennons streaming, long columns of infantry with shields slung on their backs, tall plumes of dust rising beneath thousands of pacing hooves and tramping feet. A victorious army, he thought. But whose?

Avoiding looking at the steaming, cratered top of Tor Al'Kiir, he picked his way through the huge, misshapen boulders that now littered the mountain slope. A quarter of its height had the great granite mound lost in the night, and what lay at its new peak the Cimmerian neither knew nor wanted to know.

Narus voice came to him, tinged with a bitter note. "Women should not be allowed to gamble. Almost I think you changed dice on me. At least let my buy back—"

"No," Karela cut him off as Conan rejoined his three companions. She wore Narus' breeches, tight across the curves of her hips and voluminous in the legs, with his scarlet cloak wrapped about her shoulders and his sword across her knees. The inner slopes of her full breasts showed at the gap in the cloak. "I have more need of something to wear than of gold. And I did not switch the dice. You were too busy filling your filthy eyes and leering at the sight of me uncovered to pay mind of what you were doing."

Machaon laughed, and the gaunt man grunted, attempting to pull his hauberk down far enough to cover his bony knees.

"We must be moving," Conan announced. "There has been a battle, it seems, and whoever won there will be mercenaries without patrons or leaders, men to reform the company. Crom, there may be enough for you each to have your own Free-Company."

Machaon, sitting with his back against one of the building stones that had once stood atop the mountain, shook his head. "I have been longer in this trade, Cimmerian, than you have lived, and this night past has at last given me my full. I own some land in Koth. I shall put up my sword, and become a farmer."

"You?" Conan said incredulously. "A month of grubbing in the dirt, and you'll tear apart the nearest village with your bare hands, just for the need of a fight."

"'Tis not quite as you imagine," the grizzled veteran chuckled. "There are ten men working the land now. I will be a man of substance, as such as counted among farmers. I shall fetch Julia from the city, and marry her if she will have me. A farmer needs a wife to give him strong sons."

Conan frowned at Narus. "And do you, too, intend to become a farmer?"

"I've no love of dirt," the hollow-faced man replied, snatching the dice from Karela, who had been examining them idly, "but. . . . Conan, wizards I did not mind so much, and those men who looked like a snake had been at their mothers were no worse than a horde of blood-drunk Picts, but this god you found us has had my heart in my mouth more than I can remember since the Battle of Black River, when I was a fresh youth without need of shaving. For a time I seek a quiet city, with buxom wenches to bounce on a bed and," he rattled the dice in cupped hands, rolled them on the ground, "young lads with more coin than sense."

"They had best be *very* young," Karela laughed. "Do you intend to gain any of their coin. Eh, Cimmerian?" Narus glared at her and grumbled under his breath.

As Conan opened his mouth, a flash of white caught his eye, cloth fluttering in the breeze down slope. "Crom!" he muttered. It was Boros and Julia. "I'll wring his scrawny neck for bringing her here," he growled. The others scrambled to their feet to follow him down the mountainside.

When Conan reached the girl and the old man, he saw they were not alone. Julia knelt beside Taurianus, tearing strips from her white robes to try to staunch the blood oozing from a dozen rents in the Ophirean's hauberk. The man's hair was matted with dirt and blood, and a bubble of scarlet appeared at his lips with each labored breath.

Boros flung up his hands as soon as he saw Conan. "Do not blame me. I tried to stop her, but I have not your strength. I thought it best to come along and protect her as best I could. She said she was worried about Machaon."

"About all of them," Julia said, her face reddening. "Conan, we found him lying here. Can you not help him?"

The Cimmerian needed no close examination of Taurianus' wounds to see the man would not survive them. The ground about him was already blackened with his blood. "So the nobles lost," he said quietly. A mercenary fighting on the victorious side would not have crawled away to die.

The Ophirean's eyes fluttered open. "We caught the Eagle," he rasped, and continued with frequent pauses to struggle for breath. "We left our camp—with fires lit—and Iskandrian—fell on it—in the night. Then we took him—in the rear. We would have—destroyed him—but a giant flame—cleft the sky—and the white-haired devil—shouted the gods—were with them. Some cried—it was the Staff—of Avanrakash. Panic seized us—by the throat. We fled—and his warriors cut us down. Enjoy your time—Cimmerian. Iskandrian—is impaling—every mercenary—he catches." Suddenly he lurched up onto one elbow and stretched out a clawed hand toward Conan. "I am a better man—than you!" Blood welled in his mouth, and he fell back. Once he jerked, then was still, dull eyes staring at the sky.

"A giant flame," Narus said softly. "You are a man of destiny, Cimmerian. You make kings even you do not mean to."

Conan shrugged off the words irritably. He cared not who wore the crown of Ophir, except insofar as it affected his prospects. With Iskandrian at Valentius' side—perhaps, he thought, it was time to start thinking of the fopling as Moranthes II—there would be no chance to gather more men, and possibly no men left alive to gather. "'Twill be Argos for me," he said.

"You!" Machaon snapped abruptly, and Julia jumped. "Did I not tell you to remain in Ianthe? Must I fetch a switch for you here and now? The life of a poor farmer's wife is hard, and she must learn to obey. Would you have our only pig die because you did not feed it when I told you?"

"You have no right to threaten me," the auburn-haired girl burst out. "You cannot. . . ." Her words trailed off, and she sat back on her heels. "Wife? Did you say wife?" Taking a deep breath, she said earnestly, "Machaon, I will care for your pig as if it were my beloved sister."

"There's no need to go so far as that," Machaon laughed. His face sobered as he turned to Conan. "A long road we've traveled together, Cimmerian, but it has come to its ending. And as I've no desire to let Iskandrian rummage in my guts with a stake, I'll take my leave now. I wish to be far from Ianthe before this day is done."

"And I," Narus added. "'Tis Tarantia for me, for they do say the nobles of Aquilonia are free with their coin and love to gamble."

"Fare you well," Conan told them. "And take a pull at the hellhorn for me, if you get there before me."

Julia ran to clasp Machaon's arm, and, with Narus, they started down the mountain.

"After that fool wench's display," Karela muttered, "I need a drink, or I'll be sick to my stomach."

Conan eyed her thoughtfully. "Events hie me to Argos, for 'tis said Free-Companies are being hired there. Come with me, Karela. Together, in a year, we'll rule the country."

The red-haired beauty stared at him, stricken. "Do you not understand why I cannot, Cimmerian? By the Teats of Derketo, man, you wake in me longings to be like that simpering wench, Julia! You make me embrace weakness, make me want to let you protect me. Think you I'm a woman to fold your blankets and cook your meals?"

"I've never asked such of you," he protested, but she ignored him.

"One day I would find myself walking a pace behind you, silent lest I should miss your words, and I'd plant a dagger in your back for it. Then I would likely weep myself to madness for the doing of what you brought on yourself. I will not have it, Conan. I will not!"

A sense of loss filled him, but pride would not allow it to touch his face. "At least you have gained one thing. This time I flee, and you remain in Ophir."

"No, Conan. The vermin that formed my band are not worth the effort of gathering them again. I go to the east." Her head came up, and her eyes glowed like emeralds. "The plains of Zamora shall know the Red Hawk again."

He fumbled in his pouch and drew out half the gems he had taken from the scepter of Ophir. "Here," he said gruffly. Karela did not move. "Can you not take a parting gift from a friend?" Hesitantly a slender hand came to his; he let the gems pour into it.

"You are a better man that you know, Cimmerian," she whispered, "and I am a fool." Her lips brushed his, and she was gone, running with the cloak a scarlet banner behind her.

Conan watched until she passed out of sight below.

"Even the gods cannot understand the brain of a woman," Boros crackled. "Men, on the other hand, rarely think with their brains at all."

Conan glared at the bearded man. He had forgotten Boros was still there. "Now you can return to the taverns and your drinking," he said sourly.

"Not in Ophir," Boros said. He tugged at his beard and glanced nervously toward the ruined mountaintop. "A god cannot be killed as if it were an ordinary demon. Al'Kiir still lives—somewhere. Suppose his body is buried yet up there? Suppose another of those images exists? I will not be in this country if someone else attempts to raise him. Argos, I think. The sea air will be good for my lungs, and I can take ship for distant lands if I hear evil word from Ophir."

"Not in my company," Conan growled. "I travel alone."

"I can work magicks to make the journey easier," Boros protested, but the Cimmerian was already making his way down the mountain. Chattering continuously the gray-bearded man scrambled after Conan, who refused to respond to his importunings.

Once more he was on his own, Conan thought, with only his sword and his wits, but he had been so often before. There were the gems in his pouch, of course. They would fetch something. And Argos lay ahead, Argos and thoughts he had never entertained before. If chance could bring a fool like Valentius to a throne, why could he not find a path? Why indeed? Smiling, he quickened his pace.

CONAN THE INDESTRUCTIBLE

By L. Sprague de Camp

The greatest hero of the magic-rife Hyborian Age was a northern barbarian, Conan the Cimmerian, about whose deeds a cycle of legend revolves. While these legends are largely based on the attested facts of Conan's life, some tales are inconsistent with others. So we must reconcile the contradictions in the saga as best we can.

In Conan's veins flowed the blood of the people of Atlantis, the brilliant city-state swallowed by the sea 8,000 years before his time. He was born into a clan that claimed a homeland in the northwest corner of Cimmeria, along the shadowy borders of Vanaheim and the Pictish wilderness. His grandfather had fled his own people because of a blood feud and sought refuge with the people of the North. Conan himself first saw daylight on a battlefield during a raid by the Vanir.

Before he had weathered fifteen snows, the young Cimmerian's fighting skills were acclaimed around the council fires. In that year the Cimmerians, usually at one another's throats, joined forces to repel the warlike Gundermen who, intent on colonizing southern Cimmeria, had pushed across the Aquilonian border and established the frontier post of Venarium. Conan joined the howling, blood-mad horde that swept out of the northern hills, stormed over the stockade walls, and drove the Aquilonians back across their frontier.

At the sack of Venarium, Conan, still short of his full growth, stood six feet tall and weighed 180 pounds. He had the vigilance and stealth of the born woodsman, the iron-hardness of the mountain man, and the Herculean physique of his blacksmith father. After the plunder of the Aquilonian outpost, Conan returned for a time to his tribe.

Restless under the conflicting passions of his adolescence, Conan spent several months with a band of Æsir as they raided the Vanir and the Hyperboreans. He soon learned that some Hyperborean citadels were ruled by a caste of widely-feared magicians, called Witchmen. Undaunted, he took part in a foray against Haloga Castle, when he found that Hyperborean slavers had captured Rann, the daughter of Njal, chief of the Æsir band.

Conan gained entrance to the castle and spirited out Rann Njalsdatter; but on the flight out of Hyperborea, Njal's band was overtaken by an army of living dead. Conan and the other Æsir survivors were led away to slavery ("Legions of the Dead").

Conan did not long remain a captive. Working at night, he ground away at one link of his chain until it was weak enough to break. Then one stormy night, whirling a four-foot length of heavy chain, he fought his way out of the slave pen and vanished into the downpour.

Another account of Conan's early years tells a different tale. This narrative, on a badly broken clay prism from Nippur, states that Conan was enslaved as a boy of ten or twelve by Vanir raiders and set to work turning a grist mill. When he reached his full growth, he was bought by a Hyrkanian pitmaster who traveled with a band of professional fighters staging contests for the amusement of the Vanir and Æsir. At this time Conan received his training with weapons. Later he escaped and made his way south to Zamora (*Conan the Barbarian*).

Of the two versions, the records of Conan's enslavement by the Hyrkanians at sixteen, found in a papyrus in the British Museum, appear much more legible and self-consistent. But this question may never be settled.

Although free, the youth found himself half a hostile kingdom away from home. Instinctively he fled into the mountains at the southern extremity of Hyperborea. Pursued by a pack of wolves, he took refuge in a cave. Here he discovered the seated mummy of a gigantic chieftain of ancient times, with a heavy bronze sword across its knees. When Conan seized the sword, the corpse arose and attacked him ("The Thing in the Crypt").

Continuing southward into Zamora, Conan came to Arenjun, the notorious "City of Thieves." Green to civilization and, save for some rudimentary barbaric ideas of honor and chivalry, wholly lawless by nature, he carved a niche for himself as a professional thief.

Being young and more daring than adroit, Conan's progress in his new profession was slow until he joined forces with Taurus of Nemedia in a quest for the fabulous jewel called the "Heart of the Elephant." The gem lay in the almost impregnable tower of the infamous mage Yara, captor of the extraterrestrial being Yag-Kosha ("The Tower of the Elephant").

Seeking greater opportunities to ply his trade, Conan wandered westward to the capital of Zamora, Shadizar the Wicked. For a time his thievery prospered, although the whores of Shadizar soon relieved him of his gains. During one larceny, he was captured by the men of Queen Taramis of Shadizar, who sent him on a mission to recover a magical horn wherewith to resurrect an ancient, evil god. Taramis's plot led to her own destruction (*Conan the Destroyer*).

The barbarian's next exploit involved a fellow thief, a girl named Tamira. The Lady Jondra, an arrogant aristocrat of Shadizar, owned a pair of priceless rubies. Baskaran Imalla, a religious fanatic raising a cult among the Kezankian hillmen, coveted the jewels to gain control over a fire-breathing dragon he had raised from an egg. Conan and Tamira both yearned for the rubies; Tamira took a post as lady's maid to Jondra for a chance to steal them.

An ardent huntress, Jondra set forth with her maid and her men-at-arms to slay Baskaran's dragon. Baskaran captured the two women and was about to offer them to his pet as a snack when Conan intervened (*Conan the Magnificent*).

Soon Conan was embroiled in another adventure. A stranger hired the youth to steal a casket of gems sent by the King of Zamora to the King of Turan. The stranger, a priest of the serpent-god Set, wanted the jewels for magic against his enemy, the renegade priest Amanar.

Amanar's emissaries, who were hominoid reptiles, had stolen the gems. Although wary of magic, Conan set out to recover the loot. He became involved with a bandette, Karela, called the Red Hawk, who proved the ultimate bitch; when Conan saved her from rape, she tried to kill him. Amanar's party had also carried off to the renegade's stronghold a dancing girl whom Conan had promised to help (*Conan the Invincible*).

Soon rumors of treasure sent Conan to the nearby ruins of ancient Larsha, just ahead of the soldiers dispatched to arrest him. After all but their leader, Captain Nestor, had perished in an accident arranged by Conan, Nestor and Conan joined forces to plunder the treasure; but ill luck deprived them of their gains ("The Hall of the Dead").

Conan's recent adventures had left him with an aversion to warlocks and Eastern sorceries. He fled northwestward through Corinthia into Nemedia, the second most powerful Hyborian kingdom. In Nemedia he resumed his profession successfully enough to bring his larcenies to the notice of Aztrias Petanius, ne'er-do-well nephew of the governor. Oppressed by gambling debts, this young gentleman hired the outlander to purloin a Zamorian goblet, carved from a single diamond, that stood in the temple-museum of a wealthy collector.

Conan's appearance in the temple-museum coincided with its master's sudden demise and brought the young thief to the unwelcome attention of Demetrio, of the city's Inquisitorial Council. This caper also gave Conan his second experience with the dark magic of the serpent-brood of Set, conjured up by the Stygian sorcerer Thoth-Amon ("The God in the Bowl").

Having made Nemedia too hot to hold him, Conan drifted south into Corinthia, where he continued to occupy himself with the acquisition of other persons' property. By diligent application, the Cimmerian earned the repute of one of the boldest thieves in Corinthia. Poor judgment of women, however, cast him into chains until a turn in local politics brought freedom and a new career. An ambitious nobleman, Murilo, turned him loose to slit the throat of the Red Priest, Nabonidus, the scheming power behind the local throne. This venture gathered a prize collection of rogues in Nabodinus's mansion and ended in a mire of blood and treachery ("Rogues in the House").

Conan wandered back to Arenjun and began to earn a semi-honest living by stealing back for their owners valuable objects that others had filched from them. He undertook to recover a magical gem, the Eye of Erlik, from the wizard Hissar Zul and return it to its owner, the Khan of Zamboula.

There is some question about the chronology of Conan's life at this point. A recently-translated tablet from Asshurbanipal's library states that Conan was about seventeen at the time. This would place the episode right after that of "The Tower of the Elephant," which indeed is mentioned in the cuneiform. But from internal evidence, this event seems to have taken place several years later. For one thing, Conan appears too clever, mature, and sophisticated; for another, the fragmentary medieval Arabic manuscript *Kitab al-Qunn* implies that Conan was well into his twenties by then.

The first translator of the Asshurbanipal tablet, Prof. Dr. Andreas von Fuss of the Münchner Staatsmuseum, read Conan's age as "17." In Babylonian cuneiform, "17" is expressed by two circles followed by three vertical wedges, with a horizontal wedge above the three for "minus"—hence "twenty minus three." But Academician Leonid Skram of the Moscow Archaeological Institute asserts that the depression over the vertical wedges is merely a dent made by the pick of a careless excavator, and the numeral properly reads "23."

Anyhow, Conan learned of the Eye of Erlik when he heard a discussion between an adventuress, Isparana, and her confederate. He invaded the wizard's mansion, but the wizard caught Conan and deprived him of his soul. Conan's soul was imprisoned in a mirror, there to remain until a crowned ruler broke the glass. Hissar Zul thus compelled Conan to follow Isparana and recover the talisman; but when the Cimmerian returned the Eye to Hissar Zul, the ungrateful mage tried to slay him (*Conan and the Sorcerer*).

Conan, his soul still englassed, accepted legitimate employment as bodyguard to a Khaurani noblewoman, Khashtris. This lady set out for Khauran with Conan, another guard, Shubal, and several retainers. When the other servants plotted to rob and murder their employer, Conan and Shubal saved her and escorted her to Khauran. There Conan found the widowed Queen Ialamis being courted by a young nobleman who was not at all what he seemed (*Conan the Mercenary*).

With his soul restored, Conan learned from an Iranistani, Khassek, that the Khan of Zamboula still wanted the Eye of Erlik. In Zamboula, the Turanian governor, Akter Khan, had hired the wizard Zafra, who ensorcelled swords so that they would slay on command. En route, Conan encountered Isparana, with whom he developed a lust-hate relationship. Unaware of the magical swords, Conan continued to Zamboula and delivered the amulet. But the nefarious Zafra convinced the Khan that Conan was dangerous and should be killed on general principles (*Conan: The Sword of Skelos*).

Conan had enjoyed his taste of Hyborian-Age intrigue. It became clear that there was no basic difference between the opportunities in the palace and those in the Rats' Den, whereas the pickings were far better in high places. Besides, he wearied of the furtive, squalid life of a thief.

He was not, however, yet committed to a strictly law-abiding life. When unemployed, he took time out for a venture in smuggling. An attempt to poison him sent him to Vendhya, a land of wealth and squalor, philosophy and fanatacism, idealism and treachery (*Conan the Victorious*).

Soon after, Conan turned up in the Turanian seaport of Aghrapur. A new cult had established headquarters there under the warlock Jhandar, who needed victims to be drained of blood and reanimated as servants. Conan refused the offer of a former fellow thief, Emilio, to take part in a raid on Jhandar's stronghold to steal a fabulous ruby necklace. A Turanian sergeant, Akeba, did however persuade Conan to go with him to rescue Akeba's daughter, who had vanished into the cult (*Conan the Unconquered*).

After Jhandar's fall, Akeba urged Conan to take service in the Turanian army. The Cimmerian did not at first find military life congenial, being too self-willed and hot-tempered to easily submit to discipline. Moreover, as he was at this time an indifferent horseman and archer, Conan was relegated to a low-paid irregular unit.

Still, a chance soon arose to show his mettle. King Yildiz launched an expedition against a rebellious satrap. By sorcery, the satrap wiped out the force sent against him. Young Conan alone survived to enter the magic-maddened satrap's city of Yaralet ("The Hand of Nergal").

Returning in triumph to the glittering capital of Aghrapur, Conan gained a place in King Yildiz's guard of honor. At first he endured the gibes of fellow troopers at his clumsy horsemanship and inaccurate archery. But the gibes died away as the other guardsmen discovered Conan's sledgehammer fists and as his skills improved.

Conan was chosen, along with a Kushite mercenary named Juma, to escort King Yildiz's daughter Zosara to her wedding with Khan Kujula, chief of the Kuigar nomads. In the foothills of the Talakma Mountains, the party was attacked by a strange force of squat, brown, lacquer-armored horsemen. Only Conan, Juma, and the princess survived. They were taken to the subtropical valley of Meru and to the capital, Shamballah, where Conan and Juma were chained to an oar of the Meruvian state galley, about to set forth on a cruise.

On the galley's return to Shamballah, Conan and Juma escaped and made their way into the city. They reached the temple of Yama as the deformed little god-king of Meru was celebrating his marriage to Zosara ("The City of Skulls").

* * *

Back at Aghrapur, Conan was promoted to captain. His growing repute as a good man in a tight spot, however, led King Yildiz's generals to pick the barbarian for especially hazardous missions. Once they sent Conan to escort an emissary to the predatory tribesmen of the Khozgari Hills, hoping to dissuade them by bribes and threats from plundering the Turanians of the lowlands. The Khozgarians, respecting only immediate, overwhelming force, attacked the detachment, killing the emissary and all but two of the soldiers, Conan and Jamal.

To assure their safe passage back to civilization, Conan and Jamal captured Shanya, the daughter of the Khozgari chief. Their route led them to a misty highland. Jamal and the horses were slain, and Conan had to battle a horde of hairless apes and invade the stronghold of an ancient, dying race ("The People of the Summit").

Another time, Conan was dispatched thousands of miles eastward, to fabled Khitai, to convey to King Shu of Kusan a letter from King Yildiz proposing a treaty of friendship and trade. The wise old Khitan king sent his visitors back with a letter of acceptance. As a guide, however, the king appointed a foppish little nobleman, Duke Feng, who had entirely different objectives ("The Curse of the Monolith," first published as "Conan and the Cenotaph").

Conan continued in his service in Turan for about two years, traveling widely and learning the elements of organized, civilized warfare. As usual, trouble was his bedfellow. After one of his more unruly adventures, involving the mistress of his superior officer, Conan deserted and headed for Zamora. In Shadizar he heard that the Temple of Zath, the spider god, in the Zamorian city of Yezud, was recruiting soldiers. Hastening to Yezud, Conan found that a Brythunian free company had taken all the available mercenary posts. He became the town's blacksmith because as a boy he had been apprenticed in this trade.

Conan learned from an emissary of King Yildiz, Lord Parvez, that High Priest Feridun was holding Yildiz's favorite wife, Jamilah, in captivity. Parvez hired Conan to abduct Jamilah. Meanwhile Conan had set his heart on the eight huge gems that formed the eyes of an enormous statue of the spider god. As he was loosening the jewels, the approach of priests forced him to flee to a crypt below the naos. The temple dancing girl Rudabeh, with whom Conan was truly in love for the first time in his life, descended into the crypt to warn him of the doom awaiting him there (*Conan and the Spider God*).

Conan next rode off to Shadizar to track down a rumor of treasure. He obtained a map showing the location of a ruby-studded golden idol in the Kezankian Mountains; but thieves stole his map. Conan, pursuing them, had a brush with Kezankian hillmen and had to join forces with the very rogues he was tracking. He found the treasure, only to lose it under strange circumstances ("The Bloodstained God").

Fed up with magic, Conan headed for the Cimmerian hills. After a time in the simple, routine life of his native village, however, he grew restless enough to join his old friends, the Æsir, in a raid into Vanaheim. In a bitter struggle on the snow-covered plain, both forces were wiped out—all but Conan, who wandered off to a strange encounter with the legendary Atali, daughter of the frost giant Ymir ("The Frost Giant's Daughter").

Haunted by Atali's icy beauty, Conan headed back toward the South, where, despite his often-voiced scorn of civilization, the golden spires of teeming cities beckoned. In the Eiglophian Mountains, Conan rescued a young woman from cannibals, but through overconfidence lost her to the dreaded monster that haunted glaciers ("The Lair of the Ice Worm").

Conan then returned to the Hyborian lands, which include Aquilonia, Argos, Brythunia, Corinthia, Koth, Nemedia, Ophir, and Zingara. These countries were named for the Hyborian peoples who, as barbarians, had 3,000 years earlier conquered the empire of Acheron and built civilized realms on its ruins.

In Belverus, the capital of Nemedia, the ambitious Lord Albanus dabbled in sorcery to usurp the throne of King Garian. To Belverus came Conan, seeking a patron with money to enable him to hire his own free company. Albanus gave a magical sword to a confederate, Lord Melius, who went mad and attacked people in the street until killed. As he picked up the ensorcelled sword, Conan was accosted by Hordo, a one-eyed thief and smuggler whom he had known as Karela's lieutenant.

Conan sold the magical sword, hired his own free company, and taught his men mounted archery. Then he persuaded King Garian to hire him. But Albanus had made a man of clay and by his sorcery given it the exact appearance of the king. Then he imprisoned the king, substituted his golem, and framed Conan for murder (*Conan the Defender*).

Conan next brought his free company to Ianthe, capital of Ophir. There the Lady Synelle, a platinum-blond sorceress, wished to bring to life the demon-god Al'Kirr. Conan bought a statuette of this demon-god and soon found that various parties were trying to steal it from him. He and his company took service under Synelle, not knowing her plans.

Then the bandette Karela reappeared and, as usual, tried to murder Conan. Synelle hired her to steal the statuette, which the witch needed for her sorcery. She also planned to sacrifice Karela (*Conan the Triumphant*).

Conan went on to Argos; but since that kingdom was at peace, there were no jobs for mercenaries. A misunderstanding with the law compelled Conan to leap to the deck of a ship as it left the pier. This was the merchant galley *Argus,* bound for the coasts of Kush.

A major epoch in Conan's life was about to begin. The *Argus* was taken by Bêlit, the Shemite captain of the pirate ship *Tigress,* whose ruthless black corsairs had made her mistress of the Kushite littoral. Conan won both Bêlit and a partnership in her bloody trade ("Queen of the Black Coast," Chapter 1).

Years before, Bêlit, daughter of a Shemite trader, had been abducted with her brother Jehanan by Stygian slavers. Now she asked her lover Conan to try to rescue the youth. The barbarian slipped into Khemi, the Stygian seaport, was captured, but escaped to the eastern end of Stygia, the province of Taia, where a revolt against Stygian oppression was brewing (*Conan the Rebel*).

Conan and Bêlit resumed their piratical careers, preying mainly on Stygian vessels. Then an ill fate took them up the black Zarkheba River to the lost city of an ancient winged race ("Queen of the Black Coast," Chapters 2–5).

As Bêlit's burning funeral ship wafted out to sea, a downhearted Conan turned his back on the sea, which he would not follow again for years. He plunged inland and joined the warlike Bamulas, a black tribe whose power swiftly grew under his leadership.

The chief of a neighboring tribe, the Bakalahs, planned a treacherous attack on another neighbor and invited Conan and his Bamulas to take part in the sack and massacre. Conan accepted but, learning that an Ophirean girl, Livia, was held captive in Bakalah, he out-betrayed the Bakalahs. Livia ran off during the slaughter and wandered into a mysterious valley, where only Conan's timely arrival saved her from being sacrificed to an extraterrestrial being ("The Vale of Lost Women").

Before Conan could build his own black empire, he was thwarted by a succession of natural catastrophes as well as by the intrigues of hostile Bamulas. Forced to flee, he headed north. After a narrow escape from pursuing lions on the veldt, Conan took shelter in a mysterious ruined castle of prehuman origin. He had a brush with Stygian slavers and a malign supernatural entity ("The Castle of Terror").

Continuing on, Conan reached the semicivilized kingdom of Kush. This was the land to which the name "Kush" properly applied; although Conan, like other Northerners, tended to use the term loosely to mean any of the black countries south of Stygia. In Meroê, the capital, Conan rescued from a hostile mob the young Queen of Kush, the arrogant, impulsive, fierce, cruel, and voluptuous Tananda.

Conan became embroiled in a labyrinthine intrigue between Tananda and an ambitious nobleman who commanded a piglike demon. The problem was aggravated by the presence of Diana, a Nemedian slave girl to whom Conan, despite the jealous fury of Tananda, took a fancy. Events culminated in a night of insurrection and slaughter ("The Snout in the Dark").

Dissatisfied with his achievements in the black countries, Conan wandered to the meadowlands of Shem and became a soldier of Akkharia, a Shemite city-state. He joined a band of volunteers to liberate a neighboring city-state; but through the teachery of Othbaal, cousin of the mad King Akhîrom of Pelishtia, the volunteers were destroyed—all but Conan, who survived to track the plotter to Asgalun, the Pelishti capital. There Conan became involved in a polygonal power war among the mad Akhîrom, the treacherous Othbaal, a Stygian witch, and a company of black mercenaries. In the final hurly-burly of sorcery, steel, and blood, Conan grabbed Othbaal's red-haired mistress, Rufia, and galloped north ("Hawks Over Shem").

Conan's movements at this time are uncertain. One tale, sometimes assigned to this period, tells of Conan's service as a mercenary in Zingara. A Ptolemaic papyrus in the British Museum alleges that in Kordava, the capital, a captain in the regular army forced a quarrel on Conan. When Conan killed his assailant, he was condemned to hang. A fellow condemnee, Santiddio, belonged to an underground conspiracy, the White Rose, that hoped to topple King Rimanendo. As other conspirators created a disturbance in the crowd that gathered for the hanging, Conan and Santiddio escaped.

Mordermi, head of an outlaw band allied with the White Rose, enlisted Conan in his movement. The conspiracy was carried on in the Pit, a warren of tunnels beneath the city. When the King sent an army to clean out the Pit, the insurrectionists were saved by Callidos, a Stygian sorcerer. King Rimanendo was slain and Mordermi became king. When he proved as tyrannical as his predecessor, Conan raised another revolt; then, refusing the crown for himself, he departed (*Conan: The Road of Kings*).

This tale involves many questions. If authentic, it may belong in Conan's earlier mercenary period, around the time of *Conan the Defender*. But there is no corroboration in other narratives of the idea that Conan ever visited Zingara before his late thirties, the time of *Conan the Buccaneer*. Moreover, none of the rulers of Zingara mentioned in the papyrus appear on the list of kings of Zingara in the Byzantine manuscript *Hoi Anaktes tês Tzingêras*. Hence some students deem the papyrus either spurious or a case of confusion between Conan and some other hero. Everything else known about Conan indicates that, if he had indeed been offered the Zingaran crown, he would have grabbed it with both hands.

We next hear of Conan after he took service under Amalric of Nemedia, the general of Queen-Regent Yasmela of the little border kingdom of Khoraja. While Yasmela's brother, King Khossus, was a prisoner in Ophir, Yasmela's borders were assailed by the forces of the veiled sorcerer Natohk—actually the 3,000-years-dead Thugra Khotan of the ruined city of Kuthchemes.

Obeying an oracle of Mitra, the supreme Hyborian god, Yasmela made Conan captain-general of Khoraja's army. In this rôle he gave battle to Natohk's hosts and rescued the Queen-Regent from the malignant magic of the undead warlock. Conan won the day—and the Queen ("Black Colossus").

Conan, now in his late twenties, settled down as Khorajan commander-in-chief. But the Queen, whose lover he had expected to be, was too preoccupied with affairs of state to have time for frolics. He even proposed marriage, but she explained that such a union would not be sanctioned by Khorajan law and custom. Yet, if Conan could somehow rescue her brother from imprisonment, she might persuade Khossus to change the law.

Conan set forth with Rhazes, an astrologer, and Fronto, a thief who knew a secret passage into the dungeon where Khossus languished. They rescued the King but found themselves trapped by Kothian troops, since Strabonus of Koth had his own reasons for wanting Khossus.

Having surmounted these perils, Conan found that Khossus, a pompous young ass, would not hear of a foreign barbarian's marrying his sister. Instead, he would marry Yasmela off to a nobleman and find a middle-class bride for Conan. Conan said nothing; but in Argos, as their ship cast off, Conan sprang ashore with most of the gold that Khossus had raised and waved the King an ironic farewell ("Shadows in the Dark").

Now nearly thirty, Conan slipped away to revisit his Cimmerian homeland and avenge himself on the Hyperboreans. His blood brothers among the Cimmerians and the Æsir had won wives and sired sons, some as old and almost as big as Conan had been at the sack of Venarium. But his years of blood and battle had stirred his predatory spirit too strongly for him to follow their example. When traders brought word of new wars, Conan galloped off to the Hyborian lands.

A rebel prince of Koth was fighting to overthrow Strabonus, the penurious ruler of that far-stretched nation; and Conan found himself among old companions in the princeling's array, until the rebel made peace with his king. Unemployed again, Conan formed an outlaw band, the Free Companions. This troop gravitated to the steppes west of the Sea of Vilayet, where they joined the ruffianly horde known as the *kozaki.*

Conan soon became the leader of this lawless crew and ravaged the western borders of the Turanian Empire until his old employer, King Yildiz, sent a force under Shah Amurath, who lured the *kozaki* deep into Turan and cut them down.

Slaying Amurath and acquiring the Turanian's captive, Princess Olivia of Ophir, Conan rowed out into the Vilayet Sea in a small boat. He and Olivia took refuge on an island, where they found a ruined greenstone city, in which stood strange iron statues. The shadows cast by the moonlight proved as dangerous as the giant carnivorous ape that ranged the isle, or the pirate crew that landed for rest and recreation ("Shadows in the Moonlight").

Conan seized command of the pirates that ravaged the Sea of Vilayet. As chieftain of this mongrel Red Brotherhood, Conan was more than ever a thorn in King Yildiz's flesh. That mild monarch, instead of strangling his brother Teyaspa in the normal Turanian manner, had cooped him up in a castle in the Colchian Mountains. Yildiz now sent his General Artaban to destroy the pirate stronghold at the mouth of the Zaporoska River;

but the general became the harried instead of the harrier. Retreating inland, Artaban stumbled upon Teyaspa's whereabouts; and the final conflict involved Conan's outlaws, Artaban's Turanians, and a brood of vampires ("The Road of the Eagles").

Deserted by his sea rovers, Conan appropriated a stallion and headed back to the steppes. Yezdigerd, now on the throne of Turan, proved a far more astute and energetic ruler than his sire. He embarked on a program of imperial conquest.

Conan went to the small border kingdom of Khauran, where he won command of the royal guard of Queen Taramis. This queen had a twin sister, Salome, born a witch and reared by the yellow sorcerers of Khitai. She allied herself with the adventurer Constantius of Koth and planned by imprisoning the Queen to rule in her stead. Conan, who perceived the deception, was trapped and crucified. Cut down by the chieftain Olgerd Vladislav, the Cimmerian was carried off to a Zuagir camp in the desert. Conan waited for his wounds to heal, then applied his daring and ruthlessness to win his place as Olgerd's lieutenant.

When Salome and Constantius began a reign of terror in Khauran, Conan led his Zuagirs against the Khauranian capital. Soon Constantius hung from the cross to which he had nailed Conan, and Conan rode off smiling, to lead his Zuagirs on raids against the Turanians ("A Witch Shall Be Born").

Conan, about thirty and at the height of his physical powers, spent nearly two years with the desert Shemites, first as Olgerd's lieutenant and then, having ousted Olgerd, as sole chief. The circumstances of his leaving the Zuagirs were recently disclosed by a silken scroll in Old Tibetan, spirited out of Tibet by a refugee. This document is now with the Oriental Institute in Chicago.

The energetic King Yezdigerd sent soldiers to trap Conan and his troop. Because of a Zamorian traitor in Conan's ranks, the ambush nearly succeeded. To avenge the betrayal, Conan led his band in pursuit of the Zamorian. When his men deserted, Conan pressed on alone until, near death, he was rescued by Enosh, a chieftain of the isolated desert town of Akhlat.

Akhlat suffered under the rule of a demon in the form of a woman, who fed on the life force of living things. Conan, Enosh informed him, was their prophesied liberator. After it was over, Conan was invited to settle in Akhlat; but, knowing himself ill-suited to a life of humdrum respectability, he instead headed southwest to Zamboula with the horse and money of Vardanes the Zamorian ("Black Tears").

In one colossal debauch, Conan dissipated the fortune he had brought to Zamboula, a Turanian outpost. There lurked the sinister priest of Hanuman, Totrasmek, who sought a famous jewel, the Star of Khorala, for which the Queen of Ophir was said to have offered a roomful of gold. In the ensuing imbroglio, Conan acquired the Star of Khorala and rode westward ("Shadows of Zamboula").

The medieval monkish manuscript *De sidere choralae,* rescued from the bombed ruins of Monte Cassino, continues the tale. Conan reached the capital of Ophir to find that the effeminate Moranthes II, himself under the thumb of the sinister Count Rigello, kept his queen, Marala, under lock and key. Conan scaled the wall of Moranthes's castle and fetched Marala out. Rigello pursued the fugitives nearly to the Aquilonian border, where the Star of Khorala showed its power in an unexpected way ("The Star of Khorala").

Hearing that the *kozaki* had regained their vigor, Conan returned with horse and sword to the harrying of Turan. Although the now-famous northlander arrived all but empty-handed, contingents of the *kozaki* and the Vilayet pirates soon began operating under his command.

Yezdigerd sent Jehungir Agha to entrap the barbarian on the island of Xapur. Coming early to the ambush, Conan found the island's ancient fortress-palace of Dagon restored by magic, and in it the city's malevolent god, in the form of a giant of living iron ("The Devil in Iron").

After escaping from Xapur, Conan built his *kozaki* and pirate raiders into such a formidable threat that King Yezdigerd devoted all his forces to their destruction. After a devastating defeat, the *kozaki* scattered, and Conan retreated southward to take service in the light cavalry of Kobad Shah, King of Iranistan.

Conan got himself into Kobad Shah's bad graces and had to ride for the hills. He found a conspiracy brewing in Yanaidar, the fortress-city of the Hidden Ones. The Sons of Yezm were trying to revive an ancient cult and unite the surviving devotees of the old gods in order to rule the world.

The adventure ended with the rout of the contending forces by the gray ghouls of Yanaidar, and Conan rode eastward ("The Flame Knife").

Conan reappeared in the Himelian Mountains, on the northwest frontier of Vendhya, as a war chief of the savage Afghuli tribesmen. Now in his early thirties, the warlike barbarian was known and feared throughout the world of the Hyborian Age.

No man to be bothered with niceties, Yezdigerd employed the magic of the wizard Khemsa, an adept of the dreaded Black Circle, to remove the Vendhyan king from his path. The dead king's sister, the Devi Yasmina, set out to avenge him but was captured by Conan. Conan and his captive pursued the sorcerous Khemsa, only to see him slain by the magic of the Seers of Yimsha, who also abducted Yasmina ("The People of the Black Circle").

When Conan's plans for welding the hill tribes into a single power failed, Conan, hearing of wars in the West, rode thither. Almuric, a prince of Koth, had rebelled against the hated Strabonus. While Conan joined Almuric's bristling host, Strabonus's fellow kings came to that monarch's aid. Almuric's motley horde was driven south, to be annihilated at last by combined Stygian and Kushite forces.

Escaping into the desert, Conan and the camp follower Natala came to age-old Xuthal, a phantom city of living dead men and their creeping shadow-god, Thog. The Stygian woman Thalis, the effective ruler of Xuthal, double-crossed Conan once too often ("The Slithering Shadow").

Conan beat his way back to the Hyborian lands. Seeking further employment, he joined the mercenary army that a Zingaran, Prince Zapayo da Kova, was raising for Argos. It was planned that Koth should invade Stygia from the north, while the Argosseans approached the realm from the south by sea. Koth, however, made a separate peace with Stygia, leaving Conan's army of mercenaries trapped in the Stygian deserts.

Conan fled with Amalric, a young Aquilonian soldier. Soon Conan was captured by nomads, while Amalric escaped. When Amalric caught up again with Conan, Amalric had with him the girl Lissa, whom he had saved from the cannibal god of her native city. Conan had meanwhile become commander of the cavalry of the city of Tombalku. Two kings ruled Tombalku: the Negro Sakumbe and the mixed-blood Zehbeh. When Zehbeh and his faction were driven out, Sakumbe made Conan his co-king. But then the wizard Askia slew Sakumbe by magic. Conan, having avenged his black friend, escaped with Amalric and Lissa ("Drums of Tombalku").

Conan beat his way to the coast, where he joined the Barachan pirates. He was now about thirty-five. As second mate of the *Hawk,* he landed on the island of the Stygian sorcerer Siptah, said to have a magical jewel of fabulous properties.

Siptah dwelt in a cylindrical tower without doors or windows, attended by a winged demon. Conan smoked the unearthly being out but was carried off in its talons to the top of the tower. Inside the tower Conan found the wizard long dead; but the magical gem proved of unexpected help in coping with the demon ("The Gem in the Tower").

Conan remained about two years with the Barachans, according to a set of clay tablets in pre-Sumerian cuneiform. Used to the tightly organized armies of the Hyborian kingdoms, Conan found the organization of the Barachan bands too loose and anarchic to afford an opportunity to rise to leadership. Slipping out of a tight spot at the pirate rendezvous at Tortage, he found that the only alternative to a cut throat was braving the Western Ocean in a leaky skiff. When the *Wastrel,* the ship of the buccaneer Zaporavo, came in sight, Conan climbed aboard.

The Cimmerian soon won the respect of the crew and the enmity of its captain, whose Kordavan mistress, the sleek Sancha, cast too friendly an eye on the black-maned giant. Zaporavo drove his ship westward to an uncharted island, where Conan forced a duel on the captain and killed him, while Sancha was carried off by strange black beings to a living pool worshiped by these entities ("The Pool of the Black Ones").

Conan persuaded the officials at Kordava to transfer Zaporavo's privateering license to him, whereupon he spent about two years in this authorized piracy. As usual, plots were brewing against the Zingaran monarchy. King Ferdrugo was old and apparently failing, with no successor but his nubile daughter Chabela. Duke Villagro enlisted the Stygian super-sorcerer Thoth-Amon, the High Priest of Set, in a plot to obtain Chabela as his bride. Suspicious, the princess took the royal yacht down the coast to consult her uncle. A privateer in league with Villagro captured the yacht and abducted the girl. Chabela escaped and met Conan, who obtained the magical Cobra Crown, also sought by Thoth-Amon.

A storm drove Conan's ship to the coast of Kush, where Conan was confronted by black warriors headed by his old comrade-in-arms, Juma. While the chief welcomed the privateers, a tribesman stole the Cobra Crown. Conan set off in pursuit, with Princess Chabela following him. Both were captured by slavers and sold to the black Queen of the Amazons. The Queen made Chabela her slave and Conan her fancy man. Then, jealous of Chabela, she flogged the girl, imprisoned Conan, and condemned both to be devoured by a man-eating tree (*Conan the Buccaneer*).

Having rescued the Zingaran princess, Conan shrugged off hints of marriage and returned to privateering. But other Zingarans, jealous, brought him down off the coast of Shem. Escaping inland, Conan joined the Free Companions, a mercenary company. Instead of rich plunder, however, he found himself in dull guard duty on the black frontier of Stygia, where the wine was sour and the pickings poor.

Conan's boredom ended with the appearance of the pirette, Valeria of the Red Brotherhood. When she left the camp, he followed her south. The pair took refuge in a city occupied by the feuding clans of Xotalanc and Tecuhltli. Siding with the latter, the two northerners soon found themselves in trouble with that clan's leader, the ageless witch Tascela ("Red Nails").

Conan's amour with Valeria, however hot at the start, did not last long. Valeria returned to the sea; Conan tried his luck once more in the black kingdoms. Hearing of the "Teeth of Gwahlur," a cache of priceless jewels hidden in Keshan, he sold his services to its irascible king to train the Keshani army.

Thutmekri, the Stygian emissary of the twin kings of Zembabwei, also had designs on the jewels. The Cimmerian, outmatched in intrigue, made tracks for the valley where the ruins of Alkmeenon and its treasure lay hidden. In a wild adventure with the undead goddess Yelaya, the Corinthian girl Muriela, the black priests headed by Gorulga, and the grim gray servants of the long-dead Bît-Yakin, Conan kept his head but lost his loot ("Jewels of Gwahlur").

Heading for Punt with Muriela, Conan embarked on a scheme to relieve the worshipers of an ivory goddess of their abundant gold. Learning that Thutmekri had preceded him and had already poisoned King Lalibeha's mind against him, Conan and his companion took refuge in the temple of the goddess Nebethet.

When the King, Thutmekri, and High Priest Zaramba arrived at the temple, Conan staged a charade wherein Muriela spoke with the voice of the goddess. The results surprised all, including Conan ("The Ivory Goddess").

In Zembabwei, the city of the twin kings, Conan joined a trading caravan that he squired northward along the desert borders, bringing it safely into Shem. Now in his late thirties, the restless adventurer heard that the Aquilonians were spreading westward into the Pictish wilderness. So thither, seeking work for his sword, went Conan. He enrolled as a scout at Fort Tuscelan, where a fierce war raged with the Picts.

In the forests across the river, the wizard Zogar Sag was gathering his swamp demons to aid the Picts. While Conan failed to prevent the destruction of Fort Tuscelan, he managed to warn settlers around Velitrium and to cause the death of Zogar Sag ("Beyond the Black River").

Conan rose rapidly in the Aquilonian service. As captain, his company was once defeated by the machinations of a traitorous superior. Learning that this officer, Viscount Lucian, was about to betray the province to the Picts, Conan exposed the traitor and routed the Picts ("Moon of Blood").

Promoted to general, Conan defeated the Picts in a great battle at Velitrium and was called back to the capital, Tarantia, to receive the nation's accolades. Then, having roused the suspicions of the depraved and foolish King Numedides, he was drugged and chained in the Ivory Tower under sentence of death.

The barbarian, however, had friends as well as foes. Soon he was spirited out of prison and turned loose with horse and sword. He struck out across the dank forests of Pictland toward the distant sea. In the forest, the Cimmerian came upon a cavern in which lay the corpse and the demon-guarded treasure of the pirate Tranicos. From the west, others—a Zingaran count and two bands of pirates—were hunting the same fortune: a Zingaran refugee count and two bands of pirates, while the Stygian sorcerer Thoth-Amon took a hand in the game ("The Treasure of Tranicos").

Rescued by an Aquilonian galley, Conan was chosen to lead a revolt against Numedides. While the revolution stormed along, civil war raged on the Pictish frontier. Lord Valerian, a partisan of Numedides, schemed to bring the Picts down on the town of Schohira. A scout, Gault Hagar's son, undertook to upset this scheme by killing the Pictish wizard ("Wolves Beyond the Border").

Storming the capital city and slaying Numedides on the steps of his throne—which he promptly took for his own—Conan, now in his early forties, found himself ruler of the greatest Hyborian nation (*Conan the Liberator*).

A king's life, however, proved no bed of houris. Within a year, an exiled count had gathered a group of plotters to oust the barbarian from the throne. Conan might have lost crown and head but for the timely intervention of the long-dead sage Epimitreus ("The Phoenix of the Sword").

No sooner had the mutterings of revolt died down than Conan was treacherously captured by the kings of Ophir and Koth. He was imprisoned in the tower of the wizard Tsotha-lanti in the Kothian capital. Conan escaped with the help of a fellow prisoner, who was Tsotha-lanti's wizardly rival Pelias. By Pelias's magic, Conan was whisked to Tarantia in time to slay a pretender and to lead an army against his treacherous fellow kings ("The Scarlet Citadel").

For nearly two years, Aquilonia thrived under Conan's firm but tolerant rule. The lawless, hard-bitten adventurer of former years had, through force of circumstance, matured into an able and responsible statesman. But a plot was brewing in neighboring Nemedia to destroy the King of Aquilonia by sorcery from an elder day.

Conan, about forty-five, showed few signs of age save a network of scars on his mighty frame and a more cautious approach to wine, women and bloodshed. Although he kept a harem of luscious concubines, he had never taken an official queen; hence he had no legitimate son to inherit the throne, a fact whereof his ememies sought to take advantage.

The plotters resurrected Xaltotun, the greatest sorcerer of the ancient empire of Acheron, which fell before the Hyborian savages 3,000 years earlier. By Xaltotun's magic, the King of Nemedia was slain and replaced by his brother Tarascus. Black sorcery defeated Conan's army; Conan was imprisoned, and the exile Valerius took his throne.

Escaping from a dungeon with the aid of the harem girl Zenobia, Conan returned to Aquilonia to rally his loyal forces against Valerius. From the priests of Asura, he learned that Xaltotun's power could be broken only by means of a strange jewel, the "Heart of Ahriman." The trail of the jewel led to a pyramid in the Stygian desert outside black-walled Khemi. Winning the Heart of Ahriman, Conan returned to face his foes (*Conan the Conqueror*, originally published as *The Hour of the Dragon*).

After regaining his kingdom, Conan made Zenobia his queen. But, at the ball celebrating her elevation, the Queen was borne off by a demon sent by the Khitan sorcerer Yah Chieng. Conan's quest for his bride carried him across the known world, meeting old friends and foes. In purple-towered Paikang, with the help of a magical ring, he freed Zenobia and slew the wizard (*Conan the Avenger*, originally published as *The Return of Conan*).

Home again, the way grew smoother. Zenobia gave him heirs: a son named Conan but commonly called Conn, another son called Taurus, and a daughter. When Conn was twelve, his father took him on a hunting trip to Gunderland. Conan was now in his late fifties. His sword arm was a little slower than in his youth, and his black mane and the fierce mustache of his later years were traced with gray; but his strength still surpassed that of two ordinary men.

When Conn was lured away by the Witchmen of Hyperborea, who demanded that Conan come to their stronghold alone, Conan went. He found Louhi, the High Priestess of the Witchmen, in conference with three others of the world's leading sorcerers: Troth-Amon of Stygia; the god-king of Kambuja; and the black lord of Zembabwei. In the ensuing holocaust, Louhi and the Kambujan perished, while Thoth-Amon and the other sorcerer vanished by magic ("The Witch of the Mists").

Old King Ferdrugo of Zingara had died, and his throne remained vacant as the nobles intrigued over the succession. Duke Pantho of Guarralid invaded Poitain, in southern Aquilonia. Conan, suspecting sorcery, crushed the invaders. Learning that Thoth-Amon was behind Pantho's madness, Conan set out with his army to settle matters with the Stygian. He pursued his foe to Thoth-Amon's stronghold in Stygia ("Black Sphinx of Nebthu"), to Zembabwei ("Red Moon of Zembabwei"), and to the last realm of the serpent folk in the far south ("Shadows in the Skull").

For several years, Conan's rule was peaceful. But time did that which no combination of foes had been able to do. The Cimmerian's skin became wrinkled and his hair gray; old wounds ached in damp weather. Conan's beloved consort Zenobia died giving birth to their second daughter.

Then catastrophe shattered King Conan's mood of half-resigned discontent. Supernatural entities, the Red Shadows, began seizing and carrying off his subjects. Conan was baffled until in a dream he again visited the sage Epimitreus. He was told to abdicate in favor of Prince Conn and set out across the Western Ocean.

Conan discovered that the Red Shadows had been sent by the priest-wizards of Antillia, a chain of islands in the western part of the ocean, whither the survivors of Atlantis had fled 8,000 years before. These priests offered human sacrifices to their devil-god Xotli on such a scale that their own population faced extermination.

In Antillia, Conan's ship was taken, but he escaped into the city of Ptahuacan. After conflicts with giant rats and dragons, he emerged atop the sacrificial pyramid just as his crewmen were about to be sacrificed. Supernatural conflict, revolution, and seismic catastrophe ensued. In the end, Conan sailed off to explore the continents to the west (*Conan of the Isles*).

Whether he died there, or whether there is truth in the tale that he strode out of the West to stand at his son's side in a final battle against Aquilonia's foes, will be revealed only to him who looks, as Kull of Valusia once did, into the mystic mirrors of Tuzun Thune.

L. Sprague de Camp
Villanova, Pennsylvania
May 1984